SPY BY NIGHT

SPY BY NIGHT

SPY ANOTHER DAY PREQUELS
Book Three

Jordan McCollum

DURHAM CREST BOOKS

First printing, 2014

Published by Durham Crest Books
Pleasant Grove, Utah
Set in Linux Libertine

ISBN 978-1-940096-12-4

PRINTED IN THE UNITED STATES OF AMERICA

For my children,
who mean everything

CHAPTER 1
TALIA

I DON'T DO ROMANCE. After all, when your job involves lying to almost everyone, you aren't set up for success on that front—and emotional entanglements have never helped me do said job. On a personal level, it's much, much safer to spy alone.

Fortunately, feelings have nothing to do with the allure (and lust) of Latin dance, or the fluttering in my stomach, or the guy escorting me onto the dance floor. Elliott's tall, dark and handsome enough to make James Bond jealous—and he shoots a wink my way. I skip my normal eye-roll, because I need the luck. We've been working for weeks, and if we don't look legit in these next make-or-break minutes, the whole thing will be a waste. My partner and I take our places, and the smirk passes unspoken between us.

Neither of us look at the couple to my left: Galina Isayeva and Vasily Loban, the Russian spymaster we're tracking. I know, an amateur ballroom competition in Canada might be the last place you'd expect a Russian spy, but everyone needs a hobby—and his day job as a barber in Embassy Row gives him plenty of access to prime targets. For now, I need to focus on my cover and my partner.

Most of the time, the real jobs of people like Elliott Monteith and Talia Reynolds (that would be us) look very little like the exciting lives of Bond or Bauer or Bourne, especially in Canada. But once in a while, being a spy is a scene right out of a movie. Today that scene's a ballroom dance sequence—but instead of blending into a sophisticated, glamorous reception, I'm on display to be criticized and scrutinized. I may be covered in sparkly flesh-toned spandex from ankle to wrist, and yet I feel completely naked.

I take a deep breath that smells of musty high school gym and anticipation. A couple semesters of Latin dance versus the top dancers in Canada? I'd be lucky to be naked (because nobody would be paying attention to my technique). We may not confront many direct threats in Canada, but today's biggest danger is to my dignity—and I haven't even started dancing.

"First," the melodramatic Moviefone-wannabe announcer booms over the public address system, "the cha cha."

The music starts. My heart stops. Show time.

Hyperattuned to the judges ringing the dance floor, I fasten my gaze to Elliott's. He gives his favorite signal to begin the count, an eyebrow waggle. Not hard to find the beat when the music's blasting through my bones. Two bars later, we start our steps in unison.

If I screw up, our covers are shot, and no way will we get in with the head of a spy ring. Elliott crosses the hardwood floor between us, hips swiveling in time and arms flailing in stylized flourishes. I try to forget my self-consciousness and slither and sway to the music. I'm here to protect my country, not my pride. (A lost cause in this costume.)

Grueling practice over the last few weeks has paid off. Elliott and I are usually in sync—we've worked together enough that half our conversations go without saying, and these days we're harmonized down to our heartbeats, all set to the Latin rhythm of our routines. We follow the general counterclockwise motion around the floor, but we don't have far to go. Ninety seconds in, the cha cha music fades, and Elliott spins me into a deep curtsy to finish. Next, the samba. The announcer's voice echoes through the small gym, confirming the lineup, and the whole thing starts again.

Our samba routine has the sequence that's hardest for me, promenade and counterpromenade runs, where Elliott and I take turns spinning across one another's paths. A standard skill, so I need to make this look good. I have to keep my feet up to clear his steps between mine, and the performance smile slips from my lips. I overshoot the second to last crossing, and I swear time slows.

My glittery Latin shoe heads straight for Elliott's toes like it's being reeled in on a wire. At the last second, he slides his foot two inches to safety.

"Ha," he whispers. My eyes snap to his again, and my winning grin is back.

Man, am I glad Elliott was on his college ballroom team. The dork.

Elliott spins me free and we dance, mirroring one another, ten feet apart. Another couple passes between us, also dancing separately. The woman moves behind me, and for a moment I'm dancing with a miniature cross between an athletic surfer and a Scandinavian god. Vasily.

The sheer intensity of his concentration and his effortless technique dazzle me for a minute, and I almost imagine I'm dancing with him instead. That throws me off a beat. But he wiggles out of the way, and the music winds down. Hope this doesn't make things awkward later when we're targeting him.

Samba might have the hardest step for me, but rumba's my weakest dance, where my lack of experience shows. I avoid any major gaffes through our short rumba, paso doble and jive (ugh) routines. The Jerry Lee Lewis–inspired jive music fades out at the end of our catapult (a lot less impressive than it sounds: basically me walking and spinning around Elliott). He completes the move, spinning me clockwise, then counter-clockwise, and we finish with a bow. The minutes of full-out effort catch up with me, and I'm both grinning and gasping to the thin audience's applause. Amateur ballroom isn't exactly drawing the Canadian ESPN.

The dancing might be over, but my heart rate only climbs. For all the time we've put into these seven and a half minutes of ballroom, they're just window dressing for our real mission. Get to Vasily, get his phone, get everything off it to analyze and find the rest of his spy ring.

Starting now.

We walk off the floor though the break in the bleachers at the corner, mingling with the other couples dancing in our heat. (Don't ask me how the judges do it; no idea.) Elliott and I blend in, critiquing ourselves, as if we're hoping we'll make it into the next round. Our dancing was decent, but only good enough to pass for competing on this level. We wait until we're within earshot of our targets by the bleachers, and then by a silent signal we begin the argument.

"Not saying it's your fault." Blame weighs down Elliott's words. "Just saying, if you hadn't done that, we'd be a shoo-in for the next round."

"Excuse me? We agreed the rhythm was syncopated on those beats. You can't call an audible in the middle of a heat." We're close enough now I can turn to our targets, hoping for sympathy from the female partner, Galina. "Tell him he's insane to change the routine the day of a competition."

She raises a disapproving, ornately shadowed, bejeweled eyebrow at Elliott. "Very unprofessional."

"In an 'amateur' competition," Elliott mutters. I silence him with a *look*. He pleads his case to her partner, Vasily—our target. "Don't you think the rhythm looked off?"

I shake my head before Vasily answers. "They weren't watching us. They're way too professional, way too focused." I stick out a hand. "I'm Joanne Hodges, and you're amazing. I don't know if you're naturally talented or you've worked your tails off—probably both—but you're seriously the best I've ever seen. Your lines, your technique, your connection—it's a privilege watching you, let alone dancing next to you."

Galina and Vasily break into matching smiles of false modesty while shaking my hand and introducing themselves. "Though I do have to admit," Vasily confesses to Elliott, "the syncopation *was* awkward."

"You noticed?" Elliott grimaces.

"It wouldn't be hard to fix." Vasily tries to make his tone encouraging, but the little rise of hope falls short.

I pounce on that not-so-much-an-invitation. "Are you guys around for dinner tonight? Not sure what our schedule's like, but if we're free, we'd love to pick your brain."

Vasily wavers, his eyes flicking to Galina. Elliott and I instantly tune our features to matching please-please-please looks. Galina must sense the desperation/fangirling, because after a long second, she gives Vasily an at-least-it'll-get-them-off-our-case nod.

"Why don't I give you my number?" Elliott suggests. "So you'll know to answer."

Or, you know, not. But Vasily retrieves his cell from his locker and returns to us, and I find myself holding my breath.

"Here." Elliott holds out a hand. "I'll just put it in."

This is it. Vasily hesitates, and my lungs shrink even more. Let it go, dude. Let it go.

Finally, Vasily gives up his phone. Elliott slides the icon to unlock it and types the number for his latest burner phone. He saves it under his cover, Gord Hopkins. Once he's done, he flips the phone over, admiring the expensive case. "OtterBox?"

"No, off-brand."

"Mind if I take a look?"

I try not to telegraph how badly I want him to say yes. Vasily waves his permission and Elliott pries the phone out of its case. He passes the case from one hand to the other—and then he fumbles the phone, which clatters to the floor. Perfect.

"I'm sorry!" Elliott exclaims immediately.

"Sorry," I apologize, too, and move forward to grab the phone. Except before I can take it, I "accidentally" kick the cell, and it skids underneath the bleachers ten feet away.

I glance at Vasily. His lips pinch together until they start to turn white. Galina touches his elbow, but he subtly shifts away.

"Sorry!" I say again. (Playing the part of Canadians to a T.) "Don't worry, I'll get that for you." I hurry to the bleachers before Vasily can decide he'd rather not trust his phone to people who've already abused it this badly. Elliott keeps apologizing as I drop to my knees to crawl under the half-vacant bleachers.

The flesh-toned fabric of my costume bodice hides more than my skin. I extract a tiny device from inside the elastic strap. Well, two devices—the first, a tiny flashlight. I shine the beam around the shadows. The phone's half-hiding under a metal rod, part of the bleachers, and a wheel. I crawl over, ignoring the threads and sequins popping on a dress that was made for a totally different kind of wriggling.

Elliott's apologies grow louder, and I click off my flashlight. They're coming this way. I need another minute to get what I need.

"Found it yet?" Vasily calls.

"No, I need a flashlight."

"I'll come get it."

Elliott jumps in. "You'll never get the dust out of your pants in time for the next round."

Galina's voice echoes to me, too. "He's right," she murmurs.

"I've got my phone," I claim. "I'll use my flashlight app." I turn back on the (real) flashlight and shine it around like I haven't located his phone yet. My pulse accelerates in my throat.

"What's taking so long?" Vasily again.

I still every muscle, focused on the phone lodged under the wheel. If removing it makes noise, my cover's shot. Tension tries to draw my shoulders up, but I fight it. I make up something to say over the noise, pray and pull. "There are dust bunnies the size of Dobermans in here," I reply over the slight *penk* of the phone tugging free.

I swear I can *hear* Galina and Vasily recoil in horror at the prospect of dust. (I'd better come out covered in the stuff to sell this lie.)

Okay, a few more seconds. A new surge of music covers the clicking as I pry the back of the phone's slick plastic cover off. The SD card mount is aluminum or some other silver metal, hard to miss against the backdrop of black plastic. I push the card in to make it spring free.

The size of my fingernail, the tiny memory card fits perfectly inside the second device I brought: a card cloner. A little blue LED on the side lights up, and I count the seconds. Six, seven, eight . . .

"Do you need help?" Galina's voice echoes into the dark.

"No, I think I've got it." I hope I do. Twelve, thirteen—the LED goes out. Done. I slide the micro SD card out and remount it in the phone. The music will stop any second, and adrenaline makes my fingers fly too fast. I drop the back cover. It rattles across the floor.

I clutch the phone, hoping, hoping, hoping they didn't hear. The music stops, and applause carries from above the bleachers and beside—Galina, Vasily and Elliott. For my sake, they'd better be watching the floor to see the next dance. "Jive," the announcer . . . announces. I clamp down on an automatic groan. We're already to the last dance of the heat—and after the nerves and adrenaline of four other performances, you're supposed to jump around like an overcaffeinated acrobat on spring shoes.

The bouncy music blares, and I swing my flashlight beam around to find the back of the cover again. Bingo. I snap it up, snap it on and make it out of there, snappy. My tights are covered in dust. I hold out the phone to Vasily and apologize several more times, until he frowns. He examines the phone. My costume feels like it's three sizes too small, my lungs are straining so hard to breathe. Will he buy it? Did I miss something?

"Thank you," he finally says. He takes his case back from Elliott and pops the phone in. Vasily bids us goodbye and shepherds Galina away. Elliott waits until they're clear before he looks at me, silently asking if I got the data card copied. I nod.

"That's the good news," he mutters.

"And what's the bad news?"

"We've run out of chances." He takes my elbow and turns me to the Jumbotron. The judges posted the couples from our heat moving on to the next round. I scan the list twice, but the results don't change. No 612.

Elliott, acting his cover, slips an arm around my shoulders and squeezes. "We'll get 'em next time."

Still holding the SD card copier, I pat his hand. We'd better get 'em this time.

We change and slip out as soon as we can, trying to seem laidback instead of lame. Elliott walks me through the parking lot, and it doesn't take three years of spycraft to see the hurt haunting his vague smile—again. "Disappointed with the results?" I ask, though I doubt that's the reason he's been upset for the last several weeks.

He shrugs, back to a business-casual expression. "Did what we came to do."

"Even if we have to compete again?" If this SD card isn't as productive as we'd like, we'll need to. Unfortunately.

"We'll figure it out."

I swallow an inward groan. Preparing for one competition was grueling enough; not ready to think about another.

Before I can steer the conversation to whatever's been bugging him, Elliott sizes me up, though we're both back in street clothes. "Your skirt should be shorter."

"Thanks." But I level him with a half-mock glare.

"Just saying—ballroom's all about aesthetics. Nothing wrong with playing up your most aesthetically pleasing feature."

I scoff.

"What?" Elliott holds up defensive hands. "Have I ever steered you wrong? I mean, about ballroom?"

We've established he's far more of an expert in that area. "No, just surprised you know the word 'aesthetics.'"

He rolls his eyes. "Come on. A couple weeks of practice and you got this."

A couple weeks of practice? Between the endless paper-work and agent meetings of my job, and the law internship I'm doing at Terfort & Sutter, also part of my cover, I barely chiseled out the time to prepare for *this* competition. "Let's wait and see if it's worth the trouble first."

We reach my nondescript Company car and he concedes the point. "Still with me tonight, right?"

"Of course." We're sitting on the Emirati embassy, which will probably be about as much fun as it sounds.

Elliott looks away, and I see it again—a flash of pain as his smile fades.

"Everything okay?" I ask. "In your life?"

"Yep."

I wait for him to turn to me. "Sure? You don't look okay."

He wiggles his eyebrows again, stepping closer. "I look a lot better than 'okay.'"

I groan and whack his arm. Not the first time I've tried to ask him about that expression, but like every time I try to talk about something serious, he makes it into over-the-top flirting.

I give it one more shot: "You know you can talk to me, right?"

"If I want to talk, you'll be the first to know," he bites off.

I pull back. He glances around and drops his voice. "I mean . . ." He sighs. "I want to work this out myself. I know what you'll say. I know you better than just about anyone."

Guess he does know me that well. We've worked together more than a year, and he's become like another older brother, albeit an obnoxiously flirty one—and most of all, he's one of the few people in this country or ours who knows what I really do for a living. I watch him hop in his car and peel off, marveling for a minute that the guy who can't communicate without a come-on turned out to be my best friend and favorite partner. Definitely wouldn't have guessed that the day he waltzed into my life like Langley's gift to ladies.

I shake off the nostalgia and run through a barrage of boring errands to make sure no one's following me. (Like I said, everyone needs a hobby—and mine's paranoia.) Once I'm sure I'm black—Agency slang for free of surveillance—I hit the office to hand off the card copier to my boss, Will. He'll pass it along to a courier and by tonight, it'll be waiting in some analyst's inbox at Langley.

Another surveillance detection run brings me safely to my law office for a couple hours of catch-up before rendezvousing with Elliott again.

I'm parking when my phone rings. Please don't let this be a problem at my other job. I check my phone. My mother.

Crap. If she's paying attention to me, it's way worse than work. My stress level's already spiking, ratcheting up the tension in my back. If she's suddenly remembered I exist and I don't run to answer, I'll spend the foreseeable future on my mother's hate list.

Wouldn't be so bad if I didn't have to hear about what a terrible daughter/sister/human I am from her and every mutual acquaintance until I grovel my way back into her good graces. Not worth it. Much faster and easier to talk to her for a few minutes. I may defend my country from thieves, terrorists and spies, but sometimes the best defense is not fighting in the first place. Diplomacy, meet Mommie Dearest. "Hi, Mom."

"Oh, Talia, sweetie, I was beginning to think you wouldn't answer."

I wish. I turn off the car and stay put. Not about to walk and talk—that'd leave me too distracted to watch my back. "Sorry, I'm just getting back to the office."

"Then you should've answered sooner so we'd have longer to talk."

No, what I should've done is not hope Mom could take the hint that I don't have time to talk—or, really, listen to her talk about herself.

Gotta get it over with. "How are you?" I ask.

I unbuckle and focus on the dash clock through my mom's long recitation of her latest activities. Ten minutes of nothing worth a phone call, stories of how much smarter/prettier/better than her friends she is. We take a detour for her to rail against my brother Trevor for heaven knows what. I make the right conversational noises without actually agreeing he's the worst scum to ever live until I can steer the topic back to something else she mentioned.

Apparently, she's ready to talk about me. "So, are you seeing anyone? How's work?"

"Stressful," I say. I wait a minute for her to plow ahead about herself, but when she doesn't, I dare to think she'll listen. (And care?) "This week, I spent—"

"Talia, you didn't answer the question. Are you seeing anyone?"

I cover my face. It's five o'clock on a Friday. If I'm not getting ready for a date, Mom already knows my answer. And I know what's coming—either a lecture or an announcement. "No, I'm not."

She sighs dramatically. "Aren't you ever getting married?"

I glance at the rearview out of checking-my-back habit and bite back a retort about repeating her mistakes (three of them). The point of talking to her is to *not* make her hate me. "Mom—"

"Don't 'Mom' me. I'm serious. You need to settle down."

Somewhere deep inside, I haven't learned my lesson. Eight-year-old me really, really wishes this sudden concern had to do with actually caring about my happiness. But I know she'll say something to make this all come back to her.

"It's like you don't want me to be happy."

And there it is. My existence, my purpose, my life to my mother in a nutshell: I exist to make her happy, and I never have. This is why we don't talk. I pull the keys out of the ignition and grab my messenger bag. "Sorry, Mom," I say. "But I really have to get to work."

"Is that more important than talking to your mother?"

Here comes the martyr card. I pause, one hand on the door handle.

"After all I've done for you, you can't spare ten minutes for your own mother?"

Never mind that it's already been twenty, and I haven't done any talking—and that she can barely be bothered to remember my existence half the time. "I can't drop—"

"You used to be such a sweet little girl. What happened?"

Finally, my Mom-survival instincts kick in and I shut down the emotions—disappointment, regret, and most of all, stupid, stupid hope. It's how I made it through my childhood, and if it'll help me survive this conversation, I'll do it in a heartbeat.

"Do you remember when I helped you open that bank account?"

Her leaps are harder to follow than Elliott's advanced dance steps. "I guess?"

"And the money I gave to get you started?"

Really? "You want your twenty dollars back?"

"I would never—but, you know, I'm behind on a few bills and with interest—"

Typical. Gifts, especially money, are never free in her family. "Sorry, Mom, I really can't talk now."

"Don't you care—oh, my show's on. Better go."

Wait, what? I stare at my phone's call timer, stopped and blinking. I told her how many times I had actual work to do, and the minute she had something trivial (it's July! It's rerun season!), she dropped me.

No. No. She can't hurt me, not anymore. I'm an adult. I've been through years of therapy and have control of my life and my emotions and my choices. Mom is only allowed in because she's my mom. I'd like to think she loves me, and I guess I love her. I must, since I'm still protecting her. Of all the secrets I keep for my country, none of them is buried quite as deep as my deepest: the family secret that Mom's crazy with a K.

I doubt many people will be in the office, but I'll have to endure Elliott later (not to mention the rest of the weekend—church especially), so I need to regroup. I comb my hands through my hair, smoothing it back into a ponytail and rearranging my bangs. I check my appearance in the rearview, grateful I never succumbed to the fleeting temptation to highlight my dark hair (like Mom does). My hair's fine. Game face on. Walls up. Secret safe.

Now to keep it that way.

CHAPTER 2
DANNY

I CAME TO CANADA FOR THE CHANCE TO START OVER, but some habits can't be broken—like Sunday afternoon naps. Even if it conflicts with church.

Dozing off in meetings is practically a time-honored tradition, so I don't appreciate the sharp elbow in my ribs when I nod off. Twice. Everyone else here thinks "Sassy" Beth and I are meant to be—especially Beth—but something about her is a little too far on the psycho side of the spectrum for my taste.

I've had enough psycho for four lifetimes. I'm getting out. A walk around the halls would help me stay awake . . . and give me an excuse to sit somewhere else. Maybe. Not really *that* harsh.

Three meters into the foyer, I stop short. I'm not into feet, but some shoes can drive any guy to distraction. A pair of major offenders are staring me in the face. Crisscross straps wrapped around her ankles, high heels, toes that aren't fighter-jet-pointy-scary.

More than that, I know who they belong to, because this

isn't the first time I've noticed those ankle straps accentuating those crossed calves.

Yep, totally awake.

And totally gawking at her legs. I flash my gaze to hers, fast, but she's focused on the glass doors, tapping her fingers on the armchair. At least if she catches me staring at her face, I won't look like a jerk. Not like looking at a pretty girl can hurt you.

No, but it's a start.

Stop it, brain. Stop. Those defenses are a delayed reaction not to the woman in front of me, or Sassy Beth in the chapel. My master plan for starting over didn't include dating quite yet, but when the prime opportunity to pursue the perfect puzzle presents itself, who am I to say no?

I know who she is, though I've never spoken to her. That's mostly because she seems to avoid speaking to anyone at church. Nobody knows why, and public opinion seems split along the "shy"/"stuck up" divide. In fact, nobody knows *anything* about her, and that's one reason I'm interested. I'd love to be the first to figure her out.

If she's just shy, and if it's just us in the foyer, and if she didn't just see me checking her out, then it should be okay, right?

She looks up, one eyebrow asking a silent question. As much of an invitation as I could hope for, and I'll definitely take it. I lean against the wall by her chair. "You know," I say with a nod toward the double wood grain chapel doors, "you can see better in there."

Lame.

That one eyebrow arches higher, and she points at the speakers in the ceiling. "What, does Coop have puppets and posters?"

Okay, I have to laugh. She's witty. I like witty.

"I'm not here to see," Talia says with a smirk. "Or be seen."

15

"Wish I were that smart," I mutter.

"What, the pressures of the 'meet market' suddenly too much for you?"

"That and the fact I catch an elbow every time I fall asleep." She winces.

"Talia, right?"

She blinks and tilts her head a millimeter, like she's re-calculating her estimation of me. "And you're Danny."

"That's me." Dude, she knows my name. That's better than ankle straps.

Inside the chapel, Coop pauses in his droning, and we both glance at the speakers in the ceiling, waiting for the next words. "We need to get married. Like, now."

My gaze has already fallen back to Talia, and I'm still grinning because she knows my name, so that makes Coop's pronouncement doubly awkward.

Coop's not done. "I know we all know this," he says, "and we're probably tired of hearing it, but it really is true: it's not good for man to be alone."

Footnote: sometimes, it *is* better for man to be alone.

"Oh. Marriage." Talia smirks. "Must be the fourth Sunday."

Witty again. I really like that.

"Obviously, I'm preaching to the choir," Coop continues. "But seriously, everyone I've talked to says marriage is awesome. If you get the chance, do it! If you're dating someone and it's going well, it's time to talk marriage."

Footnote 2: be extremely careful who you date. I shouldn't resent a twenty-two-year-old preaching to me like this, but apparently I'm not as mature as I thought.

Before either of us salvage that one with a clever retort, Coop launches into what has to be the conclusion of his talk. Talia gets up.

Yep, the effect of the heels is even better when she's standing. And walking. That was the first time I really noticed her, three weeks ago, walking in the back doors of the church with the sun hitting her back, lighting up her hair and dress with a coronal halo. I kind of interrupted a conversation with Sassy Beth to watch Talia walk by. At the last second, Talia looked back at me, but before either of us could react, she stopped short, narrowly missing a guy I don't know. She apologized and disappeared.

Just like she seems to be ready to do now.

"Where you going?" I call.

She looks back. "Getting a drink."

I eye the water fountain that's two meters away, 135° off her trajectory.

"Yeah, people will come out here and get a drink there during the rest hymn. And I will be—" She motions down the hall and around the corner, where another water fountain waits—"over there."

"You're taking the 'not being seen' thing to the Olympic level."

Talia smiles, and that's either subtle flirting or secretly funny. "You have no idea." She reroutes for her destination, but wheels back again before she disappears down the hall. "You know, water might help you stay awake."

A definite invitation, and a definite yes. The opening chords of the rest hymn ring out, and I have to hurry, without looking like I'm hurrying, to reach her before the inevitable string of parched people parades out the doors like she said.

The back of the building is noisy and crowded with families from our building's other congregation, which is always weird when yours is composed entirely of single twentysomethings in an attempt to get us married off. We have to wait in line for the fountain. "How's this better?" I murmur to her.

"They're not obligated to talk to us," she responds. She peeks over her shoulder to make eye contact, and I know she doesn't mean she's obligated to talk to me or vice versa. Once we've gotten water, Talia pauses to kill more time perusing a bulletin board of photos from this summer's girls camp. Or pictures of a bunch of teenagers we don't know.

In silence. I'm not *obligated* to talk to her, but I want to. I mean, I should. So . . . speak, self.

Talia glances at me again. Say something. Something.

I have nothing remotely interesting to say. Reciting tensile strengths for the top six alloys we're considering always gets the girls.

Aaand Talia turns away.

Idiot.

Apparently satisfied her chances of being spotted are zero, she leads the way back to the foyer. Even an idiot can see it makes more sense to follow her than to stare at strangers' photos. Aside from a couple with two toddlers on the couch closest to the gym, when we reach the foyer, it's quiet and abandoned.

"Brothers and sisters—guys," implores the second speaker's unfamiliar, piped-in voice, "I want to testify of the doctrine of marriage."

"Wow." I give a low whistle. "Batting zero for two today. More water?" I jerk a thumb over my shoulder.

Talia laughs with only her eyes, still hinting at those shields. "We better hunker down and take cover." But she keeps standing there, watching me.

Waiting for *me* to do something?

Okay. I take a seat at the end of the free flowery couch. Her move. Sitting across the foyer in an armchair will make it tough to carry on a quiet conversation.

She settles onto the opposite end of the couch. Yes.

I don't let the mental celebration show. "So, what's your story?"

"Hm?" That eyebrow-question mark is back.

"Why'd you move to Canada?" In the two debates I accidentally provoked with the *What's with Talia?* question, a couple guys from the ward weren't even sure whether she was Canadian. She's not—I figured that much out from the first word I heard her say: sorry.

She does the little blink-tilt-recalculating thing again. I'm beginning to like that. Or maybe I just like surprising her. "Free healthcare. Got tired of waiting for them to get it right in the US, so I came here to wait for a doctor instead."

"Oh, are you sick?" Wait, that's rude.

"No, waiting on that too."

I'd almost forgotten what it's like to talk to someone like this, joking around, not quite flirting. The brief lull allows the speaker, someone whose voice I still don't know, to butt in again. "Marriage *is* ordained of God, and He wants that for all of us, but we've got to give Him something to work with."

Awkward again. Talia and I stare at one another, frozen. There's a limit to how much embarrassment two people can endure. When did it get so hot in here?

I can play this off—I need to. So I shrug. "I got nothing."

She cracks up almost in spite of herself. Yep, I like that, too.

"What's your story?" She reflects my question back.

Oh, we're not getting into the reasons I needed this chance to start over. Not now, not ever. I give her the surface version. "Got a great job. Kind of a new lease on life."

"Life's one of those things you should definitely buy. Congrats on the job, though. What do you do?"

"I'm an aerospace engineer at National Research Council Canada."

"So you're a rocket scientist?"

We can skip the terminology lecture. Lame that I hate that phrase, but I hate it—from anyone else. From her, it doesn't sound like a joke or an insult. It sounds like a compliment. "I mostly work on planes."

"Cool. Big transition, moving here?"

"Nah, I served my mission here."

"Right here?" She points at the blue speckled carpet, teasing me.

"Mostly Québec, but actually, yeah. The Champlain Ward was my first area." That's the congregation milling around the back of the building. In fact, I probably did know those teenagers we were looking at. As children. Not that they'd recognize me

"Ah, so the hair?" She gestures at my hair, which isn't *that* long, but a lot longer than missionary standards. "Traveling incognito?"

"Hey, I like my hair."

"No, I didn't—it looks good—I mean—" She licks her lips then presses them together, like she's clamping down to cut off anything else embarrassing she might say.

She likes my hair? I lean back on the couch, getting comfortable. She can talk all day.

Unfortunately, Talia's not the one doing the talking now. The speaker's voice interrupts again. "Do online dating if you have to, but remember, there are great people right here."

I make a point not to stare at Talia after that, but you don't have to tell me twice.

"How long has it been?" Talia asks.

Since what? My last date? Oh, my mission. "Nine years since I was here."

I think Talia's in the same demographic as me, the "graduated or even finished grad school and working and STILL not married" segment, but I'm not sure. If she's younger, admitting that I'm twenty-eight might scare her off. I wait for the blink-tilt-recalculating-his-age expression.

It doesn't come. "Cool to see your mission again. Wish I could."

"Where'd you serve?"

"Mostly small towns on the border of Georgia."

"That's not the other side of the world. You know, they have these things, they're called airplanes—I think I mentioned them?"

She squints at me, like she loves and hates my logic. "What I need is a time machine. Pause my life here, then think about a vacation."

"You sound busy. What do you do?"

"I'm an articling student." She grips the edge of the couch cushion like she's bracing for a blow.

Not clicking for me. I know I *should* know it. "Sounds familiar . . . ?"

"In Canada, you have to do an internship for almost a year after you finish law classes."

"So law school's longer here?"

"Usually. If you work *really* hard and play your cards right, you can finish in three and a half years."

Talia seems like the kind of girl who works harder than anyone else and can play some mean poker. I don't think whatever blow she was anticipating came, and her posture relaxes, settling into the couch again. Was she expecting a lawyer crack? Do I look stupid?

"Has the free healthcare been worth it?" I ask.

"Oh no. Didn't they have winter when you lived here? It's like Rexburg only with humidity."

The tiny Idaho town reference pegs her as a BYU–I alum. "No," I answer her question. "We skipped it. Global warming."

She smiles at my joke. Somehow, that smile's better than watching her walk in three weeks ago, lit up and golden. Because this smile isn't the impenetrable heat shielding façade she uses at church, and maybe all the time.

This is a real person. And she's beautiful.

"So get out there," the speaker starts winding down his rah-rah-go-date-marry pep talk. "Ask people out! Say yes to dates! Be open to every opportunity for the Lord to help you find someone to share your life with."

Was I just complaining how hot it was in here? Because now I've got goose bumps, and I don't think the A/C kicked on. Not sure whether it's God or the speaker who wants me to ask Talia out, but I'm ready to go for it. "Hey," I say, drawing her attention away from the speakers overhead.

She isn't looking at me expectantly, like she thinks I'm going along with what the speaker said. I'm not. I want to take her out, take this chance to start over.

But—that wasn't my plan. I'm waiting on dating for a reason. I've had one conversation with her. There's open to opportunities, and there's stupid. Talia has no reason to say yes to me after one conversation. For all she knows I'm a serial killer or a stalker or a psycho.

For all I know, she might be, too. A "yes" today could be worse than a no. It could be the first step back into my nightmares.

The strains of the closing hymn begin, and the chapel doors swing open as a couple people jump on an early escape. Talia's shields raise. My opportunity, if I wanted it, slips away. She folds her arms, but it seems less like she's preparing for prayer and more like she's protecting herself.

That hits a little too close to home.

I thought I was an idiot because I couldn't think of anything to say before. Still an idiot, but now because I let her go.

Once the hymn and the prayer are over, the parade out the chapel doors begins again. After half a dozen people, the next guy makes a beeline for Talia. Arjay Rathee. First or second generation immigrant from India, no older than 21. Not the likeliest of crushes.

I might've passed up my chance to ask her out, but that doesn't mean I'm happy to have another guy swoop in and sweep her away.

"There you are," Arjay says to her. "Late again?"

"Hate to make an entrance."

Arjay offers a hand and pulls Talia to her feet. I stand, too. Totally not ready to give her up. I'm an idiot, yes—but not in a vegetative state. "Nice talking to you."

She glances back. "You too." Her smile's maybe half-shields.

I'll take it. Arjay tugs her down the hall, and I try to enjoy the view of Talia and not plot ways to get rid of the guy next to her.

If I'm supposed to be starting over, I'm not sure whether I saved myself or blew it.

Next thing I know, Sassy Beth's next to me. "Thought we'd lost you," she says.

"Nope, not yet." Unfortunately. Beth believes she has a claim on me because we went out once a month ago. By went out, I mean she asked me to bring food to a "party," which turned out to be her and her roommates and two other guys.

Also not my idea of starting over. But I'm not sure what is anymore, since I just let what looked like my first good chance walk away.

Maybe I should forget about Talia for a while, no matter how hot her shoes are.

Maybe I should forget about dating. Maybe there is no "starting over."

Sassy Beth reaches for my elbow, like I'll escort her to class. I maneuver over her attack, patting her shoulder and aiming her in the right direction with her roommates, AB Beth and BC Beth. They're from Saskatchewan, Alberta, and British Columbia, hence the nicknames. "I'll catch up."

"All right," Sassy Beth says. "But hurry."

I'll hurry. If only to keep my thoughts from catching up to me.

CHAPTER 3
TALIA

OKAY, I DON'T DO ROMANCE, but I don't have a lot else to occupy my mind as I watch Vasily's outdated fourplex. The '80s throwback slice of suburbia isn't where you'd expect a spy ring.

That's what makes it the perfect cover. Unfortunately, it's also perfectly boring on a Sunday evening, giving me time to roll over every second of this afternoon. I have to allow myself crushes (I'm only human), and for the last two months, that crush has taken the shape of Danny Fluker. Handsome, smart, spiritual, sincere—and he came and talked to me. I'm reliving every word, every comfortable silence, every look.

Reason #24 why Danny Fluker is one of the congregation's hottest commodities: those warm brown eyes. Describing someone's eye color with food terms is bizarre unless you're a freakish eye-eating monster, though I suddenly see the appeal. But it's not the color—it's the way that he looks at you, open and inviting and utterly magnetic.

Magnetic is dangerous. Inviting is dangerous. Open is very

dangerous. I avoid romantic entanglements for excellent reasons. All of which escaped me when I caught Danny staring at my calves (and gave him a second to look away, or I'd have to be more offended than flattered).

Okay, this is dumb. I shift in my seat to focus on Vasily's boring brick building.

I've had one conversation with the man—Danny, not Vasily. I mean, I figured he was dating Sassy Beth. I know almost nothing about him. Yet I've never been less happy to see Arjay, my one friend at church. Never mind that Arjay called me on my stupid crush within sixty seconds. At least he kept that part of the conversation in whispered Urdu. (I became his friend so I could practice my CIA-trained fourth language. Not sure it counts as real friendship.)

Gah, no—focus, Talia. I glue my gaze to apartment three's forest green door. Distractions can be deadly. No matter how much I want to talk to Danny again, no matter how smart he is (reason #17), no matter how temptingly touchable his dark hair is where it's just long enough to flip out behind his ears in little half-curls (reasons #7, 39 and 61). I don't do distracted.

Apartment three's porch light flips on, and I straighten to full attention like a Canadian Pointer. Vasily steps out, glances around. My breath stops even faster than when Danny did the same thing in the foyer this afternoon.

Unlike Danny, Vasily doesn't notice me—thank you, black shirt, black jacket, black Honda in the shadows. He jogs down the stairs to his white Subaru. He's got something small in his right hand, maybe baseball-sized judging by his grip. Definitely something I'm interested in.

He gets in his car and starts the engine. I wait until he's down the block before I pursue.

I follow him for ten minutes on a circuitous route through the suburbs and over major arteries. Watching that white car isn't enough to keep my mind totally off my favorite topic today. I'm remembering reason #95, Danny's laugh, when I realize the yellow traffic light in front of me is now red—and Vasily's down the block.

Crud. Yet another reason it's better to not let a crush get out of control.

Surveilling Vasily tonight was a long shot, especially while we're still waiting on the intelligence from his phone's memory card. He didn't do a classic surveillance detection route—no mundane stops—but he did manage to lose my (admittedly shorthanded) tail. I put another tally mark in the suspicious column and turn around to wait at his house.

Until that SD card analysis gets back, I'm keeping an eye on him. And my mind *off* Danny.

Articling students work fifty hours a week, easy—and so do spies. You can imagine I don't have a lot of time for a personal life (not to mention that whole *spy alone* thing). I have a late night of surveillance and an early morning to squeeze in seven hours of law-intern-y stuff, but even after all that I'm still fighting down a giddy grin every twenty minutes.

Just the thought stirs up a horde of hummingbirds in my stomach. (Or maybe that should be teeny, tiny planes.)

I think I've got the silly smile under control by three, when I finish up my internship at Terfort & Sutter and head to my cover job at "Keeler Tate & Associates," AKA the CIA. I file the post-action report on last night's Sunday drive: Vasily returned an hour later without whatever he was carrying, and a peek in his car windows yielded nothing the right size. Could be a dead drop.

Wish I had more to go on, but the full analysis of that SD card will take days. Elliott brings me up to date on a case I'm helping with, tracking down a source who's leaking intel from our embassy to the United Arab Emirates'. In the diplomatic dictionary, that's filed under "Not Okay."

Elliott pursues a lead: a gala for a human rights summit where our leak will most likely be. While he tries to get us—or me, on the piano—in as last-minute replacement entertainment, I move to updates on my cases. A Turkmen scientist I've been targeting is speaking in an hour on the University of Ottawa campus, my alma mater.

I'm finishing my catch-up when Elliott comes to my desk. I realize I'm smiling again—yep, thinking about Danny. What was he about to say to me before the closing hymn, and why didn't he?

I push that memory away and turn to Elliott. "You're all lined up," he reports, tapping his watch. "Seven forty to eight."

I grimace before I can stop myself. Is it bad I *don't* want to use yet another of my rusting artistic skills? "Better get practicing" is all I say, stretching those keyboard fingers. Where can I get at a piano? The church building?

Instead of a piano, though, I'm picturing the floral couch where Danny and I sat yesterday.

"What's got you all giddy?" Elliott interrupts the memory, leaning against my desk.

"Hm?" A warm tide creeps up my neck. One hand flies there almost against my will, like my subconscious automatically wants to cover a blush.

"You keep drifting back to La La Land whenever you're working, and no case is *that* good."

Crap. My mind echoes back on that innocent little phrase he said Friday: *I know you better than anyone.*

But does he? I'm not about to turn to Elliott for girl talk, and I'm going to keep my work life far, far away from a guy I've had all of one (cute) conversation with. "I—ah—no idea what you're talking about." I turn to my computer and try to type, but I have to delete the same word three times before I can get my fingers to spell it correctly. (That would be t-h-e.)

"Is this about a guy?" Elliott's tone rings with condescension. "What are you, twelve?"

See what I mean? I rub two fingertips against my forehead, not answering. Can't encourage him.

Too late. Elliott's gathered the open-source intelligence, and he's bringing it to bear on me. He leans down to mock me at close range. "You meet someone in your case files this weekend?"

Now he teases me about working hard at my cover job? "No, no—I—it's nothing."

"So it *is* a guy. New friend?"

Okay, he's caught me lying. Change tactics: feed him as little of the truth as I can. "Not exactly, not really." I wave away his interest. "It's nothing. Won't go anywhere."

"So one-night stand material?"

I fire a scowl at him. He knows me better than that. Then I see his face. He's trying to get a rise out of me. Yeah, well, congratulations.

He smirks. "You know you're going to have to tell me sometime."

I cock my head and slap on a sarcastic stare, daring him to push me. How many times have I tried to get him to talk to me these last couple weeks? Like I didn't see that "I need space" email from his fiancée. "It was just—" Defensiveness infiltrates my voice, so I try again, still on the as-little-of-the-truth tack. "I don't know—a little . . . moment."

When I look up, I glimpse Elliott's flash of a frown, like I've somehow signaled he's pushed me as far as I'll give. He shifts his weight off my desk and turns back to the case (finally!). "Okay, they'll be expecting us at seven—"

"'Us,' Kemosabe?" I quirk an eyebrow at him.

"Yeah, you and your driver." He indicates himself with a Latin-esque flourish.

Riiight. "Thursday night?"

"Yep."

"Okay." I grab my internship case files, my Sisyphean assignment, from under my desk. "Well, my Turkmen friend is holding a forum on natural gas pipelines this afternoon, and I'd better get down there to support him."

"Is that who's got you all giggly?"

That type of teasing is much safer territory. "I'm not giggly. If I were, it'd have nothing to do with him."

"I bet."

I roll my eyes and pack up for the day. "I'll practice after that. See you tomorrow." Should be able to get in to use a piano at church. And I don't let myself hope Danny will be there, too. Much.

I settle into a chair in the greenroom of the Ottawa Convention Centre Thursday night. Performance time, and the same nerves hum in my stomach as before our dance routine. I don't allow even a dash of disappointment that I didn't run into Danny despite hitting up the chapel for practice the last three nights (before going to watch Vasily). Even thinking of Danny doesn't change the fact I'm the opposite of giddy.

I can't afford to be silly tonight. I adjust my red updo wig to remind myself of my cover: Alaine Marchant. Consummate performer.

All I have to do is get through a couple songs I've known for decades—and then the real hard part begins. I've studied US Embassy rosters all week to be able to recognize any personnel here to ID the leak, and Elliott's working the Emirati angle to find his contact.

Elliott shifts in the seat next to me, but I make a point not to look at him. I still can't forget his fiancée's "I need some space" email, and he's been extra weird toward me too. Much as I want to help, my extensive experience watching relationships disintegrate can't prevent disaster.

So I run through scales on my lap. Not to be ignored, Elliott slips his hand onto mine. "You'll do great."

Whether holding my hand is supposed to be a cover or not, I pull free. "Just staying warmed up."

All I have to do is perform for twenty minutes. Then I can slide into the party and mingle while hunting for our embassy leak. The event coordinator pops in to summon me for my turn, and I focus on my breathing. That may be the only thing that gets me through the performance, classical standbys I've known for a decade. That and muscle memory.

I survive a few minor fumbles, and the longest twenty minutes of my life pass in three sonatas. I'm almost to the exit when a freckly guy steps in my path. Don't recognize him. "How did you choose the Chopin?" he asks in a nasally Northeastern American accent, smiling like he thinks he's suave.

"It's a favorite," I reply. Because I memorized it as a teenager.

"Interesting choice for the human rights summit. Polish, French, et cetera."

Is he trying to impress me with his "extensive" knowledge of Romantic composers? Not working. "Glad you appreciated the selection." I make my smile as sincere as I can and edge by.

Now for the hard part. Out of one disguise and into another to infiltrate the gala crowd. The greenroom's empty. I head into its tiny bathroom to change. I'm almost ready to down mocktails with the diplomatic set when my phone vibrates. A text message from Elliott's operational phone: *Incoming*. Then the greenroom door clanks shut.

I'm not alone. And I thought I was having a tough time breathing easy earlier.

I listen at the bathroom door, but can't hear anything. I

have to check. The door handle is well greased, and I ease it open without making a sound. Before I crack the door, I kill the light in the bathroom. Kinda hard to "sneak" with that on.

My eyes adjust to the dark and I can finally see into the room—and see the man in a suit and the woman in a burqa making out fifteen feet away. My heart drops. Think I've found the embassy leak. Now if I can get past them.

I watch long enough to see this is *not* something I should be watching before I guide the door shut. Then it hits me—the guy's the same one who talked to me offstage. If I walk out now, he could recognize me and notice my hair's a different color. Do I turn the light back on and switch to my other wig (which is pretty messy now)? Not a good option.

At least I brought help. I finally reply to Elliott's text. *Problem.*

Backup?

Maybe. Greenroom.

After a wait that makes my performance time seem like a blink, Elliott responds. *Greenroom still?*

Is he in the greenroom looking for me? Maybe he scared off the lovebirds, and I've been pacing in this tiny cell for nothing. *Greenroom bathroom.*

He asks for clarification. Guess he hasn't cleared the room after all.

Burqa and American in greenroom. That should be enough details to bring in reinforcements.

Doing what? he asks.

Seriously? *Ten guesses.*

Of course Elliott doesn't know how dangerous this might be—I haven't told him the worst part. *American chatted me up offstage. Been in here so long that it'll get weird real quick if I walk out now. IF he doesn't recognize me.*

Radio silence.

I'll kill Elliott. If I get out of here.

I inch the door open again. Don't think they'll be leaving anytime soon. The longer I wait to leave, the more awkward—and memorable—it's going to get. Time go to. I send Elliott a heads-up before I move out.

Picture, he texts back.

Um, what? *Pervert*, I respond. (Not that there's anything *that* perverted going on.) (Yet?)

I roll my feet over the carpet, shielding my phone's glow so I can snap the photo Elliott requested. They're too busy to notice me, and I make it past them. The last obstacle: the short hall to the door, with the only light in the room. Where I'll be most vulnerable.

My heart beats in my throat, but I don't have time to be afraid. I move into the light and reach for the door handle. Before I can grab it, the door swings open.

Oh crap. My pulse fills my ears.

I slide back a bit, staying behind the door as long as I can. The intruder leans into the room—Elliott.

Idiot. I tug on the handle to open the door enough for us to both escape while we can. But he lets the handle slip out of his grip, and in the silence it clatters.

I shoot Elliott a death glare. His gaze moves to a spot behind me. The couple? We're so burned.

Elliott shifts back to me, and something in his eyes shifts. He closes the last step between us, slides one arm around my waist and leans in.

The panic in my system hits the ceiling and keeps climbing, but the couple behind me suddenly isn't the only threat. I have to stop him, I have to stop him—

In an instant, I'm thrown back five years, backed into a different corner, a different coworker leaning in. Only now I have the hindsight of how badly that blew up, doubling the horror of that day.

The fear of letting Elliott do this and the fear of getting

caught collide with that echo of terror from years ago. I don't have time to stop Elliott before he kisses me. All that fear freezes me until the man behind me speaks up. "Who's there?"

"Oh." Elliott looks up, over my shoulder again, slapping on a Canadian accent. "Sorry. Didn't realize this room was . . . taken."

"It is." His tone barely leaves room for an apology—and his accent's American. I can't turn around to check his ID, though. Can't risk it.

"We'll be going, then," Elliott finishes. His arm still around my waist, he pulls me out of the room, and I don't dare look back.

As soon as we're clear, I jerk away from Elliott. I'll kill him. I'll kill him. I. Will. Kill. Him.

"Got what we need?" he asks.

"Yeah."

By unspoken agreement, we head to the garage, for our car. In electric silence.

I have nothing to say. What can I say to take back what was never supposed to happen between us? To make him understand that he yanked away the one thing that made me feel safe with him?

He thinks he knows me. But if he thought I'd be okay with this, he's dead wrong.

I know what I saw when he made this decision. I'm not safe with him.

It wasn't a cover.

I'll kill him.

CHAPTER 4
DANNY

FRIDAY IS THE QUARTERLY "LUNCH & LEARN" AT WORK, where all the R&D teams troop to the Canada Aviation and Space Museum theatre and share the latest breakthroughs in our projects. Fortunately, this time I delegated the presentation, so I get to sit back and listen. The presentations are mostly interesting—I make a mental note to talk to Bombardier's engine pod testing team—and afterwards, we file out to the picnic area for the catered lunch.

I end up in line next to Ariane, a Québécoise on the Bombardier testing team. Gotta take advantage of the opportunity. *"T'es Ariane, non?"* I ask. *You're Ariane, right?*

"Oui—Danny?"

I confirm that's me and steer the conversation to the testing design, since we'll probably have to use something similar if we ever get the perfect angle of sweep to taper AeroTechCanada's wing redesign.

We haven't made it far in the conversation when my phone rings. I check who's calling. Colorado area code.

It can't be her. It can't.

Then the rest of the caller ID finally kicks in—stupid phone. It's Steve Williams, an old coworker, and the guy I emailed this morning trying to figure out a solution to the underlying problem. I apologize to Ariane and step out of line. "Hey, Steve."

"Danny, hey. How are you?"

"Not bad, not bad." I glance at the crowd and their growing roar, and pick another route: into the museum. Right away, that choice is obviously good: quiet. I flash my NRC ID at the admission desk, since we were in here five minutes ago, and the girl there waves me past. "How about you?"

"Better than I deserve. So, why are you trying to steal our IP?" he jokes.

Technically, he's right, I shouldn't have access to any of my old employer's intellectual property—but that's not what I need. Also not completely realistic. "Well, you know, since they erased all my memories from the year I worked there."

Steve laughs. "But seriously, you know I'm not supposed to say much."

"I'm not after IP."

A couple other NRC engineers wander in after me, and I forge ahead into the museum to escape their chatter. "I just remembered a story you told me, from back when you were with Martin Marietta." Yeah, he's old—Martin Marietta merged with Lockheed when I was in grade school.

"Which one was that?"

I explain how "our client" is trying to maximize fuel economy but cutting every corner and wing possible, until Steve gets what I'm going for. "Ah," he says, "the KL-127. Yeah, I don't think this'll help. We had to redesign the entire wingtip from scratch. Took us months, plus FAA approval—or whatever you've got there in Canada."

"Transport Canada." Yep. The minor changes we've been trying to make, shaving off bits of the wing, aren't nearly enough. I've been toying with a total redesign in my spare time, but I was hoping it wouldn't come to that, not if I have to get my boss Carol's approval. I'm about out of museum: I've wandered into the farthest corner, and I'm at the last display.

"I trust you're looking into material weight and strength and all that." Steve's tone indicates he's not offering advice on those things, which is fine. We can handle that.

"Yep. Well, thanks anyway."

"Sure thing. So, how's the new job?"

"Great. You miss me?" I round the last display and start back for the entrance.

"Still cry myself to sleep every night. And how's Kendra?"

A jolt strikes my system. My feet stop, and so does my heart for a long second. So long that Steve starts to backtrack. "Um . . ."

"I wouldn't know." I finally answer his question.

"Oh. You're not . . . ?"

"No."

"Sorry to hear that," Steve says.

He's sincere and everything, but I don't want to talk about the who, what, where and especially not the why. "Anyway, I'm at a work thing. Better go."

"Okay. Good luck."

"Thanks. Take care." I gawk at my phone for a minute, slowly exhaling. I hadn't thought about Kendra today until that moment. Now my brain's scrambling as fast as I can, trying to outrun the memories, and already, my chest physically hurts.

So much for having a good day.

I look up to get myself out of my thoughts and out of this museum. Staring back at me is a CF-18 Hornet—doing my best to switch to Canadian designations—and a . . . I eye the black nose cone above my head again. I don't know this plane.

Much better distraction than trying to socialize outside.

The plane's body is a high gloss white, yellowing with age.

Just after the cockpit, empty oblong engine nacelles bear the letters: RL—and that's it. The rest of the plane is missing. I pace around to the other nacelle to find the other half of the designation: 206.

Forsaking the marked carpeted path, I edge past the shiny silver F-104 Starfighter on the other side to circle around and get a better view of the back.

Not a prototype or training model. Below the nacelles, the wiring's ripped out and roughly chopped off. Red grease pencil instructions, "Cut here," along with a guideline showed where to slice up this thing, and torch marks and burns scar the jagged edges across the entire back. I can't help it; a scoff of indignation escapes. Who would do this? Why?

"Sir?"

A man's voice draws my attention away from the carnage. Guy with a name badge—museum worker.

"Can I have you step back on the path, please?"

"Sorry." I try not to act too much like a puppy with its tail between its legs as I return to the designated carpet walkway.

"You like the arrow?" he asks.

I point to the severed plane above me. "The Arrow?"

"Yes," he says slowly, like I'm not getting it. "The Avro Arrow?"

It has a name. "Sorry," I say again. "I'm not Canadian. Should I know . . . ?"

"Oh, it's not a chapter in our history books or anything—but it *was* the most advanced aircraft in the world at one time."

Even more interesting. "What happened?"

"Program was scrubbed. Politics—military-industrial complex. Or . . ." Half his mouth flips up in a grin. "Could've been the CIA pulling strings."

I look up at the nose cone again. Is he ragging on me because I'm obviously American? The "sorry" is a dead give-away—how I could tell Talia wasn't Canadian, too.

"If you're interested." The museum guide gestures at the display and the tablet in front of the steel scaffolding supporting the plane part—none of which I've noticed until now.

"Thanks."

The guide leaves me to my reading and watching. This distraction's panning out way better than I anticipated. Don't know what it is about this plane—the indignity of chopping it up, the intrigue of why, the idea that the greatest plane in the world would end up scrapped—but I'm hooked.

I don't believe in love at first sight, but I haven't fallen for something this fast since—

Does one bright, shining moment count?

I give the Arrow one last glance. No matter how the past conspires to blowtorch my future, I'm not ready to give up. As I stride out of the museum, I add two things to my to-do list:

#1. Research the Avro CF-105 Arrow.

#2. Get to know Talia Reynolds.

CHAPTER 5
TALIA

NO IDEA HOW, but I manage to not murder Elliott the next day. Instead, I sit in a booth at Hong Den Good Food and poke holes in my sweet and sour chicken balls and Elliott's plans to ID the American with the Emirati girlfriend from the greenroom last night. We're the only patrons in the restaurant, but despite the privacy, it seems like Elliott won't mention the stupid kiss. And neither will I.

We may not have found a solid plan, but we're done sitting around a Chinese place to plan our off-the-books op. When I get up to leave, Elliott grabs my tray.

I shove down the memory of someone else always insisting on taking my tray, like I was incapable. I reach for it. "I can handle my own trash."

"I know."

"Then let me." I don't back down, waiting for him to hand it over (and acknowledge my independence, thank you).

"Listen, about last night."

I fight the urge to clench my fists. Nothing he can say now

to fix it. He doesn't know—he doesn't know me. And if he did, he'd never have tried such a stupid stunt.

I lose the battle for self-control and yank my tray away from Elliott. "We don't have to say anything else."

"No, I do."

"Don't." My tense whisper cuts off the conversation, and we both freeze there for a minute. Finally, I push past him, dump my garbage and stalk out the doors.

Elliott doesn't let me escape, but honestly, he's not what I'm trying to get away from.

And his mistake isn't the one tying my stomach in knots.

The mistake was mine. A year ago, when I met Elliott and thought we could work together. That he'd be different. That he'd understand.

Elliott catches my arm at my car door, and I wheel on him, ready to attack.

His clear blue eyes full of surprise and hurt and confusion stop me. If you can say one thing for Elliott, it's that he's never serious. But now he's close: he doesn't understand why I'm upset.

How could he? I suck in a breath and look anywhere but at him. He deserves at least half an explanation, and I can give him that much as long as I don't have to look at him. As long as I don't have to remember. "Um, when I EODed—" Agency slang for started working for the CIA—"I worked with this guy. And one day in his office, I got myself into a stupid situation, where the only thing that made sense was for us to kiss."

I push down the memories, fear echoing through my heart from last night and that day at Langley, being cornered in that office, carrying the flirting too far.

The memories fight back, surging against the firewall. I go for the shortest route. "It didn't end well, and . . . it got so bad I almost had to quit."

Elliott's quiet a minute. "I'm sorry."

Not as sorry as me. I conclude with the executive summary of the top 100 reasons Elliott's wrong for me. "I don't date people at work."

"That's not all of it."

Pfft. Not even half. I don't need to wonder how Elliott would react to the parts of the real me my persistent paranoia is supposed to protect. Not just my home, but my*self*—my family, my secrets. Someone whose favorite response to everything is flirting? I know he's *capable* of deeper thought and emotion, but when I need him to be serious, he refuses.

I trust him with my life, but only with protecting it. Not with its details.

"Get us in with the ambassador," I say, focusing on the case objective. That's all we need. All Elliott can handle.

He thinks he knows me. He's so wrong.

Maybe no one really knows me anymore.

After working with Elliott on his case through lunchtime Saturday, I have to run by Terfort & Sutter to catch up on work (law internship, not CIA). I'm almost done being the human equivalent of Quicklaw (the search engine totally let me down on finding precedents for this privacy tort) when my phone rings. Arjay calling.

We're friends and everything, but my schedule doesn't allow a whole lot of time for hanging out. Or chatting on the phone. Not something we've made a habit of. So instantly, my instincts are waving yellow CAUTION flags. "Hello?" I answer.

Arjay launches a high-speed freight train of Urdu.

"Wait, wait—" I blink to clear my mind and push away from my desk, trying to switch into my fourth language. "*Kia?*"

He repeats himself more slowly, and the words fall into place in my brain. Arjay's at a church activity—and Danny asked him about me. My heart speeds up to a swift samba rhythm.

But I can keep my head. "So you walked away and made a phone call? Obvious much?"

"I said my mother was calling." Arjay sticks to Urdu better than I do, which works perfectly for his on-the-fly cover for this phone call, since he actually does speak Urdu with his parents. "How fast can you get here? Strathcona Park?"

I don't know, so I consult the Internet. I worked through lunch, but which do I want more—food or the chance to talk to Danny? I can't lose my mind over a cute (funny, nice, gorgeous) guy.

But if I go and he looks at me with those warm brown eyes, I can pretend for a few minutes that I'm not completely alone.

Yep, Danny beats food. (Saying a lot.) *"Das minat."* It's not really ten minutes away, but I give myself extra time to make sure I haven't picked up any surveillance on the way there.

Arjay's the first person to meet me at the park, grinning like he's the cat and I'm the canary. I'm regretting responding to his teasing at church Sunday. "Over there. So he isn't into Sassy Beth?"

"Guess not." She isn't hovering around him like usual. Good. Everyone else loves her, so it's been a foregone conclusion that Miss Most Sought After would become Mrs. Fluker in short order. But I've spent enough time around her to set off my possibly oversensitive narcissist-o-meter. Arjay leads me to the knot of familiar faces eating in the shade near a picnic table. The closer we get, the higher my defenses rise. Even with Arjay, I have to be careful. More than careful. No talking about work. No talking about cases. And absolutely no talking about my life.

I fold my arms for that one last barrier and come to stand a few feet behind Danny, who's talking to a guy named Campbell (well, he's named Jonathan, but we all call him by his last name). Reason #56 Danny's our most eligible bachelor: he's so cool, the other guys forget to be jealous of the attention he gets.

Sassy Beth claps. "Okay, we've got eighteen. I'm assigning you to teams and positions. No trading!"

Oh. Great. I scan my memory for what sport we're playing, if I can remember the announcements from church. The mesh bag of mitts, bats and balls gives it away. Softball.

Danny turns back and finds me lurking there. (Subtlety, the strength of the spy.) He shoots me a quick grin. "Hey."

"Hi." I toss a pointed look at the game equipment. "Play much softball?"

"Nope. You?"

"Not really. I'm here for the food. I'm starving, and I haven't gotten to the grocery store yet today." That sliver of the truth slices between my ribs, though it's miles away from dangerous.

Danny gestures at the table, offering to get me a plate (reason #4), but first Sassy Beth and a harangued Campbell appear in front of us. "Talia, batting team. Danny, infield."

Joy, joy, joy. Campbell gives Danny a glove and a grimace.

Sassy Beth isn't done. She holds out a cardboard box. "Turn in your cell phones."

I can't stop a laugh. She has *no* idea what's on my phone (mostly my coworkers' phone numbers and CIA special apps). Not letting it off my person.

Beth flinches. She's not used to people failing to fall under her spell. "C'mon, I know you have it. Don't want the entire team browsing Facebook instead of playing and having fun."

I sidestep the Facebook issue. "Couldn't ask you to assume full liability for my phone and any damage that might occur while it's in your possession, so I'll just keep it." I shoot her an I'm-sure-you-understand smile.

Beth opens and closes her mouth a minute, then shoves the box in Danny's direction. Geez. She's couching it nicely, but pushing us like this could cost her Canadian Card.

"Yeah, same," he says with a sorry-I'm-not-sorry shrug.

"Ugh." A scowl flashes across Beth's face. At least one of us just got on her bad side.

"That was awesome," Danny murmurs as soon as Beth's out of earshot. (Reason #78.)

Effective, yes, but awesome? Obviously not winning me any friends. "That's why people hate lawyers."

"I'm a fan right now." In some imperceptible way, Danny shifts closer to me.

Maybe it's winning me one friend. But I'm not here for that. Right?

Yeah. Right.

Beth roars, "Okay, play ball!" from directly behind us. (Where did she come from?)

Yeeesh. Danny and I exchange an expression like we'd both rather stay here, but I march off to join my team. Not exactly surprised Beth assigned me and Danny to different teams. Ten guesses who's team Danny's on.

Hers? Bingo. She wouldn't put them side-by-side in the batting lineup and force the teams to sit in order—but Beth does assign him first base while she plays second like her life depends on every pitch.

Reason #11: he sees through Sassy's subtle scheming. Reason #82: he still manages to be nice to her without leading her on.

At the top of the second inning, we share an amused look in passing. "Beth got you to first base, eh?" I tease him.

Danny laughs (slightly uncomfortably). "No, but if she could walk me, I think she might."

We both grin, and my silly heart soars like a pop fly.

That's when it hits me: if I let this go on, I stand to lose a whole lot more than a softball game.

CHAPTER 6
DANNY

I MANAGE NOT TO EMBARRASS MYSELF through the first inning, and it's not my fault Arjay made it to first. Now the real pressure's on: Talia steps up to bat. Another piece to the puzzle: what does "not really" playing softball mean?

The answer seems apparent fast. Talia pops AB Beth's first pitch up behind home plate. She winces and ducks away, though she's well clear of the drop zone. Joel at catcher doesn't bother running for the ball.

"Strike one!" Apparently Sassy Beth's both second base and the umpire now.

"Foul!" Joel shouts back. He tosses the ball to AB Beth.

"Softball rules," Sassy Beth screeches. "Fouls count as strikes!"

That tone must wear on everyone's nerves, but I doubt many other people are fighting down revulsion and panic because of the memories it brings back.

AB Beth throws two balls and then a good strike. "Strike two!" Sassy Beth looks back at the outfielders. "Easy out! Bring it in."

The outfielders reluctantly trudge forward ten feet.

Talia moves away from the plate. "That the best you can do?"

"Swing, batter, batter," I call, totally devoid of enthusiasm.

Her lips twist, but she's fighting a smile in her eyes. She steps to the plate, takes a serious stance and nods to AB Beth. Beth lobs her best pitch today. Talia swings hard—and *PING*.

The ball sails way, way out into left field. Um, whoa. Jenny jogs after the ball.

And Talia's still at home, watching in stunned silence.

"Run, Talia!" I beckon for her to get moving.

She drops the bat and takes off for me, running a little faster than Jenny. I can't help myself again: I hold out a hand as she runs by, and she slaps my palm. By the time Jenny's got the ball, Talia's rounding second.

Then they both hit the accelerator. Jenny stops and fires the ball to Joel at third—the girl can throw.

"No!" Sassy Beth shouts. "Home!"

Joel catches the ball a couple yards from base and goes for the double play, swiping at Talia with his mitt. She drops to one hip, out of range of Joel's tag, and slides the last feet to the base.

Joel pivots to throw to Campbell, waiting by home, but it's too late. Arjay crosses the plate. He and Talia hoot in celebration.

"Batter up!" Sassy Beth tries to keep the game moving over Talia's team's noise.

Talia doesn't make it home after the next batter strikes out now that Jenny's pitching, and the last guy pops up a fly ball that Sassy Beth catches. She hasn't noticed everyone else would rather talk than play by now. At the inning switch, Talia marches off the field.

"Where are you going?" Beth shouts.

"To eat." Talia has the same smile from earlier, polite to the point of almost condescending. "I'm partial to not dying."

Talia passes me, then she calls my name. I turn around.

"Thanks. I always perform better under pressure."

I swear she winks before she heads for the food again. I'm done with softball, and I don't care how obvious this is. I'm following.

"Danny, where are *you* going?" Beth hollers.

I look back to repeat Talia's excuse, but keep moving in her direction. "To eat."

"You ate before we started."

She's watching me. That's cool. Not. "I'm a guy. Gotta eat every twenty minutes."

Before I turn around, I see a couple other people coming this way, too. Didn't mean to lead a mutiny against Sassy Beth.

Oh well. By the time I catch up to Talia, she's already tearing into a bag of tortilla chips. I gesture at the three open bags on the table.

She dismisses them. "They'll be stale, sitting out this long." Apparently that rule goes for everything, because she also twists the lid off a new jar of salsa instead of using the open one. She dumps half the bag of chips and plenty of salsa onto her paper plate, then rips into a new package of chocolate chip cookies.

I can't stand girls who don't eat.

"You don't really play, huh?" I ask.

"Nope. Didn't ask if I can hit the ball." Her shields are down, and I get another glimpse of the real Talia.

Someone I want to get to know. Know what's a good way to get to know someone? A date.

Before I can work up to that, her phone rings. She looks at the full table, then around. Nowhere to put her plate.

"Here." I take it. She smile, another real Talia smile, then pulls out her phone. She sees the screen, and her whole countenance changes. Not shielded. Serious. She angles away, but I can still hear her side of the conversation. "Hi. . . . Yeah? . . . Now? Yep, ten minutes."

Talia glances back at me and mouths, "Work," then motions toward the parking lot.

She's leaving.

I nod, like I'm okay with ending this so soon. She gestures to the plate I'm holding for her, then motions for me to take it.

Hooray. Consolation corn chips.

I'm not quite obvious enough to watch her leave. I turn to the group gathering around the food table.

"Guess you *were* hungry," Sassy Beth mutters, eyeballing my plate.

I shrug and don't bother correcting her. "A guy's gotta eat."

She maneuvers closer, her eyes saying, *Isn't this the perfect coincidence?* "I love to cook."

Another warning light flashes in my mind: she'll make herself into whatever she thinks I want. Like she doesn't have a personality of her own, doing whatever it takes to keep me around.

Can I get away fast enough?

Before I literally *run* from her, I stop myself. Desperation isn't necessarily a sign of psychopathy. It's actually sad, and I should be nice to her. So that's what I do. "That's cool."

"I could make you dinner some time."

"Oh." I hunt for a way to make this rejection nice. Or an exit strategy.

Campbell bounces over just in time. "Hey! Danny!"

"We need to dial down your caffeine drip, dude." I take the opportunity to extricate myself from Beth's grasp and walk away with Campbell.

"Do you play Xbox?" he asks.

"Used to, before mine broke." No mentioning who did that. But it definitely wasn't me.

"Joel and I need someone else to play. Want to jump in?"

"Sure—I'm busy next week, but if you want to bring yours over after that, I've got a huge TV."

He beams like someone in a manic cycle. "Sounds like fun!"

He starts away, but I speak up first. "Hey, thanks for . . ." I jerk my chin over my shoulder in Sassy Beth's direction.

Campbell shakes his head, mystified.

"Never mind." Lucky timing then.

The activity devolves into sitting in the shade chatting. Joel breaks out a guitar, so girls are hanging on him for a change.

Arjay strolls over to plop down by me. "You should ask her out."

I raise an eyebrow. If anyone else came to talk to me about my love life, they'd probably mean Sassy Beth, but considering I barely finished his friend's food, I don't think I have to ask who Arjay's talking about.

"Seriously. Here." He fishes a piece of paper and a pen out of his pocket and scribbles something. He offers the paper to me. "Her number's wrong in the ward directory. You should text her."

That would be weird. I accept the paper, a phone number. My mind takes off at Concorde speed. Is he telling me this because he thinks I'm cool, or because Talia and I are both old— or because Talia said something to him?

Too much to hope for the last one?

Maybe it's too much to hope at all. Yeah, she's got the whole international woman of mystery, puzzle I need to solve, yet totally out of my league appeal. But what will I do if it turns out I like her even more than I already do?

There's obviously more to her than what she shares willingly, but I have no idea whether that's caution because she's reserved, or she's crazy.

I'm supposed to be starting over—but not starting the same ordeal over.

CHAPTER 7
TALIA

I AM SO NOT HAPPY to be sitting in this van again. It's not cabin fever or awkwardness at being in close quarters with Elliott. (Hint: it's because he dragged me away from Danny. And my dinner. I'm doubly grumpy.) We don't even have anything to watch, strategically parked halfway between our two potential leaks' houses. Just waiting on Langley to tell us which one's guilty, but that's not why tension's tightening along my vertebrae.

"So," Elliott starts, "who's this guy?" His cajoling makes it clear he doesn't mean our target.

Oh, great. "A guy."

"A guy that's got you blushing after one conversation."

And my face gets warm. "Two."

Elliott grins. "Come on, give me something to work with."

"Yeah, that's a big no." My tone kills the conversation, a little more heavy-handed than I really mean to be.

Okay, maybe the whole close-quarters-with-Elliott thing's grating on me more than I want to admit. I've made it through two days with him, but stilted conversation and focusing on work won't get us through a couple hours in a van, let alone the rest of our week. Our careers.

Elliott is my closest friend—was. Now it'll never be the same. And for what?

I have to know.

"Why?" My voice scythes through the quiet.

"Why what?" Elliott keeps his tone light, but he'd have to be brain-dead to not understand.

I'm not giving up that easily. "Why'd you do it? The truth."

He looks into my eyes, and I backpedal. I shouldn't have asked. I shouldn't care. I should pretend none of it happened. My barricades fly up, and suddenly I realize exactly why I hate what Elliott did.

Because it means he doesn't know me like I thought he did. It means I'm alone.

"It was nothing," he says at last. "Part of the cover."

I can't turn away. I don't dare. Because even in the dim streetlight, I can see he's lying.

He hides the lie with that don't-you-love-me? grin. "Don't tell me you're developing a crush on me."

"When are you going to get over yourself?"

"But there's so much to love."

The tension twisting along my spine begins to dissipate. He's flirting, but the joking gleam in his gaze says this is his usual over-the-top silliness. I don't know exactly what he was lying about, but we'll make it through . . . whatever this was.

Elliott leans across his armrest, turning more teasing. "Seriously, what's his name?"

I make a sound between a sigh and a groan. Anything to get him off my case. "Danny, okay?"

"Told you you'd have to tell me. Sounds like a geek."

I roll my eyes. "Shut up," I say, teasing him right back.

"How'd you meet him?" Elliott presses. "Work?"

"Church."

"And you're sure he's not a geek?"

I shove his shoulder, and he shifts back into the driver's seat. "Shut up," I repeat.

"Come on, throw me a bone here. Your eyes locked across the crowded chapel? Your hands brushed when he passed you the plate?"

"We don't have collection plates." Should've known better than to even give up a first name.

After a minute of silence, Elliott grumbles again. "Seriously? That's all you're going to tell me?"

What does he want to know? I focus on our first conversation. "I was sitting in the foyer during church, and he came out and talked to me."

"Coincidence? I think not." He waggles his eyebrows.

"I think *so*. He couldn't have seen me from the chapel."

My phone chimes, saving me from the rest of Elliott's interrogation. I check my cell: a text message. From Langley. We've got our leak. "Voiceprint match. Marcus Lee."

Elliott starts the van, and we head out to get the last evidence to nab our leak.

We're halfway there when my phone dings with a new email. I'm so excited to be tying up this case that I can't conjure up a specter of worry about any of my other projects. Until I see the subject line: *FEATHERSTONE analysis.*

Our ballroom dancing spymaster. I cast a clandestine glance Elliott's way. Not sure I'm ready to go back undercover as his dance partner. We might've made it through this time, but what would another hundred hours of one-on-one practice do?

I'll tell him Monday. I slide the phone back in my pocket. Elliott navigates into a quiet neighborhood. We cruise past our target's brick house and park down the block. It's getting dark, and his car's out front. After a few minutes of silent surveillance from the back of our van, Elliott hops on the phone to line up his Arabic translator for the last evidence to implicate Lee. (She owes Elliott a favor. I bet they all do.)

Elliott finally gets her on the line and directs me to cue up the latest recording on the laptop. I help him, then scoot out of the way so he can get at the computer. But as I move, I spot it—Lee's porch light is on now.

Is he going somewhere?

Yep. Leaving right now. I don't know if he suspects anything, but if he slips away now, he could keep passing along diplomatic intelligence. (Again, Not. Okay.) We've got to stop him.

I grab an earpiece, a red wig (pays to be prepared) and my leather jacket, and run out the van's back doors. If Lee notices me, we're out of luck, so I duck behind the van to slip into the wig before I cross the street.

Lee's concentrating too hard on sorting through his key-chain to see my approach. I come even with him as he opens his car door. "Oh, hey!" I exclaim.

He looks up and smiles, rearranging his freckles. "Hi. Remind me how we know one another?"

"I played Chopin, and you admired it." I'm a little too far away to shake hands. "Alaine Marchant. Just moved in around the corner, down the street about three blocks." I point in that direction.

"Oh, that's great. I'm Marcus Lee."

In case I had any doubt, identity confirmed.

"So, how are you liking the neighborhood?"

Better get my flirt on. "Kind of quiet, but getting better all the time."

He laughs, giving that line way more credit than it deserves.

Back to business with a natural getting-to-know-you question, just like with Danny. "What do you do for a living?" I ask.

"I work for the American Embassy." Marcus makes it sound as though he's a lot more than a secretary, propping his elbow on his car roof like he owns the entire diplomatic corps. (Wonder if he knows Galina.)

I can play this game. I make a little noise like *I'm oh so impressed tell me more about that* (sad how often this works), and edge closer. "That sounds major league."

Marcus shrugs one shoulder, pretending he's not all that important. Even he isn't buying his modest act.

An ego this size always needs more to eat, so I feed it. "Do you know the ambassador?" I ask, like I've heard he's the Wonderful Wizard of US.

"I do, actually." The smug grin returns. Does he think that works? "Would you like to meet him?"

I kick up the flirting another notch. "I bet you say that to all the girls."

"Just the really cute ones."

"Oh yeah?" I've reeled him in. Elliott should have his evidence translated by now. Time to drop the hammer, maybe startle him into an admission. "Like Leyla al-Fulan?"

Marcus's smirk falls faster than a tech stock in a bust, and he turns pale. "Who?"

I move up his driveway two more steps. "You know, the Emirati Deputy Ambassador's wife. Did you introduce her to Ambassador Rhodes?"

"Who are you?" The horror dawns in his voice.

"Alaine Marchant." My tone reminds him he has no reason to freak out. "The pianist from the reception? Where you both were?"

"But—how—" Marcus raises his hands in defense, not surrender. I halt, but it's not enough for him. He backpedals into his car door. "You don't—you can't—"

"Oh?" I pull out my phone and tap through the menus until I pull up a recording Elliott took of him and his Emirati girlfriend talking a couple hours ago. (Lucky he sent me this.)

"You need to be more careful," Leyla says softly.

"And me getting caught carrying your phone around is careful?" His New England accent rings through his sarcasm.

Marcus stands there, every muscle tightening with tension.

I put away my phone. Elliott still hasn't come through on the evidence and Marcus clearly isn't confessing. Marcus isn't the only one tensing up. I need to work him harder. "I know how these things go. Maybe it was an accident."

"What do you mean?"

"It starts off so innocent. Smiles at those functions. Small talk by the bar. You didn't mean to cross any lines."

"I have no idea what you're talking about," Marcus insists. "You need to go."

I've got to get him talking. "Crossing one line made it easier to cross another, huh? And you had to help Leyla, help her people."

He moves toward me, but I stand my ground and he stops. "You don't know anything."

"Why shouldn't the Emiratis be allowed the same rights as other countries? And of course, it only makes sense for you to help a friend."

Finally, Elliott comes through: "T," he says over my earpiece. "Hook him."

Trying to. Marcus advances toward me again. "I couldn't care less about landing rights."

A flash of fear bursts in my brain, and this time I do fall back. "Then what do you care about? Why are you selling out your ambassador?"

"*My* ambassador? He's my *boss*. He's a career diplomat. The Emiratis needed my help. They needed me."

I shake my head pityingly. "Your country needed you."

"Okay, we got him," Elliott says. "Now get out of there."

Perfect timing. I turn and stroll away from Marcus.

"When you're clear," Elliott tells me, "get out of sight." I pass the hedges and he signals that's good enough. I can go back to the van, and I do, taking out my earpiece.

I'm in the middle of the street when it registers: that's not a normal engine noise. I jerk around to the sound—Marcus's little red car, coming straight for me.

My heart barely has time to stop before the impact. But it's not two tons of metal colliding with me: it's Elliott.

Everything happens at once. We're flying through the air and hitting the ground and rolling and the headlights pass all at the same time. Then time catches up to us, lying on the cement, clinging to one another—and the Earth pauses with Elliott an inch from my face.

I'm still not over the fear from the car, but am I about to get another reason to be afraid?

Elliott doesn't make a move.

"You okay?" I ask.

"Yeah." He lets me go and helps me up. "Let's get out of here."

Definitely. I recover my breath after that double scare. Maybe I don't have anything to worry about with dancing.

Maybe.

There's one welcome distraction at church the next day. I drift to a stop in the foyer after our meetings, casually observing the giggling gaggle of girls surrounding Danny, his smile hiding an edge of discomfort.

I'm used to being a woman on a mission, driven toward my objective at all costs—just not at church. Especially not when that mission's talking to a cute guy (who isn't a client or target).

However, I'm also not desperate enough to tackle him

between meetings. Reason #2 why Danny's the most eligible bachelor in the congregation over twenty-five: he's new. Everyone's still getting to know him, even the girls in the younger age bracket. Short of throwing elbows, I don't have a chance, even after church, unless I want to loiter in the foyer for a suspicious amount of time.

"Scoping out the goods?" Arjay ambles up to where I stand by the doors, apparently not being all that discreet.

"Gotta get home," I murmur. "I need to eat."

He offers a sympathetic frown, because nearly everyone here has skipped the last two meals (monthly fast). But I don't just mean, "I'm hungry." Between catching up on work and helping Elliott, I skipped two meals before that, too, so I'm on the shaky-knees, massive-headache, when-did-the-sun-get-this-bright end of the spectrum.

"There's a break-the-fast." Arjay eye-points past Danny and the flirting girls to the gym where a diligent few are setting up round tables and folding chairs for the monthly potluck—all that unprotected, unmonitored, ripe-for-tampering food.

I glance at Danny, who seems almost as uncomfortable as I feel. I should rescue him. I probably could, if my blood sugar weren't somewhere south of the basement. (Then again, some of those girls are vultures, so I dunno.) "You go ahead," I tell Arjay. "I'll be there in a minute."

"Ask him out. Get it over with."

I shoot Arjay a spearing look. "I think you're more into this than we are."

"Come on. You're both old and still single. You obviously need the help."

I groan. What I need most is food. I back up for the doors. Before I reach them, my phone buzzes in my purse. I check who's calling: my mother.

Our last conversation was almost okay, but I don't have the strength to deal with her now. I tap the icon to ignore her.

"Talia?" comes a voice next to me.

I freeze on instinct, though I have nothing to be afraid of here. I turn to the guy speaking to me. Average height, average brownish-blondish hair, higher than average energy, even while fasting: Campbell. He and Joel, the blond dude standing two feet to his right, are my "home teachers," assigned to visit with me every month and make sure I'm doing okay. (Everyone at church has these assignments. In fact, AB Beth is also assigned to me.)

"Got a minute?" he asks.

My stomach tightens, reminding me how hungry I am. (Not to mention that it's still home to more than my share of hummingbirds at the prospect of seeing Danny, and extra anxiety at having to talk to my mom. It's a wonder my stomach feels empty.) I want to get out of here and eat, but Joel and Campbell will be after me to meet all month if we don't get it over with.

"Sure," I force myself to say. At least I've convinced them they should never try to visit me at my apartment. Nobody at church has my address. Yet another thing I have to hide. I follow Joel and Campbell through the chapel to the quieter foyer on the other side of the building. I juggle the small talk and awkwardly-wedged-in-the-conversation spiritual thought, ignoring the persistent buzzing from my bag. My mother, working herself into a fit because I won't answer. Not because she's worried something might've happened to me—I'm legally allowed to tell her what I do for a living, but I'd have to be seven shades of stupid to trust her with that information.

Nope, if Mom's upset, it's more likely because I'm not acting as her adoring, on-demand audience. I'm desperately, deeply torn: draw out the conversation with Joel and Campbell to leave my mother hanging that much longer or shut them down to tend to her before they get suspicious?

Option B, keeping the family secret, always, always wins. I

invite Joel to pray to end our little meeting. They head to the gym to descend upon the potluck buffet like locusts with passable table manners. Once they're through the doors, I turn on my heel for the parking lot. I've got my phone out before I even reach my car, but I wait until I plop into the seat, my window open, to read the messages.

i ned to talk 2 u, says the first text. But what she means is she needs me to pay attention to her. Ignoring the fact she has the typing skills of a two-year-old, I scroll through the rest of her messages to assess the damage.

i miss u. Possible, but I'll believe that when I see it.

why arent u answering? Yes, heaven forbid I do anything but wait for her next message.

The time stamp shows three minutes before her next text. *why cant u just talk 2 me? ur being realy ungrateful.* (Which isn't true. I'm grateful she didn't type "gr8ful," for example.)

i no we used to have problems, but i dont no why we dont talk. dont u love me any more?

Does she really want to talk? Including listening? I doubt it, but I can't stop the lift of hope in my heart. Before I gather my dwindling strength to dial her, another message comes in: *troy came to visit but ur allways 2 busy.*

Ooh, comparing me to my brothers already. Maybe it's not such a great time to call. We're barely skirting the edges of her brand of crazy, and I can already tell I'm better off in my usual role of invisible kid.

Then my phone rings. No need to check who's calling, but I answer because it's obviously the only way to end this. "Hi, Mom." I smooth any trace of annoyance out of my voice.

"Hi?" replies someone who's obviously a guy.

Oh, man, what did I do? I check my phone display—Arjay. "Sorry, what's up?"

"Thought you'd like to know *someone* here is scanning the crowd. And there's lots of food that you won't have to make yourself."

I glance in the rearview at the building behind me. I know almost nothing about Danny except he seems like a really good guy (a really attractive, really good guy). For all I know, walking in there would be pointless.

"I'll get you desserts," Arjay offers. Like he knows exactly how to sweeten the deal (literally). Plus what he doesn't know: the other reason I didn't eat dinner last night is because I don't *have* any food at home, and I didn't have enough energy in the post-op-and-brush-with-death adrenaline crash to get something.

Before I can answer, a car door slams behind me. I whirl around and lean out my window. Two rows away, Sassy Beth hoists her glass pan of brownies higher, and her roommate, BC Beth, pulls out a tray of Nanaimo bars. (I resist the urge to tackle her and steal them.)

"Is my lipstick okay?" Sassy asks BC.

"Yep." BC Beth winks. "Danny won't be able to resist."

"He'd better not."

I can't see her expression, but there's man-killing in her tone. They don't notice me as they walk back in the building.

"Talia?" Arjay pipes up in my ear.

"Okay, I'm coming."

I can practically hear his triumphant smile. "I knew it. You owe me."

"Yeah, yeah, I'll make it up to you. How about a nice mug?"

"That says 'World's Greatest Wingman'?"

"Greatest, most obvious, something along those lines."

He snorts. "Just get in here before the Beths get to him."

Believe me, I'll try.

CHAPTER 8
DANNY

AM I NOT SO SUBTLY SCANNING the break-the-fast crowd for Talia? Yep. I wanted to get to her after church, but by the time I spotted her, hugging herself like somebody's out to get her, Joel and Campbell had marched Talia off. She looked like she was facing a firing squad instead of her home teachers.

At this point, my observation efforts are getting ridiculous, but I've spent the last twenty-four hours working up the courage to ask her out. Like her best friend told me to.

Unless this is a really, really stupid idea.

Twenty minutes into the meal, Joel and Campbell walk in. They're done meeting with Talia. So where is she?

The taco salad's mostly demolished, though the dessert table is still doing swift business, freshly restocked by the Beths. Do girls think that's the only way to get a date?

I don't care if Talia can't boil water. I'm going to figure her out.

As if thinking about her is a telepathic beacon, Arjay carries his second plate to the seat next to me. "Asked her out yet?"

I cast an eye at the four other people at the table, including Sassy Beth, though I'm not sure I care if she hears. On cue, Beth hops up to toss her barely touched plate of less taco, more salad. Footnote: I really don't get girls.

I finally answer Arjay. "She's in stealth mode."

"She's quiet."

That isn't it. Even Arjay hasn't figured her out: this level of avoidance goes deeper than being quiet, and it doesn't explain the heat shields and protective postures.

Arjay finishes his tortilla chips and heads out. Campbell and Joel take the other two seats at the table, and we pass the time talking. I manage to not ask them if Talia mentioned me, where she went, what she likes to do on weekends, or any of the other questions circling my thoughts.

Arjay re-joins the table after a minute, carrying a plate loaded with eight of BC Beth's Nanaimo bars and three of AB Beth's butter tarts.

He's got good taste. Apparently coupled with a strong desire to develop type 2 diabetes.

Or maybe not that strong of a desire. He doesn't touch his food, and not because we're too busy talking. Not stopping Joel and Campbell on their second helping of taco salad.

I turn back to check on Arjay and find Talia sitting next to me in his place.

And I jump. Because I'm cool like that.

She frowns. "Sorry to scare you."

"No, you didn't—I just—you're good at sneaking up on people."

Her frown becomes a smile tugging at the corners of her mouth. "Lawyer trick. Only way we can make friends."

"Not everyone—"

Before I can reassure her I don't hate all lawyers, someone throws an arm around my shoulders—and hers. Arjay leans between us. "'Friends'? You should add him on Facebook."

"I'm not on Facebook," I say at the same time Talia says, "I don't do Facebook." We both catch what the other's saying and trade a look like we're second-graders sharing a secret.

"You're not on Facebook?" Campbell interrupts. "How is that possible?"

"Believe it or not, there's an entire world out there, outside of the Internet," I joke, sweeping a hand in front of me. "I call it 'The World.'"

"We could show you," Talia offers. "But you'd have to step away from the computer."

Campbell snorts good-naturedly. "In that case, no thanks."

Talia turns to me. "For the best. He probably can't process anything without sharing it online first."

"That's the hardest part of quitting. Now I don't know what to do with every inane thought that crosses my mind." I sigh like this weight is too much to bear. "Will you please look at my food?" I ask Talia, gesturing at my paper plate.

"Like." She gives it a thumbs up, though it's empty.

"The other day, I saw this picture of a kitten that was so! Cute! I almost died because I couldn't share it." I'm making fun of Campbell, but somehow I end up telling that entire joke to Talia, who fights back a laugh.

"Kittens, huh?"

"What can I say? I'm powerless against the cute."

"I have an idea," Arjay interrupts, leaning between us again. "Send each other your cute kittens."

"And spare the rest of us," Campbell mutters.

"Good idea." Talia's not so much agreeing as shutting down the subject. Her gaze falls to the table, then her eyes widen at the sight of the plate at her place. "Wow."

Let's see. Arjay came to talk about asking Talia out, disappeared for a minute, then stocked a plate which he gave to her when she showed up.

Yep, Arjay's definitely coming in handy.

Talia stares at her plate, biting her lip.

"What?" Arjay asks. "Better offer waiting at home?"

Yesterday she said she hadn't gotten to the store yet. I'd share my pantry—but that's weird. She's gone shopping in the meantime, right?

Finally, her shoulders drop like she's giving into something, and she picks up the first Nanaimo bar. Silence falls over the table as Talia proceeds to eat every single thing Arjay got for her. Half a pan of Nanaimo bars and three mini butter tarts, gone in less than three minutes.

I said I like a girl who'll eat, right?

Talia polishes off the last bite and settles back in her chair with an expression of satisfaction.

"Don't go into insulin shock," I say.

Lame.

She shakes her head. "If I were diabetic, I'd probably be dead. I haven't eaten since breakfast yesterday."

No wonder. Now I feel bad for taking her food at the park.

Talia smiles at me. And I realize we're the last people at the table.

Time to ask her out.

Unless—unless that would be the worst idea ever.

"Hey, Danny?" Sassy Beth calls. She almost seems sorry for interrupting my moves on another girl. "Can we get your help with chairs?"

"Sure," I say. Not sure whether I just dodged a blow or took one, but I start folding the metal chairs at our table. Talia hops up to toss her plate and help with cleanup, too, folding chairs at the next table. On my second glance back at her, our gazes cross paths and she casts me an expression of *look what we got roped into*. Heat shields down.

I'm being ridiculous. I like her. Definitely asking her out.

Before I finish at my table and move to help her, Beth intercepts me. "You know, I can't help thinking that we've just been dancing around one another since our party."

"Oh. Yeah." Tricking me into a triple date doesn't count as "our" party. I keep my tone noncommittal, searching for the best way to sidestep what's coming.

Maybe it was an oversight, but dating via trickery is yet another warning light for Sassy Beth. Being this close to her is triggering that old panic, even if she's secretly desperate, not manipulative and mentally ill.

And she has something else to say. Gotta get away. Finally my escape passes in front of me—Campbell, again. I grab him by the shoulders. "Hey, man, help me get this table?"

Campbell agrees, and in seconds, I have a solid shield between me and Beth.

"So," Campbell murmurs as we roll the table to the storage rack. "Are you *not* dating Sassy Beth?"

I sigh. "No—but I'm not sure she knows that."

"Have you tried, 'It's not me, it's you'?"

Sure, now he gets it. "Yeah, that'd go over well."

"How about, 'Actually, I'm interested in Talia. What do you know about her?'"

So I'm not subtle at all, though I hardly need Campbell announcing it. I shoot him a warning glare. But beyond him, I don't see Talia putting up chairs anymore.

She's way too good at that disappearing thing. Campbell and I head back to tackle the next table. As soon as we've got the legs folded, Arjay reappears.

Which one of them taught the other this materializing-out-of-thin-air routine?

He doesn't say anything, just nods at the nearest corner. The doors? Worth a look. I stack the table on the storage rack and head for the doors, narrowly missing an incoming Beth.

Yep. Subtle.

In the hall, away from the bustle of clean up, it's almost

creepy quiet. After half a second, I hear her voice. "I got the email last night, but I figured it'd wait until Monday."

On the phone?

My well-trained brain says I should give her privacy, but she rounds the corner before I can retreat. I signal that I'm backing off.

"We'll hammer it out tomorrow. Gotta go," she tells the phone and clicks the icon before the caller protests. "Hey," she says to me.

"Hi. Feeling better?"

"Eh." She waves a so-so hand. Shields nowhere in sight.

Suddenly I want to ask dozens of questions—about her life and her family and just *her*—but only one seems right. This is sending a huge, HUGE message if she saw me dodge Beth. And I don't care.

Is this a good thing or a bad thing?

If I don't ask, I'll never know. "Would you like to go out Saturday?"

Blink-tilt-recalculating-smile. Real Talia smile. "Yeah. That sounds like fun."

Didn't say what we'd do. I don't even know.

"Let me get your number." She holds up the phone she was just using. "In case something comes up."

"Here." I hand over my cell. "Wouldn't want to accept full liability for your phone."

She shoots me a fake glare. "Ha."

"You work Saturdays?"

She types in her number and mutters, "I work anytime they call, day or night."

Sounds . . . fun. Dedicated, at least. I give her phone a ring and hang up so she'll have my number too. Now texting wouldn't be weird. Mostly. "Anything you'd like to do in particular?"

"You did the asking," she teases. "You'd better be prepared

to do the planning."

"I will," I reassure her. "Just making sure we don't end up doing something you hate."

"I'm not worried."

"Man, Talia, you—" Arjay stops abruptly when we both turn to him, standing in the door to the gym. "Oh, sorry."

"That's okay," Talia says. Though it's not. She points at the exit, then presses two fingertips to her temple. "Better get home. Need some painkillers."

"Hooray, free healthcare," I try a lame joke.

She snaps her fingers as if to say *aw, shucks*. "Still have to pay for OTC drugs." She looks at me a minute longer, a smile instead of shields in her eyes. "See you Saturday."

"See you." I watch her the whole way out. Luckily Arjay retreated so I'm alone for my silent celebration.

I have a date. With Talia.

I'm still beaming when I reach the gym again, and I'm feeling so good I don't even try to escape Beth. Smiling. "You know, it's so nice of you to reach out to Talia, but just a heads-up: it's probably a lost cause."

Yeah, right, I buy that. "Oh?"

"I mean, she's got Arjay, but she still doesn't come to church hardly ever."

"Strange, I've seen her here pretty much every week."

"Well, sure, it *seems* that way, but she's not so much *here* as lurking in the corner, you know?"

Not okay. I don't know Talia well enough to defend her with facts, but really, all I can see is Beth fixating on appearances, reinterpreting reality and manipulating me with it. More than ever before, I want—I *need* to get away from her.

I take a second to scrape together enough tact to admit some bit of the truth. "Can we clear something up, just between us? I know everyone else seems to think we're dating, and you're great, but I don't want to lead you on."

"Oh." She giggles, nervous. "Yeah." Her gaze falls. Though I don't know if she really believes the "It's not you, it's me" line, Beth drifts away to help finish the clean up.

If only she were bitter about this, if only she turned spiteful because I turned her down, if only she'd scream I was the worst person on the planet, it'd be so much easier not to feel bad.

Duh, naturally I feel bad.

It's insane to wish she'd flip on me. That might make it easier to shut her down, but I've been there. Never want to go back. Don't even want to start.

And dating could be the start.

If I don't want to date, why did I ask someone out? Isn't going on dates "dating" by definition? A one-way ticket to destination: dating?

I know *nothing* about Talia. The protectiveness could be hiding her psychopathic tendencies. She could kill bunnies and puppies as a hobby. She's a lawyer, for crying out loud.

Or the protectiveness could mean she's been hurt worse than I have.

Whoa. Calm down, self. Let's be logical. It's one date. Not that big a deal. Even if Talia's secretly a serial killer, I'm not signing my own death warrant. I want to start over. Talia doesn't have to be Ms. Right, but moving on with my life is right.

If I can just figure out how.

CHAPTER 9
TALIA

AS SOON AS I GET TO WORK Monday afternoon—Keeler Tate (CIA), not Terfort & Sutter—Will, my boss, steps out of his office. Ironically, in an organization that thrives more on relationships and people skills than rocket-propelled grenades, most managers in the CIA basically suck. Not Will. No head games, no manipulation, no nonsense.

To prove my point, Will spots me and gets right to the day's agenda, beckoning me with a single crook of two fingers. He extends the invitation to Elliott with only a meaningful glance.

My something's-up-o-meter creeps into "caution" zone. If this were a run-of-the-mill report on our dancers, he'd tell us at our desks instead of behind closed doors. But close the door he does, once we're all in the office, and he jumps in before we have time to sit. "Vasily Loban's phone records have contacts with dozens of MPs, government officials, diplomats—"

"Russian diplomats?" I interrupt. Could be his contact to hand off intelligence to the Motherland.

Will gives a single grim nod.

"How much access does he have to these people?" I ask. "Isn't there a barbershop on the Hill? I mean, like, in their offices?"

"Vasily's an *artiste* with more than stage makeup," Elliott says, settling into a cheap office chair. Do I want to know how he knows that? "Likely has a lot of regulars."

Will rounds his desk and takes his cushy seat. "Even if he hasn't recruited from Parliament and Embassy Row, you know how people talk to their barbers."

Other women supposedly talk to their stylists; do men do the same thing?

"Also, we partially decoded at least one encrypted transmission. If the analysis was correct, he has seven agents in his ring, minimum."

"Anyone outside of his clientele?"

Will checks his monitor. "Possibly another dancer."

I ignore my sinking stomach. (Is it bad I was hoping to *not* dance again?) His partner's the most likely suspect. "What does Galina have access to?" Elliott asks.

I run through my mental case file. "She's a translator, part-time at the US Embassy."

"And Vasily was dating a secretary from the embassy until recently," Will adds. "So we've got a lot of leads. Do whatever it takes to get into his next competition and on his friends-and-potential-agents list."

If we can do that, we'll be able to feed the Russians whatever misinformation we want. Will's charge sounds like a get-to-it dismissal, and Elliott and I both start for the door.

"But . . ." Will starts again, hesitant. "Keep it quiet. If CSIS caught wind . . ."

Uh yeah. We try hard to play nice with our Canadian counterparts, and between Vasily's connections with Members of Parliament and American embassy employees, I'm not sure which of us wants at him more. No one here would purpose-fully betray us, but we all know what loose lips do. (Aside from kissing on a first date.) (Is that still considered bad?)

By silent agreement, Elliott and I head to an unoccupied office down the hall to strategize. He closes the door behind us. A few spare computer chairs are our only company. "First thing, we need to know when their next competition is."

"Okay, I'll get on that, see if he or Galina updated their blog."

"I'll check Canada DanceSport's website." He turns for the door. "Should we get food? Pizza?"

I actually trust the pizzeria across the parking lot from our office building, but—"I'm not walking today."

"You like walking."

Less "like" and more "can't avoid." "Not in these heels."

"And I do love you in a skirt."

I roll my eyes. "You love anything in a skirt." I plop into one of the empty rolling chairs in the vacant office to reinforce my decision to stay. "Next time I have to appear in court, I'm bringing a change of clothes."

"Fine, no food. Can you tackle Galina?"

I doubt he means physically. (Still, she's tiny.) "Sure."

"Let's split up the list of phone calls—"

"Double-check they're sorted by frequency. Remember last time?"

He grunts. "That woman still drunk dials me sometimes. Never calling blind again."

We both shudder.

"Need to increase surveillance on his shop," Elliott adds.

Our strategy session reaches an abrupt halt as we've run out of things to say. "So." Elliott draws out the word and settles in another office chair, but the casual note in his voice and posture is obviously fake. "How's your boy toy?"

"Huh?" Is that supposed to mean Vasily?

He swivels around to face me. "You know, the one who passed you notes during the sermon yesterday?"

My cheeks flush. (Stupid cheeks, stupid cheeks, stupid cheeks.) "We weren't passing notes—I mean, I didn't see him during church."

"Ah, an illicit meeting beforehand? Getting fresh in the 'foyer,' making out in the choir loft?"

"Only you would think of a church as a make-out spot. And we don't have choir lofts."

That doesn't throw Elliott off the trail. "After church?"

My cheeks turn up the heat. I stand. "Better get on the phone."

"Wait, wait, I'll stop. Business: do we need to prepare for another competition?"

"I guess so." Yippee.

"Oh, almost forgot—our friends at the embassy picked Marcus Lee up. He's back in the States. Never working in the foreign service again; may even stand trial."

The US Embassy leak from his case? Who tried to kill me? We probably would've been better off calling in the Ottawa Police for attempted murder. But the CIA isn't in the business of justice. "That'll ruin his week."

"Let's hope so."

Elliott updates me on his meager progress with the Lebanese scientist, a colleague of my Turkmen professor. We haven't tapped into their motivations and values, so prospects aren't good with six weeks before they head home.

He manages to stay on business for four entire minutes. I'm about to go get to work when he changes the subject. "Danny, right?" Elliott asks.

I clamp down on the blush as much as humanly possible and fix him with a mock glare. I point to the window. "Did you want to practice rappelling without equipment?"

"T, relax. Just making sure he's good enough for you."

Not sure I buy that. He thinks he's teasing me, and with any other topic, I'd play along. But the way my face burns whenever he mentions Danny, I can't play this cool. "Thanks, but I already have three big brothers."

"You do?"

We have definitely discussed this before. "Let's keep focused—next step with Vasily: find the date for the next Canada DanceSport competition."

Elliott persists. "And what's your next step with Danny? Do you two have a date yet?"

I cover my cheeks with my hands, but it's too late.

"You do," he crows. "When is it?"

"Saturday," I mutter.

Elliott laughs and jumps out of his seat. "Fast to be getting married after two conversations."

Ugh. I punch him in the shoulder for that stupid joke. But in the split-second pause before Elliott's next volley, the idea sets in, sending a cold front through my bones.

Stranger things have happened, especially when it comes to sometimes-marriage-happy Mormons. I don't fall in that category, but Danny—no, Danny's not insane. He'd have to be more crazypants than Mom to make that leap. I lived with her long enough to key into crazy a kilometer off.

"I know how you Mormons are," Elliott breaks into my thoughts to rag on me again.

Sure, *now* he remembers/cares about my religion for the first time? "Almost as crazy as the perpetual engagement?" I toss off the parting barb, maybe a little crueler than it sounded in my mind, and escape the office before Elliott can respond.

Remind me never to tell Elliott anything personal again—not even something as innocuous as the first name of a crush.

Elliott's great for hunting down spies and moles, but when it comes to relating to people, the man needs serious help.

CHAPTER 10
DANNY

I WAIT UNTIL A DECENT HOUR to call Talia Saturday morning. Last minute, I know, but it's taken me all week to plan and work up the nerve to do this. I won't let the sweaty palms deter me now, though I'm glad she can't see me rubbing my thumb over my knuckle. No way am I sabotaging this before it starts by looking stupid. I hop on the kitchen counter and dial.

"Hey," she answers. "Still on for tonight, right?"

"Oh—actually I was thinking earlier in the day. Like eleven."

"Mm." The pause on the line does not bode well. "I'd love to, but I have to go into work this morning."

Before I can even think about being disappointed, she continues, "Can we do . . . whatever a little later?"

"We can try, but I was planning around the weather."

"You like to live dangerously, right?"

I let some sarcasm sneak into my tone. "Yeah, that's why I'm designing the planes instead of flying them."

She laughs. "I think I can get away by one. That work?"

"Sure." Maybe. "Then I'll pick you up around one? What's your address?" I'm smooth—the street she has listed in the ward directory doesn't exist on any map.

"I'm already cutting it close. Can I meet you there?"

"Yeah. Hang on a minute." I grab my laptop to read off the bike rental place's address. "Know where that is?"

"Like, downtown?"

I double-check the map. "That's the place."

"Yep, I can find it. So we'll be outside? What kind of shoes should I wear?"

Random. An image of her calves and those ankle-strap heels flashes through my mind, but those aren't really practical. "Tennis shoes will work."

"Okay. Good thing nobody cares what I wear to work on a Saturday."

"They should be grateful you're willing to come in at all."

She sighs. "Less 'willing' and more 'unable to get out of it.' But I'll work as fast as I can. One o'clock."

"Good."

I get to the sidewalk in front of the bike shop a couple minutes early, just enough time to worry about whether I'll do something stupid. Been a while since I've ridden a bike, but you're not supposed to forget how. I don't have long enough to go completely out of my mind, because Talia's right on time, wearing tennis shoes as promised, and khakis short enough to show off her calves. "Hi," she says.

"Hi." Silence. This is where the conversation is supposed to happen.

Suddenly it hits me: been a long time—years—since I've been on a first date. Even then, it wasn't like I was *good* at being cool and confident and putting a cute girl at ease. My temperature is already rising, and not because of the sun.

"So," Talia says at last. "Bikes?"

"Yeah." The relief is a little too evident in my voice.

"Sounds like fun."

We head for the rental shop. A bike ride isn't just something cute and easy. If things get weird, we can always focus on pedaling, and if it takes a turn for the worse, built-in escape, right?

Once we've got bikes, I lead the way up to the street and over the Rideau Canal. We take the path down to the locks where the canal meets the Ottawa River, pausing to watch the water cascading over the gates.

I should say something. The silence is sliding from comfortable to cold.

Say something, self.

Please, please say something.

Talia finally attempts to restart the conversation. "You like biking?"

"Seemed nice, riding along the river trail." I'm hoping she's okay with it. She didn't object.

"Plus we have to take advantage of summer while it lasts," she adds.

"Hey, Ottawa has four seasons, Miss Rexburg."

Talia cracks a smile. "Yep. And three of them are winter."

"The fourth is road construction."

Her smile converts into a laugh, and I know we can keep this up. "Do you come here often?" I ask before I realize I'm echoing a lame pickup line.

"First time. You?"

"Mine too."

She turns back to the locks, and the wooden paths running across the tops over the little waterfalls. "Can we walk on them?"

"Guess so." I indicate the handrails.

Talia turns to me, a question hanging in her eyes: *shall we?*

I hold out a hand, inviting her to go first. We walk our

bikes across, only to find the concrete landing pad on the other side doesn't extend into a sidewalk to the next gate.

"Oops," Talia mutters. She checks with me, chagrined. Like we should have looked before we leaped.

At least I'm not the only one worried about screwing this up.

"We'll manage." I take the lead to put her at ease, walking my bike down the dirt path beaten to the next gate. She follows. Once I'm back to the fully paved side, I turn back and catch a glimpse of Talia, paused in the middle of the gate. Her bike leans against her hip, and she's pulling her dark hair back into a long ponytail.

Without thinking, I get out my phone to take a picture.

"What are you doing?" she calls over the rushing water.

"Need a picture of you for my contacts," I ad lib. "Since I can't get one from Facebook." She smiles before I capture the photo, the Château Laurier looming behind her like a castle.

"Does it look okay?" she calls again.

"Perfect."

Her gaze drops to the walkway in front of her, and she grabs her bike handlebars before I realize maybe I said too much with that word. I gulp hard and stick my phone in my pocket, scanning for where the river parkway begins.

Be cool. Please be cool, self.

"Oh." I point across the greenway between us and an asphalt path, and we walk our bikes that direction. Yep, this is the path we were supposed to be on. Definitely should've figured that out sooner. I sneak a glimpse of Talia. She isn't staring at me like I'm an idiot. She gets on her bike and starts off, and so do I.

In silence. It was a lot easier to talk to her last week. Focusing on pedaling is looking good. Except this is downhill, so we're coasting. We reach the bottom lock, and the path turns to parallel the Ottawa River. Talia stops at the fence marking the parkway entrance. "Think we should read the map?"

I'm about to say maybe when I see the teasing in her eyes. "Guessing we'll find our way back."

"Let's hope so." She starts off again. I hurry to keep up, reaching for a conversation ploy less lame than my last pickup line. "Where are you from?"

"The States?" She isn't checking her facts; she's checking to see if I remember them.

Naturally. "There are fifty of them, you know."

"Oh, I lived all over. How about you?"

"I grew up in Missouri and Michigan. Lived in Colorado for a while, too." Then back to Michigan, but I really don't want to talk about why.

She nods. "Cool."

"You a military brat?"

"Nah, just had to move a lot." Talia stands up on her pedals and glances back. "Oh, hey." She stops and motions behind us. I turn back to see the glass towers jutting above the trees.

"National Gallery." She pans around to the steel cantilever truss bridge spanning the river. "Alexandra Bridge." Finally she points to a building with white columns supporting a rounded green roof. "Museum of History."

"How long have you lived here?" I ask.

"Three years."

"Right, law school."

"Yep." She hops back on the pedals. I hang back, watching her a minute. Even knowing her this long, I can tell the shields are still up.

We round a bend, and green-roofed Gothic towers rise above the trees in front of us. "Parliament Hill," we announce in unison. Talia smiles over her shoulder.

"How have you coped with not sharing cute kittens with anyone this week?" she jokes.

It takes me half a second to catch up with her physically and mentally, remembering that from our Facebook-free conversation at Sunday's break-the-fast. With the teasing her tone, I definitely want to play along. "Honestly? I'm dying."

Talia's gaze turns distant, like she's thinking of something. I echo that contemplation in my grin. "What?"

"Putting the clues together." Her tone matches her gaze.

"About me?"

"Mm hm."

Funny, I'm trying to do the same, but she's not giving me much to work with. "What did you get?"

"Kitten-loving, Michigander rocket scientist who hates Facebook."

"Me in a nutshell." The green hill to our left has grown into a cliff, and a sign warns us to dismount for the tunnel ahead, so I obey.

Talia stops too, eying me. "That's a profile of you. It's not you."

I arch an eyebrow. "Okay, tell me more about me."

She barely hesitates long enough to focus on the middle distance. "You're always thinking, probably analyzing and criticizing things, especially yourself. You're good at recognizing patterns and making connections. You like answering questions, especially if it seems like no one else will. You'd rather do something solo or individual than a team sport. You're not totally comfortable being the center of attention, so I bet you haven't done it a ton, except maybe at work, where you're brilliant, though you'd never say that."

With every phrase, she nails something else about me, not everything I've really consciously thought about, until I almost expect her to list my relationship with Kendra next.

Fortunately, she doesn't strike quite that close. She stops, expectations in her half-raised shields. "How'd I do?"

I make a face to say *not so much.* "Eh."

She rivets me with a look of *I'm not buying that for a minute.* "Forgot to mention your killer sense of humor."

"Got me there."

Talia leans away from her bike. Toward me. I'm not thinking about kissing her—well, I wasn't—but my pulse picks up anyway. Her voice drops to a dramatic whisper. "And I don't think you like kittens half as much as you claim."

"That's where you're wrong. Everyone loves kittens."

A couple other bikers zip past us before they dismount to pass through the tunnel, ruining the moment. Talia mimics my *meh* expression. "We'll see about that."

"Try me."

"No, you try me." She starts walking her bike down the path for the tunnel. "Or can you?"

"Give me a minute." The pieces are already there, but after everything she's noticed about me in a couple months of sitting through the same Sunday School class, I want to make this good. We reach the tunnel, a series of cement boxes with breaks to let the light in, and I have to maneuver closer to her. No objection here, and Talia doesn't move away.

That gives me all the courage I need to answer her. "You aren't at church for the social scene, which says a lot. Arjay's your closest friend, and I think he's the reason you came to the break-the-fast. I'm guessing he's either your matchmaker or your wingman."

In the half-shadow, her laugh echoes.

"When you want to do something," I continue, gaining momentum, "you do it, no matter how hard you have to work. You perform better under pressure. You don't know how to give up. I don't like being the center of attention, but you *hate* it, and you work hard to avoid being noticed at church. But you'll talk one-on-one, so you're not shy. I think it's a defense mechanism."

We're closing in on the end of the tunnel. "Defense from

what?" Talia murmurs.

"You've been hurt." In the second-to-last stripe of light, she turns to me, shields down. Instead, her eyes are full of fear.

She blinks and it's gone. "Everyone has."

"True." Truer, apparently, than either of us like to admit directly.

"Race you to the end of the trail." Talia hops on her bike and launches herself out of the tunnel.

I add *not as subtle as you think you are at avoiding touchy topics* to my description of Talia and take off after her. "The trail runs to the Pacific," I shout.

She looks back long enough to reply, "Better get pedaling."

I answer with a wry smile and try to keep up with her. Too many people around to really race, but we cruise past the back of some Parliament building at a decent speed, the crowd slowly thinning, until it seems to hit us at the same time—it's getting dark. We make eye contact and slow down by a silent signal, both scanning the sky. Heavy clouds are rolling in, fast.

"Not supposed to rain until three," I say.

"Don't think those clouds are wearing a watch."

"Time to head back."

Talia agrees, and we head back. The crowd hasn't just thinned: we round a corner and we're the only ones in sight.

Then the storm breaks. I slow down to let Talia pass me, and then we both pedal hard, though it's too late to stay dry. The speed makes the pelting rain sting more.

The tunnel comes up fast, and she doesn't dismount like we're supposed to. "Talia! Stop!"

She plunges into the shadow. I follow, focused on her silhouette. She stops pedaling and coasts to a halt in the last block of the tunnel. I roll up next to her, drawing deep breaths after that race that turned real. Talia stares out at the rain, breathing hard, wiping away the water running down her cheeks.

"You okay?" I ask.

She flashes me a smile. "Yeah. Just thinking how glad I am I decided not to wear that white shirt."

She laughs, and I have to join in. "Well," I say when our laughter subsides, "we're already soaked. Do you want to brave the rain or wait it out?"

"Let's wait. Can't last that long." She leans her bike against the cement tunnel wall and sits on the dry patch of ground in front of it. Once again, I follow suit, taking a seat facing her.

"Lovely weather we're having," Talia begins.

"Yeah, torrential downpour is my favorite biking weather."

She appreciates the joke, and though my fallback topic is one of those stupid standard questions you always ask, it feels totally natural to continue the conversation. "Any siblings?"

"Too many brothers."

I make a face like I'm afraid they'll come after me, and she dismisses that concern with a wave. "They're far away; you're safe. What about you—any siblings?"

"Little brother and sister."

"Did you always want to be an aerospace engineer?" she asks before I come up with another question.

A small thing, I know, but I really like that she remembers the real name of my job, instead of "rocket scientist." We fall into conversation, and I don't miss the potential distraction or escape the bikes offered. When the rain slows after fifteen minutes and stops completely after thirty, neither of us make a move to get up—definitely not because this asphalt's comfy. It's not until the shadows start to grow longer that I realize the bike shop might close soon.

I stand and help Talia up, and we retrieve our bikes. The conversation slows down to match our pace walking back, but now the occasional quiet is a lot more comfortable.

My original plan was a short daytime date to ease into . . . everything. But this date is just starting to hit its stride, and I'm not ready for it to be over. I need a Phase II. An early dinner?

Where?

I glance at Talia, and she's looking at me. Waiting. Oh, crap, my turn to say something. "You know, I don't think I asked you why you wanted to be a lawyer."

"Oh." She waves the question off. "You know, the usual. Save the world, make enough money to pay off student loans while doing it."

Once again, I get the distinct impression there's more to say, but I'm willing to let her tell me as much as she's comfortable with.

Okay, my turn again. I should ask her to dinner. Maybe we'll find something to do after that. Marathon first dates are okay, right? Sure. They even count as two or three, and that makes kissing at the end totally acceptable.

I just have to say something. Talia's watching me again, this time like she knows what I'm working up to.

So say something, self. Say something. Just say it.

The silence ticks past. The trailhead grows closer by the second.

Say *anything.*

Then her phone rings, stealing my opportunity. She checks to see who it is. "Sorry, work," she murmurs. I signal for her to take the call, of course.

"What is it?" she answers the phone. I take it she knows the person on the other end pretty well.

"Yeah. . . ." She stops walking abruptly. "Can it wait? Can't you handle it?" Her face says it all: major crisis. "Where should I meet you?"

Well, there goes the second half of my date plan.

"Okay." Talia ends her call and looks to me. "Danny, I'm so sorry—"

"Major crisis at work. It's okay. Obviously it's out of your hands."

She smiles her thanks, but picks up the pace to get back to

the bike shop. "I hate to run off," she says for about the third time.

"I know."

"I had fun," she says, like I doubted. "Thank you."

"Thanks for coming." Before I can suggest we do this again, Talia's already backing away for her car. "See ya," I say.

She waves and finally walks away. I watch her until she reaches her car, mentally cataloging the new entries in my Talia file. Youngest, bunch of brothers, kind of a daredevil as a teenager, lived in Florida, went to BYU–Idaho, never seen the Great Lakes, likes her dad, no mention of her mom, super dedicated to her job, evasive about why exactly. Though most people can hide this for a few hours, I do have to note Talia shows no signs of being a complete psycho.

Only thing I regret: letting her get away. At least I'll see her at church tomorrow. Too soon to sit together? Too soon to ask her out again? Too soon to kiss her?

Whoa, wait, what? We've spent like four hours of our lives together, ever. It's way too soon for just one thing: thinking about all that.

Suddenly, I'm colder than when I was soaked from the rain. We've been on one date—one half of a date—and I'm losing my objectivity over Talia.

Yeah, I like her, but maybe it's smartest to take a step back.

CHAPTER 11
TALIA

I CUT MY DATE WITH DANNY SHORT—and it was going *really* well, we were really connecting—for this? The World's Worst Tacos (we're here solely because this dive has outdoor seating for the summer) and watching Galina and Vasily rehearse through the plate glass of their street-level studio? Elliott's basket of chips conceals his long-distance listening device, but even I can tell our dancing friends aren't passing sensitive intel.

To make matters more frustrating, Elliott and I are the entire surveillance team. Normally, you'd want two or three people per target at a minimum—a dozen would be ideal—but we're still not supposed to talk the rest of our team about this.

They're not the only people I have to be careful around. The defenses rising in my mind don't have anything to do with the spymaster across the street. They have everything to do with the guy munching cold, greasy chips at the next table. The guy who should be my best friend.

I hate feeling like I can't trust myself around him, but with everything going on lately . . . I can't. I don't dare mention Danny or church or my mother, and the list seems to grow every week.

Funny how much more comfortable I was an hour ago, talking to a guy I barely know. Reason #43: Danny's a good listener. Maybe too good—I still things have to be careful about some things. My job, yes, but most of all, my mother. The less I say about her, the better.

As if he's reading my mind, Elliott pipes up once the waiter ducks inside. "Sorry for making you miss your date."

I think he means that, so I offer him the smallest reassurance. "We already went out."

"A daytime first date?" Elliott rearranges the chips in his basket and munches on one. "Bigger geek than I thought."

"Takes one to know one." Okay, sometimes our relationship is less obnoxious flirting and more grade-school insults.

"Or maybe he's just not that into you."

"Oh, shut up." We might be alone, but I still want him to be careful about what he says.

Especially about Danny. Because I'd hate to have to punch Elliott.

Before he can launch another round of teasing my way, Elliott clears his throat and coughs—the signal. I turn back. Beyond the enormous poster of Galina and Vasily in full costume, beaming beside a trophy as tall as them, the real-life dancers are taking their shoes off.

Their work's over, but ours is beginning. Elliott leaves a couple dollar coins ("loonies," as they're called) for a tip and starts for his car. I take a minute longer, hooking up my Bluetooth earpiece/comms cover so I can get away with talking to Elliott without looking like a crazy bag lady (been there, done that).

Inside the studio, Galina stands. Vasily gives her something small—a USB drive? The likelihood of them exchanging sensitive secrets that way might be low, but it's so easy to dismiss the handoff with that reasoning that they might be able to get away with it. If it were anyone but me.

Galina heads out, and I'm ready to pursue. I wait until Galina chooses a direction and follow her on my side of the street. At the first corner, Harper Street, she crosses toward me. I backtrack to avoid bumping into her. Not so stealthy.

Did she park this far away? The street's not that crowded.

Galina continues down Harper and I keep her in my sights.

"FEATHERSTONE's getting in his car." Elliott apprises me.

I return the favor, pressing two fingers to my earpiece. "Yeah, walking down Harper. Be there soon."

"We're on Worcester, heading the other way."

Galina turns through the glass doors of a stucco building. Nice, probably ten to fifteen years old, and close to her studio and her job downtown, translating for the US Embassy.

Could this be her apartment building? I note the street number, 277, and tail her into the lobby. High cream walls, wide white trim, everything trying to be elegant and pretty. Galina's ten feet ahead, waiting for the elevator. My sunglasses will have to suffice for a disguise, and I give her more of a lead.

Something gnaws at the back of my mind as I repeat the address to memorize it: 277 Harper Street. Why does it seem familiar? Was it already in her traces?

Then an image of seeing that address flashes through my mind—not on the building, but on my phone. In my church directory app.

Oh, no. I pull out my phone, zip through the password to my personal stuff and open up the church directory. Campbell is the first listing that jumps out—nope, not him. I scroll through the names.

Danny? Have I checked Danny's address before? (Of course.)

Oh, please, please, no.

The elevator dings to announce its arrival from the basement, and my head snaps up. The doors slide open. My breath seizes in my throat.

I've known him a couple months and yet I'd recognize Danny anywhere. Plus, it's only been an hour. He's still wearing the blue shirt with a fighter jet/maple leaf logo (Winnipeg Jets; looked it up during dinner)—and the same mask of not-quite-concealed disappointment.

Galina steps onto the elevator, and Danny nods to her, like you'd nod to someone you've seen in the laundry or the lobby, not your next door neighbor. So much for riding up with her.

"Hold the elevator!" a woman's voice calls, and for a split second, I'm afraid it's mine. Fortunately, high heels echo over the black and white checkerboard tile behind me. I duck my head, holding my earpiece to shield my face. But I can still see Danny stick out a hand to stop the doors, a Loblaws' plastic grocery bag dangling from his wrist.

I automatically take stock of what I can see: loaf of bread, blue package inside the bag—Oreos? (Compared to the American kind, they're just not the same.)

Crap, no, Danny's not the one I'm supposed to be profiling.

"Don't you have any reusable grocery bags?" Galina asks.

"Yeah, just tired of buying new ones because I forgot 'em."

Galina nods sympathetically. The running woman breezes past me and practically leaps onto the elevator. "Oh, hey, Danny," she pants.

"Hi, Megan." He releases the door and it slides shut.

Even if I followed her up now, I can't let her see me (and I won't sneak into her place without a solid plan). I make my way back to my car and report to Elliott via comms. "Have we bugged Galina's apartment?"

"No, only a tracker on her door."

"We need to figure out what he gave her."

Elliott grunts in agreement. "Still on FEATHERSTONE,

going for his shop."

I drive over there for support. "Is this everything you're planning?" I ask as I park down the block from the barbershop.

"No, tomorrow's his busy day at the barbershop, and we need to bug Galina's."

And those sounds like all-day engagements. "Tell me you've got support lined up."

"Yeah, you."

My heart sinks. That means I'll be stuck doing this instead of seeing Danny at church tomorrow.

"Are you pouting because you're missing church or Danny?"

"I'm not pouting."

My passenger door opens. My pulse rate hits the roof. I scramble to grab a pen from the console, the best I can do for a weapon.

Elliott plops into the passenger seat. I throw my pen at him. "Is your face not scary enough? Now you have to sneak up on me?"

He smirks. "You're pouting."

"I'm not pouting."

"No, it's cute."

I shoot him an oh-please look. But a nagging voice in my mind whispers he's right. Not only do I want to see Danny (and go to church), but I don't like the one-two punch of cutting our date short and ditching church.

I have to send him a clear message to say the opposite. And I think I know exactly how.

Kittens.

CHAPTER 12
DANNY

MY TIE'S OFF THE MINUTE I WALK IN my apartment after church. I had to run to duck the usual flirt-fest, because I'm in no mood. Talia ran off at the end of our date—before the end—and then she wasn't at church today. Even if I need to be more rational and take a step back, I'm not trying to drive Talia away from the church.

Realistically, a couple hours of talking to me shouldn't be enough to do that when we've established she's not there to make friends, but I'm still pacing.

Because I'm worried about her? Or worried about me?

No. Nothing to panic about. She's not insane; she's just not interested. That I can survive. Way better than if she was crazy.

Heck, I could be dodging a bullet. Or a full-fledged air strike.

I'm changing my shirt when my phone rings. My stomach bounces like a plane in the midst of a bad landing, though it's probably not Talia calling. Nope, my mom.

Once the pleasantries are done, Mom cuts straight to her

big news: "I'm coming for a visit!"

I sink onto the bed. I'm not ready for this.

"That's great, Mom." Except that she'll be on my case from the minute she gets off the plane. *You should be dating, you should get a roommate, you should move here, you should get your PhD there, you should cut your hair.*

Because apparently I don't know how to run my own life.

"And I have a surprise for you," she continues.

I go for the least-likely scenario. "You're having a baby."

Mom laughs. "Cute, Danny. With your sense of humor, you should really—"

"Consider stand-up?"

"Be dating."

Yesterday, I could've claimed to be working on that, *if* I wanted to use Talia as a shield with my mom, which I don't. Today, I don't have a defense. I sink back onto my quilt made of T-shirts from high school—one of many things I do have to thank my mom for, I remind myself—and use Mom's tone that says *my patience is wearing thin.* "So you keep telling me."

"Have you at least spoken to any nice girls lately?"

"Yep, I talk to nice girls every day."

That puts her on pause. "Nice girls you'd take on dates?"

"I don't think their husbands would like that."

"Ah. Stand-up?"

At least she can be funny. And hey, she's my mom. I love her. I just don't always love to listen to her.

For now, I dodge her usual badgering by asking about Carrie and Sam. My younger siblings are off in newlywed- and new-parent-land, not really running for my calls. Mom doesn't make any direct comparisons about how I'd be so much happier if I just followed their lead and settled down, because I *am* getting on in years, and soon nobody will ever want to marry me.

Apparently she doesn't need to give the lecture. Got it

memorized.

Once I'm up-to-date on Carrie and Sam, and Mom and Dad, and half a dozen of my mom's friends I don't remember from home, we're running out of things to say.

"When will you be here?" I can sacrifice a weekend to spend time with Mom. Not like I'll be doing anything else.

My phone buzzes with an incoming message, but I don't want to miss Mom's answer. "August thirtieth through September seventh."

I check my mental calendar—that's two weeks away. I press two fingers to the bridge of my nose. "Generally when people 'drop in' for more than a week, they actually okay it with you first. Like before buying their tickets."

"Stand-up again?" But I hear the undertone of hurt in her voice.

Guilt gathers in my gut. Great. "Sorry, Mom."

"It's okay. Do you want me to bring ketchup and Oreos?"

Don't think I've mentioned the differences between Canadian and American foods recently, so she must remember this from sending packages when I was a missionary nine years ago. "Thanks, that'd be great."

I tell my mom I love her and get off the phone. I scrounge in my kitchen for a halfway-decent meal—okay, a sandwich and some cookies—and it's half an hour before I remember I got a message during Mom's call. Once I'm done eating, I retrieve my phone from the charger in my room.

The text's from Talia. My stomach takes another bad-landing bump before I park myself on the bed again. *How was church?*

She must think I'm ignoring her. *Okay*, I text back. *No talks on marriage.*

She doesn't respond—probably busy. Maybe her major crisis is ongoing. Man, am I glad to have a job I can leave at the office when I want.

I don't know how long it is before my phone vibrates, jarring me from the nap I hadn't meant to take. Another text from Talia. *Then I'm sorry I missed it.*

Work still?

Always.

That response makes me frown. I know she's dedicated to her work, but what does a lawyer do that takes twenty-four straight hours on a weekend?

Then again, if she's avoiding me, she's doing a crappy job. Unless this is all part of her head games.

Before I realize it, I've set the phone down and picked up my laptop. I start reading through the lesson I'm supposed to teach at church next week.

Wow. Been a long time since I've been this desperate to distract myself.

What, about nine months? Since my last crash-and-burn?

Now I have something else to distract myself from. I scroll through the lesson, highlighting a quote or two, until my phone buzzes again. And again. And again. Before I touch my phone, I jolt to sitting up straight. Urgency floods my bloodstream. I'm supposed to be somewhere. I need to go, I need to get to—Kendra's. Because she'll lose her temper if I take too long to change clothes after church.

Calm down, self. I take a breath to release my tensed muscles. That's not what a flood of texts means anymore. But suddenly I'm a lot less excited to hear from Talia.

She won't say, *Where are you why don't you love me anymore don't I mean anything to you?????* Talia's not that unbalanced. Right?

Four texts. *Anyway, this is just a heads-up*, says the first one. *Because . . .*

A picture of a tiny kitten yawning and stretching, with the message *You're!*

A kitten hopelessly tangled in yarn, looking forlorn, with

93

the text *Gettin!*

Three fluffy kittens curled up together, sleeping, with the text *Kittens!*

Another breath. The joke's lame, but in a "so bad it's good" way. I can play along with this. *I should contact the ASPCA*, I type. Before I send it, I switch it to the CSPCA, though I'm not sure that's a thing.

? is all she says.

Canadian Society for the Protection of Cute Animals. I smile at my own cleverness, but the smile fades. We're playing a game—the good kind—but I need this to be real. I need to know she can be real, too. We're old enough to be real. So I drop the pretense, while still trying to keep up the game.

But first, Talia texts back: *You're the one dying without pictures of cute kittens. This is a mission of mercy.*

You're exploiting those poor little kittens, using them to flirt with me.

Feels like an hour ticks by before she responds. *Is it working?*

Did I say it wasn't?

Whew.

All right. Awesome. We're both totally upfront about our flirting. She likes me, I like her, and the kittens could be a cute inside joke for months.

Now's the part where I ask her on a second date. All I have to do is say something.

Wait—months? I'm getting way ahead of myself here. If I'm not careful, I could fall for her way too easily.

I scroll back to the kittens pictures. Remind me why shouldn't I fall for her?

Then I see the time stamps, in quick succession—and remember the reaction they triggered. Ice creeps through my veins, and I set my phone down. Why shouldn't I fall for her? Seriously? I know exactly why not. I already like her—a lot. If I fall for her, I'll lose all rationality. All objectivity. I'll ignore my good judgment, justify all the warning signs, sweep them under the rug or dismiss them, until I wake up one day, married to a vicious banshee.

I turn back to my lesson, even when my phone buzzes again. It takes every gram of self-control I have—and then one flash of a memory, a pair of raging eyes. Not Talia's, but they did belong to someone else who I thought was sane. Those eyes went from normal to nasty in less than a blink—could Talia's?

Could Talia turn into that? I don't know. And I don't want to find out.

CHAPTER 13
TALIA

OUR MISSION SUNDAY WAS RIVETING. Half an hour to lure Galina's upstairs neighbor out long enough to place the bug and six hours of watching men walk in Vasily's shop with shaggy hair and walk out with slightly less shaggy hair. Americans, Russians, Canadians, etc. Between surveillance there and dance rehearsals with Elliott (and that pesky law internship), I haven't had a whole lot of time to brood over Danny's disappearance from our texts. Or the two other times I've tried to text him this week. Still, I wasn't planning on spending Friday night with Elliott. Especially not for his little "surprise" that requires me to dress up.

Exactly how stupid is Elliott? What would he spring on me? We park in front of a brick church, and I start recalculating his idiocy.

"Seriously?" I ask. Please, please tell me he isn't here to drag me through some sort of wedding rehearsal torture to tease me. "When you said surprise, this wasn't what I had in mind."

"That's what makes it a surprise." Elliott grins; I glare.

Okay, dancing may not be the real reason I'm grouchy today. I won't blame Danny for the crappy mood I've been in all week, but ever since he ditched our text conversation Sunday night, nothing's seemed to go right.

Elliott clears his throat, dragging me out of my thoughts. "You okay?"

I heave a sigh, but I'm not about to lay out my dating problems to Elliott's mercy. "Depends on what we're here for."

"We're performing."

I wheel around to the church again. "Performing what?"

"Just a little exhibition. Rahim has one every week. Good way to practice with an audience—for fun."

"Who's Rahim? An agent?" Meaning *is he spying for you?* and *do you trust him?*

"A DJ. You've never heard of Rahim's Salsa Fridays?"

"I gave up dance after college. Haven't done a lot of clubbing between my two full-time jobs."

"And your uptight church."

Now that's out of bounds (and ironic, given where we are). Both my eyebrows raise along with the mercury in my temper thermometer.

"Hey." Elliott slaps on his don't-hit-me-you-know-I'm-just-kidding smile. I suck in a cool breath and remind myself this guy's my best friend, the person I turn to when I need help, the man who's saved my life.

And he's also the guy who loves to get a rise out of me—he's just discovered a new way to do it. Two, if you count Danny.

But maybe neither of us should be counting Danny. My gaze falls to my black skirt.

"You're fine," Elliott reassures me. "Well, maybe a little overdressed. Last time I was there, the girl performing wore those short-shorts . . . Spanx?"

I do not think that word means what he thinks it means. "Spanx?"

"I'm good, thanks," he says, like I'm not asking but offering.

I groan. Hard to believe Elliott has ever spoken to a woman, let alone gotten one to agree to marry him.

He glances at my legs. "If only we had that view to distract people if you mess up."

He doesn't pull the grin defense fast enough, and I punch him in the arm. (That's gonna leave a bruise.) "Thanks for the vote of confidence."

"Let's get in there and arrange the music."

The prep time for the performance flies by with one quick run-through while they teach a lesson for beginners. As the regular start time approaches, the audience streams in, filling the room the same way nerves fill my lungs. I focus on the rafters overhead, like that'll amplify my prayers.

Elliott appears by my side. "Stay by the DJ's table."

I follow him over there, trying not to scan the crowd gathering around the dance floor (and failing). Elliott turns to the DJ—and then one man, short and blond and red-shirted, edges through the crowd. My blood slows in my veins.

Vasily.

I grab Elliott's arm, but Rahim cuts me off with his opening announcements. Next he'll introduce us. Please tell me Elliott gave Rahim our cover names.

Okay, damage control. Vasily knows we're Ottawans too. As long as we've got our covers, we're good. If Vasily has any reason to think he's drawn suspicion—like other dancers using two names—he'll roll up his spy ring and escape.

Rahim booms his intro for the guest DJ, Lance. He takes the mic and pumps up the crowd. "Tonight," Lance continues, "we're happy to have new performers with us, fresh off the amateur competitive circuit!"

Applause interrupts him. My tongue goes dry, but my

palms are sweaty. Did Rahim pass along the right names? As long as Lance announces us with our cover names, we're good.

Please, let us be good.

"Do you want to see some cha cha?" Lance shouts to cheers. "Samba?" He increases the volume and so do the on-lookers. He drops to a trying-to-be-sexy rumble. "Rrrrumba?" The crowd *oohs*.

Nausea crawls through my stomach. Yeah, if we don't get through this introduction fast, I'm going to give them a different reason to *ooh*. Or, more likely, *ew*.

"Tonight we'll see all three and more! Here with their amazing Latin medley, Joanne Hodges and Gord Hopkins!"

Relief floods in so fast, all that's left is the adrenaline. I gulp down air. Performing's easy compared to the stress of waiting for our intro. I hit my poses, keep good lines and remember to smile—especially during the split second I glimpse Vasily in his trademark red shirt.

If nothing else, we're seriously selling our cover. My rumba could still use work, but I'm hardly worried about that. After our final spin into a not-competition-approved dip, my smile turns real.

Elliott turns me loose and the crowd begins to edge in, our performance space becoming the full dance floor. Lance gets the party started and picks the first song. If anything, casual practice could undermine the discipline I've worked so hard to regain. But I wait, observing the crowd, keeping tabs on Vasily. I can't imagine he'd meet with an agent or his handler here.

After only two songs, it's suddenly a lot easier to track my quarry. Because he's heading for me. We make eye contact—yep, definitely headed for me. Too suspicious to run away now. "Haven't we met?" he asks as soon as he's close enough.

"DanceSport competition a couple weeks ago."

"Of course. You saved my phone."

Did he notice we did something to it? He doesn't seem to

suspect anything, but he *is* holding out a hand. I look at it and back to him. "Would you like to dance?" he asks.

I place my hand in his, and he leads me onto the floor. I manage to keep up—he's taking it easy on me. Salsa isn't technically one of our competition dances, but he mixes in steps from other dances anyway.

"You and Gord did well with your exhibition." Vasily's looking over my shoulder, though. Might be making sure we don't bump into anyone—or he might be lying. About the compliment?

"We could've been better. I didn't get much advance notice."

"That explains it."

I fight back a frown. I thought we did okay, actually. But I change the subject. "Do you come here a lot?"

"When I can. You?"

"Not really." My cover wasn't originally designed to hold up to close scrutiny, so we're still scrambling to fill out the details. I need to be very careful what I say.

Before I can say anything else, Vasily flinches. I know that's not my fault. He's still looking over my shoulder. The song ends, and he releases me too quickly. "Thank you." He bows slightly and turns away, weaving through the crowd as the next song begins.

Yeah, that's not obvious. I move to the edge of the floor, subtly scanning the area Vasily was watching when he weirded out. A bulky guy towers over the dancers, fixated on something—or someone—in the direction Vasily went.

Big Guy edges along the outskirts of the dancing crowd. Pursuing Vasily. I search for Elliott, but he's off dancing. I'm on my own.

I track Big Guy from a distance, trying to ignore the tug-of-war between my dropping stomach and my rising pulse. Vasily ducks out of the rear doors of the gym. Big Guy sees and gives chase. I hurry to reach them in the hallway, in time to see Big Guy leaving the building. I catch the fire door before it latches behind him.

Is this guy competition (in a non-ballroom sense)? Not very well trained. But random street crime doesn't follow you into a dance. He's after Vasily.

I prop the door open with my foot. I can just get an angle to see Big Guy through the narrow opening. He quickens his pace to catch up to Vasily, a good fifteen feet away. Vasily jerks around like someone called his name. He spots Big Guy and shoots off at a run.

I take it they know one another.

Buy Guy pursues, and so do I. Vasily ducks around a corner of the church, but now he's in the shadows of the streetlights. Big Guy outpaces Vasily easily, grabbing him by the collar of his red dress shirt. I'm getting too close for comfort, so I hide behind the church.

"The money!" Big Guy concludes, punctuating his with a thump against the brick. (Made by Vasily?)

"Soon," Vasily pleads. "I almost have it."

I can't make out any words in Big Guy's growled response, but I peek around the corner to see him give Vasily one more shove. I duck back before Big Guy walks by without noticing me. When he passes under a streetlight, I snap a quick photo.

I peek around the corner once more—man, I wish I had my mirrors. Vasily slinks toward me. I hurry back the way we came to slip into the dance before he notices.

He owes someone money. Someone with enough connections or clout to command an enforcer.

That could be exactly why he's engineered this spy ring. He needs the Russians' money to pay off whoever this guy is. Money, after all, is a great motivator—a great manipulator. (Right, mother?)

We may have Vasily's motivation. But we've got a ways to

go before we stop him.

Vasily doesn't see me as he passes, headed for the parking lot. I slide back into the gym. Of course nobody noticed I left. I want to get Elliott and update him, but he's still nowhere in sight.

I finally spot him twirling another woman. I'm not jealous—that should probably be Shanna's job anyway—but I still feel . . . jilted? I glance at the people having fun, dancing. I'm not the only person without a partner, but now, I'm the most alone.

Guess I'll tell him Monday. I text Elliott that I'll take the bus back and slip out, the music fading behind me as soon as the door shuts.

After yet another Saturday of catch-up at Terfort & Sutter (great face time with more torts), I *need* to go to church. Yeah, it's healthier for me to occasionally be around non-CIA, non-lawyer people, though I don't want to talk to most of them (not sure whether Danny falls into that category). But more than that, I need to feel . . . connected. One of the things that I love about church—those moments where you just *feel* part of truth and light and knowledge and a higher power and everything.

The times I know, no matter how I feel most days, I'm not completely invisible.

I make it to church on time for once, and as soon as I take a seat in the chapel, Arjay's at my side. "Well?" he asks, as if I've been withholding information and food for the last two weeks. "When are you and Danny getting married?"

A pop of panic flashes in my brain at the M-word. I check the pews immediately around us—empty. But I'm not scared someone heard Arjay. Even the idea—just no.

Yeah, Elliott teases me about it, but deep down, I know he's trying to bug me. Arjay's not teasing, and that's the scarier.

Let's put this to rest. "I haven't heard from him in a week."

My voice sounds rusty—because I haven't spoken to anyone since I thanked the bus driver Friday night.

This is getting just sad.

"He didn't ask you out?" Arjay asked.

"He did; we went out last Saturday."

Arjay's eyes widen to satellite dishes. "Well?"

"Like I said, I haven't heard from him in a week."

Arjay's gaze shifts behind us, and I start to follow, but he grabs my shoulder. "Don't look. He walked in."

My breathing picks up, but I have to play it cool. "Seriously, you're more invested this than we are."

He smirks. "I won't be dating for two years. I'm trying to live through you."

I'd forgotten he was leaving on a mission in a few weeks, that he's so much younger than me. "Don't you have more important things to do? Like that whole mission prep thing?"

"This takes five minutes of my week." Arjay watches Danny. (Watching Arjay's *so* much more subtle than me turning around, especially since Danny's pegged him as my wingman.) Arjay tracks with him down the aisle, and I draw in a breath, steeling myself to see Danny pass my pew, for him to not turn my way, for that one little link to be gone.

And that's a good thing, right? Not like he'd be my "happily ever after." Those don't exist, especially not if your last name is Reynolds.

(Hint: my last name is Reynolds.)

I wait, monitoring the aisle in front of me, but Danny doesn't pass me. Arjay pivots, as if he's watching Danny take a seat in a pew behind me. Now I really can't breathe. Is he directly behind me? Do I acknowledge him? Wait for him to say something?

Here I was, thinking that admitting we were flirting would

help cut out all this stupid overanalysis. Nope, apparently I'm still a girl.

"Two rows back," Arjay says. Before I settle on a course of action, the bishop steps to the pulpit and begins the meeting.

I don't know if I could tell you a single word said in the meeting. (Okay, other than "Jesus" and "Amen.") This is why dating someone at church is stupid. What if we'd let it go longer? Once we flamed out or drifted apart, what would we do? Change congregations?

When Sacrament meeting ends, everyone stands to move to the classroom for Sunday School. Everyone except me—and Arjay. He waits until most people have left. Including, I assume, Danny.

"Okay, what went wrong?"

I offer a palms-up shrug. "No idea." I give Arjay the ten-thousand foot view—or maybe the postmortem—of my brief relationship with Danny.

He frowns at the unsatisfying conclusion. "You can't give up yet. Unless that's why you're still single."

One of Danny's spot-on assessments of me: I don't give up. I can't. And I won't, because as much as I like to be left alone, it's dawning on me how very alone I am. Especially after that one brilliant hour of connection on our date last week.

That doesn't mean I can march up to Danny and plant one on him. (Although that doesn't sound like a bad idea. I'm completely okay with kissing on a second date. Actually, I wouldn't have complained if Danny kissed me last week. Stupid Elliott. Stupid work.)

I get ready to stand, but Arjay shifts on the pew, pensive. "I don't want to be weird about this." Not a good beginning.

"Okay . . . ?"

"Look, I know you don't hang out with anyone else at church. I don't want leave you with nobody. You and Danny would be good together."

Guess that's why Arjay's so eager about this. Danny's such a good guy I can only take that as a (somewhat deluded) compliment. "Thanks. I'll be okay, either way."

"Just want to be sure." He finally stands, and we leave the chapel.

By the time Arjay and I make it to Sunday school, the only available seats are on the front row. Rather than parade through the class, we stay standing by the back door. If I want to talk to Danny, I can't gamble on getting to him after church. I've got to act.

I halfway pay attention to the lesson from the book of Acts. (I should feel guilty, but then again, Joel seems to delight in dwelling on the verses about circumcision, so I don't feel bad for ignoring him.) The other half of my brain's in spy mode: zero in on the target. Map out his routes out of the classroom. Run through possible interaction scenarios. Outcomes: he's not that into me, and I let him go; he's just been busy, and I ask him out.

My palms turn clammy at the thought, but I'm going for this. Because I don't give up.

With ten minutes left in Sunday school, Danny stands up. Doubt he's offended by Saul/Paul's preaching against Jupiter worship, and I didn't see him dozing off. I glance at Arjay; he shrugs.

Danny grabs a sheaf of papers from under his chair and heads for the door—where I'm standing. My chance is coming sooner than I'd planned. I swallow, but my dry mouth doesn't cooperate.

"Need a drink," I whisper. Arjay grips my arm and doesn't let go, like I'm trying to get out of talking to Danny.

I pull free a half-second before Danny spots me. I don't think he actually stops, so maybe it's time or the Earth that pauses as I wait for his face to reveal . . . anything.

"This is the man who had scales fall from his eyes," Joel's

voice carries right on cue. I don't know if Danny's paying attention to the lesson anymore, but it *is* like his thoughtful, distracted expression falls away—and he smiles.

Reason #1 why Danny is the most eligible bachelor in this room full of single guys. That smile, like he doesn't care who's watching, like he doesn't care who sees exactly how happy he is, like he's smiling with his soul—it does more than crinkle his eyes. It lights up his face, the room, my heart, and its sheer genuineness melts any resistance I might've had.

Go time.

I back up, opening the door for him. Totally unsubtle, I follow him out (but not fast enough to miss Arjay's encouraging fist pump before the door closes). "How was your week?" I ask Danny, like our last conversation didn't end abruptly.

"Pretty good. Project at work is going well, working with SinclAir."

"Awesome."

Danny pauses in the hall, looking both ways. "Where's the library again?"

"I'll show you." I pretend I'm not freaking out and start down the hall, hiding the mental happy-dance at the excuse to walk with him. "Teaching next hour?"

"Yeah, substituting."

"Good luck."

"Thanks. Not too worried." But he's not looking at me.

You'd think after spending well over an hour talking last Saturday, we could fall into a conversation more easily. Instead, something about this is all surface-level.

When in doubt, kittens. I feign concern. "How have you managed this week?"

Now he turns to me. "Okay . . . ?"

"Without kittens?"

"Oh." He shakes his head, teasing. "Been hard. Sometimes I

didn't think I'd make it."

I choose not to read too much into that, though we did kind of say kittens = flirting. Before I continue in that vein, though, we reach the library. Danny gets a Ziploc bag with two stubs of chalk and a battered eraser.

Now my excuse to walk with him is gone. Nobody else in the hall. Time to go for it (and no, not the kissing option). "So, you doing anything this weekend?"

"Um." Danny pauses. Can't tell if he's thinking or just hesitating. "Nope."

"Then would you like to do something?"

He pauses again, subtly regarding me. My lungs flinch in a silent gasp. Yeah, that seems like hesitation. I immediately backpedal, literally and figuratively. "Oh, you know, if not, that's fine. No big deal. I just had a good time last week, and—"

"No, I—yeah, I did too." He nods, more like he's trying to convince himself instead of me. "Let's do something."

"You sure?"

"Definitely. But it's your turn to plan."

I flash a smile. Well, I mean to flash a smile, but I can tell the smile's lingering way longer than a "flash." "Frolicking with kittens it is."

Danny laughs. "Perfect."

"Good luck teaching," I bid him again.

"Thanks." He backs up the first few feet until he finally has to turn away.

I manage to rein in the celebratory dance. Not that I have a chance before someone slaps me on the back. My heart leaps out of my chest, and I jump to a defensive posture—but it's Arjay.

"Atta girl," he says, not bothering to keep his volume down. "You're totally marrying him."

Now my heart's racing faster than when he scared me. No, we're not—so, so not—and I really hope Danny didn't hear.

So much for celebrating.

And when my phone chimes with a text message, I have twice the reason to not celebrate. Mom again. I never called her back.

talia (again, texting skills of a two-year-old) *i dont know what i did rong.*

A silent groan sinks in my lungs. I know she's not asking for a list of her crimes, but instantly one springs to mind. I shove down the memories of her neglecting me, screaming at my brother Troy, smacking Tyler for an A–, mocking Trevor.

but watever it is im sorry & ill always b ur mother. i just want ur love. can we put the past in the past?

I wish, I wish, I wish I could cut her off, that I could trust all my memories of her. But sometimes I'm not sure what to trust about my memory, since Mom always tells a very different version of events—and she's right about one thing for sure. She's my mom. She *must* love me, right?

Danny gave me a second chance. I can do that for my mom, right? I walk to my car, roll down my window, then hit the icon to call her and take a bracing breath.

"Talia," she gushes. "You called!"

Emotion slaps me in the face at her voice. I shouldn't believe her, but she sounds so . . . sincere. Like she really has been dying to talk to me. Like she cares. "Of course."

"How are you?"

"Fine," I say automatically. For half a second, I debate telling her more. Where do I start? My internship, my coworkers, Danny?

"Well," Mom says, breathless, "we just had the worst tragedy here."

Oh. It's about her again. Mom lacks a true sense of proportion, so "worst tragedy" might mean an unexpected bill. I'm guessing this time she's using other people's drama to get attention. For now, she has it. "What happened?" I ask.

"Remember my neighbor's daughter, Ashley? She's about nine."

Last time I went to my mom's house, she lived somewhere else. "Sorry, no."

"Well, she had this dog—kind of annoying—but it ran out in traffic and was killed! Right in front of my house! Can you believe that? I still have to pass the blood every day, Talia. Every single day."

"Oh. Do you?" Let's see. A child loses a beloved pet in a tragic accident, but the real problem is that nobody's hosed off the street yet. "How's Ashley holding up?"

"I don't know. What difference does that make?"

"No idea, Mom." Yes, why would any child's feelings matter? If we'd ever been allowed to have a dog—*Are you kidding? You're too irresponsible! Remember what happened to Twinkie?*—I can't say I'd be surprised if she ran over it herself. (I swear to you, she poisoned that goldfish.)

"Anyway." Her tone's sharp enough to cut off any further interruptions. She steamrolls on. I let my head loll back against the headrest, and I pack away everything I might have told her, everything I might say, everything I might feel.

Yep, it's my childhood all over again. She runs rampant, and I'm hiding.

CHAPTER 14
DANNY

I SURVIVE MY MEETINGS with Patrick from AeroTechCanada all Monday morning, until they turn us loose a little before lunch. We haven't made much progress with on the wing re-design, unless you count finding four methods that don't work.

The putative Thomas Edison quote about discovering ten thousand ways *not* to do something didn't go over so well, either. If my boss Carol hadn't been in the room, I might've gotten desperate enough to pitch the really outside-the-box solutions I've been contemplating. And drafting. And calculating.

Unfortunately, Carol ran the meeting—into the ground. Fortunately, my job security isn't on the line with this one task: I've got five others ahead of schedule or better than spec. I've earned a minute to chill once I've got my white pizza in the cafeteria.

Carol strolls over to my table, and I try not to let my tension around my boss show. So much for relaxing. I like her—I try to like her—but the feeling doesn't seem mutual. "You're not on the de-icing team, are you?" she asks me.

Isn't it her job to know that? "No."

"Would you like to be?"

"Um." At my hesitation, Carol frowns. My schedule's pretty full, and from what I've heard, Carol isn't interested in trying anything new or different on de-icing. Without that draw, I'm ready to plead off.

"Oh, hey." Another guy I know, Lucas, strolls up with his tray. "Talking about de-icing? We could really use you."

Flattery isn't enough to sway me, but the *for real* look Lucas and Carol are giving me might be. Guess I'm not *that* busy. "Okay, I'll try to make room."

"Great." Carol beams, but I recognize fake enthusiasm. She sits down at the next table, like we'll prolong this deal-making discussion.

Yeah, I'm gonna finish lunch at my desk. "Oh, just remembered—need to get an email out ASAP." I grab my pizza to go and retreat to my office.

Once the door shuts behind me, I puff out a breath. After the AeroTechCanada meeting this morning, and a whole new project where I can spin my wheels, I need to de-stress. And my new favorite way to relax at work is researching a particular plane.

I find a site offering an online rental of a documentary on the Arrow and sit back to enjoy the show. While it's loading, I check out the other comments on the page. One mentions a Facebook group for Arrow fans, and I pause the video to click through without a second thought. The public files have some interesting stuff—specs, models, etc. I'm almost tempted to reactivate my old account.

No matter how sneaky I am, Kendra would find out.

What am I afraid of? Having to ignore her again? Finding out she's doing worse? Doubt it gets a whole lot worse than her mother in tears, begging me to save her daughter's life.

I definitely don't love her anymore—hard not to hate her some days—but I don't want her dead. So I do the thing I'm never, never supposed to: I click in the search box at the top of the page and type her name.

The public version of her profile comes right up. Her picture's the same flower she always used. The first post on her page is a photo of a sunrise. Dated eight weeks ago. That seems hopeful.

I scroll past the messages of support and bewilderment through March—I'm sure dozens more are visible to her friends. I keep moving past the memories until I reach the next photo. A selfie of Kendra in a white fur-lined hat, in front of a snowy neighborhood.

Takes a second to click—that neighborhood is my parents'.

The memories surge back. I know what day that was, though I never saw her. I don't want to fall back into those memories I've worked so hard to forget; I can't—

My phone buzzes. I pull my eyes from the monitor and check the text message. From Talia.

She has no idea how much I needed rescuing. Without looking at the monitor again, I hit the keys to kill the browser tab and turn to Talia's message.

Time for your daily kitten!

Another message comes through, a kitten in sunglasses and a Hawaiian shirt. I glance around, like somebody's going catch me grinning at a goofy picture.

How do you respond to a kitten? Send one back? Say it's cute—implying that Talia and her flirting are cute? She must know I'm into her, but I still want to be careful.

Maybe more than careful. To be honest, I've been a little . . . worried about our next date. I want to go out with her—who wouldn't? But as soon as I accepted, Arjay popped up, and everyone within twenty meters had to have heard him shouting we were "totally" getting married.

Just like yesterday, my stomach clenches. Is that what Talia expects? Because aside from the fact it's ridiculously early in the relationship, I don't know when I'll be ready to think about that, other than not for a long time.

I've tried so hard to start over, to get past Kendra and all the crap I went through with her. It hasn't been all that long, but . . . what if I can't?

My gaze falls on my computer screen. The Arrow documentary's back up, paused on the dramatization of blow-torching the only five Arrows in existence into pieces. Some things you just can't undo.

A knock at my door interrupts my thoughts' spiral dive. "Come in," I call.

"Hey, Danny?" Brad, one of my team members, pops his head in my office. "The wind tunnel tests for that SinclAir engine pod are back. Do you have a minute to go over them?"

"Yeah." I take stock of my now-cold pizza, my unanswered text, my unfinished documentary. The documentary will wait. I shove two more bites of pizza in my mouth and stand.

Only one thing undone: the text. Definitely not a decision I wanted to make with an audience.

I've got to be reasonable. Objective. Losing my ability to think rationally to Kendra once again doesn't help anything. I need to keep trying. Moving forward. Starting over.

Perfect timing, I text Talia. *Thanks for the fix.*

I look to Brad still standing in the door. "Let's go."

I'm going out with Talia this weekend. We *will* have fun. I might even kiss her.

I just need to make sure she knows I'm not on the marriage market.

CHAPTER 15
TALIA

SOME DAYS, it's not so hard to juggle a law internship and a CIA job: you get up, you go into the (law) office, you work your day, you meet with an agent or two at night, you eat, you sleep.

Some days, you get up, you go into the office, you get a call, you fabricate a ridiculous yet believable excuse to run away, you pack up the depositions you'll be annotating all night, and you go break into someone's house while he's home.

Some days, being a CIA officer looks a lot like being a cat burglar.

Could be worse, though. I could still be in the skirt and heels I wore to the office. Fortunately, I've learned to keep a spy-emergency outfit hidden in my trunk: breathable black shirt, form-fitting black pants, shoes designed to muffle my footsteps. Vasily can't even hear me creeping over the hardwood floor through the open doorway to the living room.

Seeing me might be another story. I can't afford to mess with a disguise when I need stealth. If Vasily catches me, not only are our dance covers blown, but he'll hand off everything he knows about us to the Russians—it could end our careers. (Like a lot of risks we have to take.) But bugging Galina's apartment yielded nothing so we've got to go to the source.

I pull a slim mirror from the pack on my belt and ease it around the doorframe in slow motion, careful not to reflect a direct beam of light. Vasily's on the couch, hunched over his laptop, his back to me.

Some days, things totally go your way. That laptop's a definite win. We're looking for copies of anything he's fed to his handler, beyond the limited comms we've intercepted. I feel my belt pack again, checking for another device I packed: a hard drive cloner. (Like an external hard drive, but smaller and faster.)

There it is—plastic case the size of thick credit card. I push the slider to extend the USB plug. Doubt Vasily's logged his next visit with his Russian handler in iCalendar, but there's got to be something on there we can use, if only to figure out the next time to target him. Now I just have to get at his computer.

I rub my fingertip over my minimicrophone at my collar, signaling Elliott: brush brush tap, brush brush brush. Go.

In under a minute, Elliott knocks at the front door. (Another reason I came in the back.) I sneak back to the kitchen. Not a great plan—no other escape routes—but it's out of sight of the hall. I wait, listening.

"Sorry to bother you, sir," Elliott begins when Vasily answers the door. That's when I remember—Vasily and Elliott have met before, and Elliott didn't detail a disguise for me in the mission rundown.

He's smarter than that. Right? Or did we blow this?

"How can I help you?" Vasily asks. No sign of recognizing him.

"Luke Chambers with Ottawa Public Works. We've had reports of some damage to the pipes to your building." Elliott keeps his tone perfectly polite—perfectly Canadian. "I'd like to test your water, if that's possible? It'll only take a few minutes."

"Well . . ."

I hold my breath.

"We just need to make sure there's no sewage leaking into your drinking water," Elliott explains. Yeeeah, even I'd let somebody in for that. (With a reasonably convincing uniform.)

"All right," Vasily says.

Whew.

"Thanks. Shall we start in the kitchen?"

I.e., where I am. Crap. I glance around, like a door into another room magically appeared in the last ten seconds. Nope. I tap the microphone almost as fast as my heart is beating, and roll my feet to noiselessly hurry to the pantry door.

"Oh, actually," Elliott says, "could you show me to the restroom? Sometimes we get interference with kitchen appliances."

If I were Vasily, I'd be gearing up to evict this liar. (Of course, I'm also a girl, so strange guys in my house telling lies would be three strikes, get out.) Fortunately, Vasily's not me, and he's buying Elliott's nonsensical line. "Yes, this way."

I'm curious to see how Elliott's selling this, from disguise to props, but I don't have time. He's given me maybe three minutes to get out of the kitchen and on Vasily's computer. Fortunately, he didn't shut it down. I plug in the cloner. The blue LED lights up, and I crouch behind the gray suede couch, out of view of the hall. Elliott's small talk focuses on keeping up his lie—something about pipe problems upstream, water testing kit spiel—and keeping Vasily pinned down. I watch the LED flicker, waiting, waiting, waiting.

Funny how fast this device seems when we test it in the office. I feel like I could do this faster copying the files manually. As in writing them by hand.

Elliott's voice grows louder. Another advantage to his running commentary: locating him and Vasily. I drag a finger over my mic slowly, hoping he gets the signal to draw it out.

"Let's test the water in the kitchen next."

"It's over there," Vasily says. Like he's not coming with Elliott.

Elliott's no fool. "Sorry, could you show me which switch runs the garbage disposal?"

Vasily doesn't respond aloud, and in the silence, my pulse thumps in my ears. I realize I'm clutching the arm of the couch, like it'll protect me (or hide the cloner) if Vasily comes in. The seconds crawl by until I hear two sets of footsteps on the kitchen linoleum.

My heart rate returns to normal. I check the LED—green. All done. I pull the cloner out and slip it back into my belt pack. The hardware was always the easy part. Now I just have to get out.

The water runs in the kitchen and I take my opportunity to cross the room and slide my mirror around the doorframe again. Elliott, in a blond wig and I'm guessing a fake scar or something, holds up a tiny plastic cup. He tears open a black packet and pours in a white powder, then picks up a black plastic pod and squirts in a dark liquid. He adds tap water and offers it to Vasily. "Can you shake this for me for sixty seconds?"

"Sure," Vasily says, hesitation hanging in his tone. But he takes whatever it is and starts shaking.

"Hold it up to the light. Let me know when it turns yellow." Elliott points to the window—facing Vasily away from me. Elliott flips on the water and the garbage disposal, and I've got cover and a distraction to escape.

I creep to the front door, not bothering to wait for Elliott to finish "testing" the water.

Half an hour later, I beat Elliott to the rendezvous, a Tim Hortons/Coldstone Creamery, though I've taken my time in making sure I'm not being watched. I settle at a table to watch the sanitized weather and headline reports while I wait. (I'd get ice cream, but the food security at these restaurants is pretty lax.)

Elliott cruises through the parking lot in a gold Company car, and I meet him around back. He rolls down his window. "You didn't get me anything?" he asks, a hand on his chest like he's wounded.

"You were late. I ate it. Sorry." I smile extra brightly to show I'm not sorry at all. I get in the passenger side, moving aside the stuff on the seat: a condiment cup with a lid, one of those liquid drink mix pods and . . . a packet of salt. "Your 'water testing kit'?"

"I know you're impressed."

Okay. Maybe a little.

"You got it, right?" Elliott asks.

"Yep." Anything sensitive will most likely be encrypted, and we'll have to send that back to Langley =, but now we've got a lot more than the fragmentary messages we've been able to intercept so far. We might even have enough to figure out the identities of the rest of his spy ring.

We head back to the office, with a few more stops to make sure we haven't picked up any tails, though we were both clear when we met. After our final stop, we get on the Queensway.

"You know," Elliott begins. He's trying to sound casual, but he's walking down a path I do not want to follow. He drags me along before I change the subject. "I haven't heard anything about Danny lately."

"Nothing to report."

He glances at me—though his eyes aren't teasing (like they normally are). Is he actually . . . concerned? "No second date?"

Though I contemplate not answering, I feel bad about leaving Elliott hanging when he might care. "Not until this Saturday."

Elliott punches me in the shoulder. "What are you doing

this time?"

"I don't know. I have to figure it out—I asked him."

"Hm."

I can't tell whether he's thinking about that or worried I had to ask Danny. (It's the twenty-first century. I can do that.) Or maybe just driving.

Elliott waits until we're off the Queensway before he returns to that topic. "Been to the Rockcliffe Park pond?" he suggests. "Wait, I think that's only open in the morning. You could try a ghost tour—or they do Shakespeare in the park."

I frown, and he catches my skepticism. "What?" he says. "I have culture."

"The bacterial kind?"

Elliott glares at me. "You've got to give me something to go on, unless you guys are going to pass the time planning your wedding."

I ignore a minor jolt of shock. (Stupid W-word.)

"Any hobbies?"

Aside from kittens? "Not that I know of."

"Local?"

"American."

Elliott stops at a red light, pondering. "What does he do for a living?"

"He's an aerospace engineer—"

"Aviation museum," he cuts me off.

Have to admit, not a bad idea. Maybe boring for me, but most museums try to appeal to the layman, right?

"What's his last name again?" Elliott asks.

"Fluker," I answer—then I realize he slipped one past me, just when I was starting to trust him. He doesn't need that intel to figure out a good date, and I haven't told him before. I can only imagine what he'll use it for.

Before I can backtrack, we reach our office parking lot and switch back to business mode (or as close as Elliott gets). A couple coworkers are in the bullpen once we pass the reception area and security swipe, so we divvy up the intel from the hard drive cloner, and I get stuck with Vasily's old emails.

Nothing looks suspicious, dance and trading shifts with another stylist (which is why he's home today). After half an hour of scrolling through his social life, I'm out of leads.

"Hey, T," Elliott says without moving from his desk. Rashad's the only other guy in the office now, but he looks up, too. "When's the last time we updated your call sign?"

"Maybe a year?"

"Time for a new one." He turns to Rashad. "You need one?"

"Hit me."

We're supposed to use an approved list and pick something at random, but sometimes we get creative. "OTIS," Elliott declares.

"Otis," Rashad repeats. His scoff says *you can't be serious.*

"Sure—wasn't there a kid named Milo on *The Cosby Show* with Phylicia Rashad?"

Rashad pops up an eyebrow. "No Milos on that show."

"Sure there were. Right?" He falls silent for a minute. The lack of an actual connection is good, though. Nobody else would ever make the logical leap Elliott did. "Well, whatever, *Milo and Otis*: OTIS."

Rashad shakes his head like he can't believe this white boy and goes back to his computer. Elliott looks to me. "Anybody call you Tally growing up?"

"No," I lie. Nobody I want to admit to knowing.

"Perfect. Now you're FOXHUNT. Tallyho!"

Rashad and I exchange an is-he-for-real? look. "Why do we put up with this?" I ask.

"We take whatever they give us. We're the tokens."

I furrow my brow in a question, and he explains: "You're the token woman and I'm the token Black guy. We're just trying to not be the first to die."

Not sure that's very "PC," but it's pretty funny.

"FOX," Elliott says, "c'mon, do me."

I turn back with an expression of *excuse me, what, now?* But that's not an overt come-on. Elliott beckons for me to come at him—he wants a new name, too.

I narrow my eyes and fold my arms like I'm thinking deeply. "You're named after Eliot Ness, right?"

Elliott flinches. "You remember that?"

"Yeah. And he was the leader of the Untouchables."

He waits for my conclusion.

"HAMMER." I lean back in my desk chair like that seals it.

"Hm?"

"You can't touch this."

Elliott mock-rolls his eyes. "OTIS was better."

"No way." Rashad jerks his head in my direction. "She's doing mine next time."

"Hey." Elliott holds out a hand to go along with a give-me-some-credit-here face. "You like yours, don't you, T?"

"Almost as much as I like yours."

"C'mon, what's more fitting than calling you 'FOX'?"

I grin. He totally set himself up. "Calling you 'HAM.'"

Elliott laughs with the rest of us, and we drift back to work. I'm about done with my report when Elliott drops a manila folder on my desk. A couple papers fan out across the desktop. I look up. "Done already?"

"Yeah." He slides the folder closer, like he doesn't want to give a high-level report first.

Fine. I flip it open—and stop. The top page is a scan of a passport, and smiling up at me is a photo of Danny.

I slowly raise my eyes to meet Elliott's. "What is this?"

He purses his lips as if to say I'm smarter than that.

"This is a total misappropriation of resources—"

"It's not his *real* traces; just something I threw together." Elliott waits for me to accept that argument, and when I don't, he tries again. "We'll do a background check when you get married anyway."

I slap the folder shut, forcing my climbing heart rate to slow. "I know you're all tied down, but we're just going on a second date. Don't get excited."

I expect Elliott to attack back. Instead, he raises his hands in surrender. "Okay, okay. But never hurts to be informed."

Right. To make my point, I shove the folder into a desk drawer. Elliott heads back to his desk. But he only makes it a few seconds before he's on my case again. "Wait, T—your date is *this* Saturday?"

I swivel back on him, ready to let into him, but then I see his face. He isn't teasing again. He's still sincere.

Always bad news. "Yes, this Saturday. Why?"

The apology in his tone is 100% real. "That's Vasily's next competition."

Of course. Of course. Of course.

Some days, I hate my life.

CHAPTER 16
DANNY

WEDNESDAY EVENING, Campbell brings his Xbox 360 and Joel over for pizza and the chance to use my bigger, better flat screen.

Yeah, yeah, I'm a single guy with disposable income. I buy stupid electronics. Sue me.

I can only play video games for an hour or two before it starts to get monotonous. Shoot the bad guys, more come back, etc., etc. But this passes for my social life, so I play along. Half an hour after I'm really thinking about AeroTechCanada's wingtips, Joel pauses the game to grab more soda, and then my phone rings. Out of nowhere, my throat instinctively tightens, random PTSD that has nothing to do with this war game. I'm not expecting a call.

Could be Kendra.

No, I know it's not her. Can't be. She doesn't have this number.

Unless my mom gave it to her.

I push down the panic and pull out my phone. The display

reads *Talia.*

Now I'm nervous for a different reason—but a good nervous. I hope. Without any explanation to the guys, I duck into the spare bedroom to answer. "Hello?"

"Hi, Danny? It's Talia."

"Hey, how are you?"

"Um, could be better, because . . . I've got bad news."

I don't allow my pulse to rise. No other response. "What's that?"

"I was really excited about our date, but—"

Was? But? Oh, this'll be good.

"I just got three huge cases dumped in my lap, and I'll be stuck putting out fires all day Saturday."

Now my heart sinks. I try to keep the disappointment out of my words. "That's too bad."

Could this be a tactic to get out of a date? To control me? I remember that moment that almost made me turn her down when she asked me out, when she backpedaled and that little voice in the back of my brain screamed Talia was manipulating me into going out.

That little voice sounds a lot like Kendra.

"I'm so sorry," Talia cuts into my thoughts. "Can I get a rain check?"

"Yeah. Sure." I silence the screaming in my mind and try to keep my tone on the safe side of flirting. "But I was looking forward to kittens."

"Bet you've done nothing but daydream about running through the wildflowers with some adorable little furballs."

"Exactly."

"Sorry to disappoint you."

She might be kidding, but my chest does feel hollow. I *was* looking forward to our date. "I'll need, like, six or seven pictures of kittens to get over this. Or to retain the will to live."

I can just see her doing the blink-tilt-recalculating thing

and practically hear her smile. "I'll see what I can do."

"They'll have to be extra cute. Cuteness overload."

She laughs, but her keyboard clicks in the background. Not ready to give her up to work yet. "What kind of cases do you handle?"

"I'm a litigation intern—so mostly scut work and whatever else they want me to do. Couldn't go into too much detail anyway; confidentiality, you know. Plus, it'd bore you to death, and that'd probably double my kitten debt."

"Maybe triple."

"Exactly. Better avoid the topic of work. Although I bet that aerospace gig isn't boring."

The tension in my shoulders releases a little. She's not trying to cut and run or play games. She actually sounds like she doesn't want this conversation to end.

Only logical to settle in and talk. "I don't think it's boring, but I won't make you listen to the ins-and-outs of the latest fluid dynamic trials."

"I dunno, I'm already racking up a massive cute-debt. Might need help working it off."

I glance around the room. Crud. Unless I want to plop down on a cardboard box of stuff I hauled nine hours and six hundred miles to not unpack, there's nowhere to sit. Why couldn't I have picked my room? Yeah, it's ten feet farther away, but—great.

Talia sighs. "I should get back to work."

"Don't sound so excited."

"Believe me, I'm not." But she gets off the phone anyway—before I have a chance to hammer down when that rain check would be. Something tells me it'll be harder to cash that check than it was to get out of Beth's reach.

Just when I was getting my hopes up.

I return to my living room, but only one of my friends is still there. I know I wasn't gone that long. "Where's Joel?"

"His girlfriend called." Campbell mimics cracking a whip.

No comment on why I left.

"Been meaning to talk to you," Campbell continues. He points past me, down the hall. "Did you say you have a spare bedroom?"

"Yeah . . . ?"

"What's your rent like?"

I tell him, but I'm not hiding the eyebrow of skepticism. "Why?"

"Landlord's doubling my rent. Looking for a roommate?"

Hard to say no to halving my bills every month, and Campbell's a cool guy. "Sure. When do you want to move in?"

"I have to be out by the end of the month."

"That'll work." I think. "Oh, wait—my mom will be in town that weekend."

"Is she staying here?"

"Not sure. Maybe."

Campbell considers that. "We'll figure something out."

"Cool."

Then the freight train traveling at sixty kph from New York collides with the ninety kph train from Boston. I really hope Talia doesn't try to cash that rain check while my mother's in town. Don't see that ending well. For all the pressure she puts on me to date, nobody's good enough for her son. Nobody except one girl.

Not going there.

I pick up my controller again, but I'm hardly paying enough attention to do well in the game. When my phone buzzes, I'm grateful for the distraction. A text. From Talia. I open it to find a picture of a tiny cat asleep in a teacup. *This has got to count for at least two kittens. Right?*

I press my lips together to hide the smile from Campbell. *I dunno*, I text back. *It's so small, it might only be a half a kitten.*

At this rate, I'll be in cute bankruptcy before I can use that rain check.

I text her back: *Just be sure to cash in by Aug 30. Limited time offer.*

Yep, manipulation. Awesome. I learned from the best, but it's not a lesson I want to pass on.

On the other hand, Talia and my mom will not mix. I'm doing this to protect them both.

Talia doesn't seem too concerned. *I'll see what I can do. I understand you're in high demand.*

I text one last time: *Ha.*

You know, it's totally rational to be this excited to go out with her. Now to make sure we cash that rain check.

CHAPTER 17
TALIA

ONCE AGAIN, I'm spending the weekend away from the man I'd like to be getting to know. Plus, the last time I was in a poofy, froufy, sparkly dress was supposed to be *the last time*. But here I am, waiting in the wings at another ballroom competition, nerves battling in my middle.

I was anticipating nerves today, but they were supposed to be over my date with Danny instead of trying to get in with the head of a (so far untraceable) spy ring so he'll recruit me.

"You got this," Elliott whispers to me. He massages my shoulders. "Gord" and "Joanne" might interact like that, but I have to jerk away. Too tense to enjoy that (and still a little strange).

If Danny were here, he'd know better than to reassure me. He knows I perform better under pressure and I'd rather be pushed to do my best than reassured. And he'd know better than to try to touch me. Or maybe I wouldn't mind him trying.

Though if Danny were here, I'd be hiding in the bathroom, figuring out how to get him out of the building.

Fortunately, he's not even in the same city—we drove to Montréal for this—and Elliott and I have already made it through the first round. They announce the first half of the Latin semi-finals, our event, and Elliott holds out his hand. My palms are sweaty but oh well. Gord and Joanne are on.

We strut to the floor, and I slap on a smile over the nerves. I've got this. I've got this. I've got this.

Stupid how scared I am to mess this up, when winning isn't our objective today. In fact, messing up's our strategy: get me closer to Vasily, whether that means me flirting or me falling.

He and Galina are in this heat, too, which hurts our chances at the finals. Elliott and I reach our spot on the floor and do a double underarm turn, him releasing me into a solo spin to take our positions. I strike my pose for the first dance, the cha cha, and make eye contact with Elliott. He glances in the direction of Vasily's red shirt and gives me the subtlest nod.

Yep. I'll be taking a fall in this heat.

Having a concrete objective calms my nerves a little, and the music blasting over the loudspeakers covers up the rest of the jitters. Here we go.

The first song is too soon to make a move on Vasily, so I concentrate on the performance. I catch the beat, catch my breath and catch my skirt. I swish the neon green poofs around my legs and strut in a circle. In any other context, this would look totally bizarre, but here, I'm anxious about not exaggerate-ing the movements enough. Elliott starts for me and I sashay away, only to reverse the chase on him in the next count. Finally he takes my hand, spins me, and pulls me into the closed formation for the dance. I concentrate on hitting my marks with my feet, hips, hands, posture, smile.

Another turn rotates us into an open formation, following the steps side by side, until we freeze in a mid-step pose for a second. Before we start into motion again, the music fades.

"Samba," the announcer echoes. Elliott checks his shoe

soles. (Don't worry, his sequins are all in place.) We take our positions. When the beat booms through my rib cage again, I arch my back, circling my hips wide.

Again, this would be bizarre anywhere else.

Although keeping up this snake-like movement takes more concentration than the cha cha, I glimpse of Vasily's red sparkly shirt. Not close enough to make our move.

Samba runs long, it seems, but Elliott made sure our routines covered an extra minute. (Each dance only lasts ninety seconds, and no, there's no "overtime.")

We bow for the samba and move to our positions for rumba. For some reason, these routines always seem to begin with posing, gesturing and posturing. I go through my poses as Elliott slowly advances on me with his own stylized steps.

Rumba is even harder for me than samba, but that has less to do with the footwork and more to do with how we're supposed to stare into one another's eyes with *passion*.

I have a hard time staring into Elliott's eyes without laughing. Especially seeing him dance. In spandex. And stage makeup. And—glitter?

Don't get me wrong—he's good—he's way better than me. But to see a guy I know like Elliott swiveling his hips, spinning, kicking . . . yeah. Laughter is the right response.

Fortunately, I'm also supposed to tease and reject him in this dance, and that I can do. But just as we're getting to the good part, I see a flash of red in the middle of a turn.

Vasily's right next to us.

"Time," Elliott says. That's all the warning I get before he spins me out—and directly into Vasily.

I bounce off him, sending me sprawling on the floor. A collective gasp rises from the room. Vasily stumbles, but barely breaks rhythm.

The music fades before Elliott reaches me, and as soon as he's done with his own hip wiggling, Vasily's kneeling by me.

"Are you hurt?"

Phase one: check. Now to suck him in. I shake my head without making eye contact.

"What did you do to me?" Elliott demands. Those words hit like a slap. I flinch away from him—and that's not acting. Because for a split second, it's not Elliott standing over me.

It's my mother.

Vasily helps me to my feet, glaring daggers at Elliott. "Do you need any help?" Vasily asks me.

I don't trust my voice, but I manage to shake my head, still staring down. Elliott steps up to pry me from Vasily's grasp and push his arm away. "She's fine."

Finally I shove all my emotions into the right places. This is Elliott. He's supposed to act this way to help me draw Vasily in, playing Gord as my high-handed partner. Not an eerie imitation of my mom.

A judge, a middle-aged woman in a floor-length glittery dress, reaches us. "Can you go on?" she asks me.

I let my eyes grow wider, flicking between Elliott and Vasily and back. Elliott sends me a not-so-subtle signal, *tell the nice woman yes*, and I nod, my gaze locked on his.

"The paso doble," the announcer interrupts, exaggerating his pronunciation. Elliott grunts, which probably means the announcer said it wrong anyway.

The judge backs off, and I shuffle to my position to start the second-to-last dance. The dance is supposed to imitate a mata-dor (Elliott) and his cape (me). Elliott casts a pointed look at my feet—no, my knees.

Got it: fake an injury.

The music starts. Within eight bars, my feet are slow, my hips are off, and I'm obviously favoring my "good" leg. As soon as Elliott's got me in the closed formation, he bows closer to me (poor form). "You okay?"

I grimace to cover my wink and follow his underarm turn.

But again, I'm too slow. Instead of meeting him at the end of the turn, I trip on his foot.

And bump into Vasily again. "Sorry," I murmur. He doesn't look my way, absorbed in his own dance, but I know he heard.

Probably enough. I hobble off the floor to the stands. Elliott plays his role to the hilt, continuing our paso doble routine alone. He looks extra ridiculous waiting for no one to spin and turn with him.

The paso doble ends, and Elliott strides from the floor in my direction. I shift a fraction of an inch to see Vasily watching him.

"Jive!" the announcer calls the last dance.

Before the music starts, Elliott reaches me. He seizes my upper arm and drags me to half-standing. "Dance," he barks.

"I can't—"

"Because you're embarrassed?"

"Because I'm hurt!"

He drops my arm. I slam down onto the wooden bleachers, and Elliott marches off.

Through the last song, I fold my arms and let my head hang. Feels like ages pass, though it's only a few minutes before the music's done, the announcer's pumped up the crowd, and the dancers are filing off the floor—past the bleachers where I'm sitting.

Let Vasily approach me. Let Vasily approach me. Let Vasily approach me.

"Excuse me," comes that now-familiar accent. "Are you hurt?"

I look up, sniffling conspicuously. "I'm fine."

"Because it seems like you're injured."

"Joanne?" Vasily's partner, Galina, takes a seat next to me, her skinny arm across my shoulders. "No man should treat his partner this way."

Vasily settles on my opposite side, and I look to him, like

I'm verifying Galina's reassurances. He agrees.

I drop my gaze to my knees again. "But he's my partner."

"That does not make him right," Galina says. "It was his fault you hit Vasily."

I shrug a shoulder, still staring at the wood grain of the bleachers showing between my neon green skirt and Vasily's black pants. "Doesn't matter to him."

"You need a partner who respects you," Galina insists.

"No, I can't stop now. Gord's taught me so much; I'll lose everything if he drops me."

"You should drop him," Vasily says. "Not the other way around."

I finally meet Vasily's eyes. "Then what would I do? Who would I practice with? I'd have to give up everything I worked for. He's made me everything I am."

"Have you not worked hard?"

"Of course I have."

Vasily pats my knee—my "injured" knee. If he's testing me, I'll pass. I suck in a breath through my teeth, and he draws back. "Sorry."

"You've worked hard to get here," Galina repeats. "Don't waste it all on an idiot."

The realization solidifies in my chest: I've got them. This is my chance. Just one more little nudge in the right direction. "I can't. How would I ever find another partner?"

"Don't you live near Ottawa?" Vasily asks.

"I have to." I toss out one little bit of bait, showing Vasily I could be a valuable asset. "I work in Parliament."

"Then you must come to our studio. We'll help you find someone."

Almost there. "Auditioning new partners while I forget everything I know? I'll stick with Gord."

"I'll help you." Vasily holds out a business card for an Ottawa dance studio.

I take it, allowing a smile to infiltrate my features like I just infiltrated Vasily's good graces. "Thank you."

Vasily pats my knee again, again initiating the flinch-gasp cycle before he pulls away.

Mission accomplished—or, really, the first step of the mission. Now to convince him I know something he wants to pass on to the Russians (and my knee's all better).

Easy, right?

The victory finally sinks in on the drive home that evening. A big move in the right direction for our case.

"Well," Elliott says, "that wasn't so hard. If only you could hook Danny that easily."

I shoot him a look of *do we really have to go there?* But of course we do, because he knows it bugs me.

"Thought about what kind of ring you want?" Elliott fishes in the backseat and tosses papers my way—a jewelry catalog. (Why does he even have this?) "I have ways of dropping hints, you know."

"Number one, no, you don't; you're a guy. Number two, if you give this to him, I will hurt you. Seriously."

He gives me a wicked grin. "Think he'd buy into a cryptic message scrawled on the front: 'You just met the girl of your dreams; what are you going to do next?' Mailbox or doorstep?"

I groan. "That would freak any normal person out."

"How about if it's in your handwriting?"

I whip around to face him again. Danny wouldn't recognize it, but—"You can forge my handwriting?"

He grins again, and I'm not sure he's joking. A chill trickles across my skin. What if he really did that? What would Danny think? I'm sure he's not into obeying cryptic anonymous messages, but some guys are desperate to get married, especially

Mormon guys once they get to our age.

Is Danny desperate to get married?

"Have you read his file?" Elliott asks.

That manila folder's still sitting in my desk drawer, screaming at me every time I come in the office. Doubt Danny has anything to hide—but then, it's always the ones you least expect, isn't it?

I dodge the question, turning the tables on Elliott instead. "Would you have read a file like that on Shanna?"

I don't know the timeline, but they were already either living together or engaged when Elliott joined the CIA, so he knew her before the Agency did (officially).

"Dunno," he admits. "Would've been nice to have her credit report before I proposed."

"Like you're ever getting married."

"December nineteenth."

For a long minute, I wait for him to crack a smile, but Elliott's totally calm. And totally serious. After *years* of being engaged, the guy who kissed me not three weeks ago—as a cover, but while he and his fiancée were "on a break"—set a date?

"That's four months away," I point out.

"Shanna's been planning for years. Only hard part is getting the place she wants."

The place *she* wants. Red flags are flying all over the place in my brain, but I watch Elliott for his reaction. (No, I'm not going to ask a guy how he *feels*.) No tension in his forehead, no worries in his eyes, no frown sneaking onto his lips. I'm gripping my seatbelt way too tight, practically panicking by proxy, but he's not freaking out or resigned. He's at peace.

He's crazy.

"Congratulations." Wish I sounded like I mean it.

"Thanks. It'll be good."

For an incurable flirt to marry a woman who thrives on

drama? Clearly we have different definitions of "good."

"You should try it. You and Danny could still beat us to the altar."

I ignore him and lean down to get my case full of even. More. Legal research.

"Come on," Elliott continues, "I know how you Mormons operate. You'll be married with a kid before the year's out."

No, no, nonono. I draw in air against my closing ribs and try to play it cool. "Hello? It's August. That's physically impossible."

Also, just plain impossible. Me? Married? I'd die first. Really. I push aside the fear, grab a green highlighter from my case's pocket and pull out the first book to get started. Yes, my law firm's trapped in the last century, but I still remember how to use one of these book . . . things.

"Seriously." Elliott's not dropping it. "I had a Mormon friend in college—proposed to a girl on their second date."

Sadly, this isn't the first or the craziest story I've heard like this. Though they knew each other slightly from serving as missionaries in Finland at the same time, my own parents officially dated for three weeks before they got engaged. Two months later, they were married.

Look how well that worked out. (That's sarcasm, if you can't tell.)

I realize my breathing has grown shallow again, and I force myself to take slow, deep breaths.

After a minute of silence, Elliott tries once more. "You're coming to the wedding, right?"

Maybe. Before I ask where it is, Elliott follows up, "You need to catch the bouquet. You're next."

Ugh. I clamp down on my panic, whack him with his jewelry catalog, and flip to the index of my book.

He's wrong. He has to be.

CHAPTER 18
DANNY

THIRTY-SEVEN. Over the last week and a half, Talia's sent thirty-seven kittens—thirty-eight if you count the picture of a kitten pushing an impossibly small, identical kitten in a tiny shopping cart as two separate animals. Animated, sleeping, frightened; black, gray, tabby; wearing hats, wearing sweaters, wearing socks. Kinda curious how long she'll keep this up.

I might find out. I look over the guest bedroom one more time. The borrowed air mattress is sad—I might end up sleeping here instead of Mom—but at least my stuff's out of the way. Ready as I'll ever be.

My mom arrives in a few minutes, and Talia and I still haven't set a date for this date. As I'm heading out the door, my phone buzzes with a text. From Talia. No kittens. *It's the 30th, isn't it?*

That's today, I reassure her.

Sorry! Wanted to cash that rain check last night, but wild-fires were spreading. Like . . . wildfire.

Okay, she does want to go out, and she's funny. Two

pluses. *Let me know if you need a bucket brigade,* I reply.

She doesn't text back until I'm halfway to the airport to pick up Mom. Once I'm safe in the park-and-wait lot, I read it. *Digging a firebreak today. That rain check would really come in handy. Esp the rain part.*

Thirty-eight times this week I'm trying to hide a goofy grin after her texts. I'm definitely giving her extra humor credit because I like her, but if she wants to go out tonight . . . I can't immediately ditch my mom, and them meeting would send them both the wrong message.

If not tonight, when? Mom's supposed to be in town for two weekends. If by some miracle Talia avoids her at church, it'd still be a long time to put off our date. With the way I hesitated when she asked, even kittens may not be enough to convince her I'm interested—especially when I have to tell her I'm not looking to get married soon. I need something to let her know I'm into this.

If that's the price, how bad could it be? *When?*

Tonight?

I hesitate, twiddling my thumbs over my phone. Can Talia endure—or maybe avoid—my mom?

My phone rings: Mom. She's bursting with excitement, so maybe I shouldn't go running off quite yet. She directs me where to meet her, and I roll up to the right pickup spot. She's waiting under the shade on the sidewalk, tall and tanned, like a retired beach volleyball star. I get out to greet her. "Hi, Mom."

"Danny!" She grabs me in a big hug, then leaves me to lug her over-the-weight-limit suitcase to my trunk. What are sons for? I load her bag and hop back in the driver's seat. "How've you been?" she asks once we're on the road.

"Good." I keep my tone light, like I wasn't just having a major philosophical debate about whether or not to go out with a girl I'm really interested in.

"Seeing anyone? Or 'hanging out'?" She says it with derision, like she didn't hang out back in the day.

I don't buy it, and I don't buy into her ploy. "Yes, I've been hanging out."

"Oh?" Mom lifts her eyebrows, but she looks a lot less curious and a lot more disapproving. "Is it serious? What's she like?"

"Well," I say, borrowing a line from an old commercial Mom loved, "she's a guy, so . . ."

Mom imitates a rimshot. "I'm not trying to harp on this, but you won't not be happy by yourself forever."

Ouch. Time to change the subject. "You said you had a surprise?"

Her eyes light up. "Yes. Are you sitting down?"

I glance at the steering wheel, the car seat, and her, letting that stand for my answer.

She purses her lips, but continues. "It's a gift—a graduation gift. Belated."

I graduated three years ago. Guessing that's code for *you're still not married, and we're tired of sitting on this, so here.*

Mom drops the bomb. "Your father and I are giving you fifty thousand dollars."

"Wait, what?" The shockwave echoes through me. I mean, yeah, my parents are well off, and they like to make big gestures—LASIK after high school graduation, a car and an undisclosed "nest egg" for each of my siblings' weddings—but this is by far the biggest.

Then the shock turns cold. Those big gestures come with big "ifs" attached. LASIK *if* I was preparing for a mission—like I wasn't planning on it anyway. A car *if* I stayed in-state for grad school—which worked out, since U–Mich was my first choice.

But can those strings work out so conveniently yet again?

"To buy a house," Mom concludes.

Oh. That's doable. More than doable. It's a big deal. My parents are admitting I'm an adult, capable and independent, even if I'm *still* so sadly, desperately single.

But she isn't finished. She flips down the visor and combs her hair into place, dropping the last two words of the condition like an afterthought. "In Michigan."

Those strings cinch around my throat. The light in front of me turns red, and I hit the brakes a little too hard. "You want me to move back to Michigan?"

No way. No. Absolutely not. Never.

"I wouldn't want to buy you a house to keep you away from us, would I?"

I shake my head, shaking off her attempt at logic. "I have a job here."

"Don't make this into an argument."

"I'm not arguing."

"You're not agreeing, either."

I look at her like I can shoot lasers from my eyes—not how LASIK works. "Mom. You expect me to walk away from a really good job—"

"You had a job in Michigan, too."

"I telecommuted part time from your basement. I have a career here."

"What else? The friends you've made in the last four months? Come on, sweetie. You have a good job, but waiting for you back home is a real life."

I flinch, then puff out a breath. For a second, I thought she said "a real wife." As if I didn't already get the subtext. Because Kendra's in Michigan.

The biggest reason I'm not there.

Mom waits until I look at her to throw in her guilt-trip kicker. "We just want you close by. There's more to life than work."

I bury a sigh. The thing about mothers: in the end, they're trying to do what's best for you. Usually, she's right. About my mission, about grad school—but not about this.

But she's my mom, and I do love her. And I know she loves me. Just wish she'd find another way to show it. "Okay. I'll think about it."

I don't need to buy a house. Hadn't even crossed my mind until she brought it up. I'm liking the idea, but I won't die if I don't.

Moving back to Michigan? Not so sure about that survival rate.

The light finally turns green, and Mom moves on to telling me about her last visit with Gracie. My niece is cute enough to get out of any trouble, and that free pass extends to my mom for now.

When we get back to my apartment, I put Mom's suitcase in the spare bedroom, while Mom stops in the bathroom.

As if Talia were watching me to see when I could respond again, my phone buzzes the minute I'm alone.

So . . . not tonight?

Disappointment curls up in my stomach like a sad little kitten. Again, if I don't go out with her soon, she'll think I don't want to go out, or I'm playing mind games.

And if she gives up, I lose one little reason to stay here, bringing me one short step closer to taking that bribe to move back home.

I check the time. Almost five. I could take Mom to an early dinner and make it back in decent time for a date, appeasing Mom and still getting to see Talia.

I'm already doing something for dinner, but I'm free after. Does 8 work for you? I text Talia.

Hm. "Doing something." That doesn't sound purposefully vague.

Pick you up at 8, she replies. *The kittens will be sleepy though.*

Perfect. Now I have a completely different reason to hope my meal with Mom goes fast.

CHAPTER 19
TALIA

MY STOMACH'S DOING A JITTERBUG even bouncier than the dance I sat out last week. Didn't know I could *get* more nervous than I was at the competition, but as I walk in Danny's apartment building, the nerves of last week are a pale memory.

The mixed signals I'm getting from Danny aren't helping.

I'm in the lobby when suddenly I remember there's something else I need to be worried about here—and she's headed my direction. Galina.

So far, she hasn't seen me. We haven't been able to figure out whether she's part of the spy ring or not, since most of our efforts have been centered on Vasily, and her apartment bug hasn't turned up anything. Right now, Galina's walking like a woman on a mission, and she's carrying a black leather tote.

My interest is instantly piqued. Who knows what kind of intelligence she could have in there? The Illegals spy ring in the States (you know, Anna Chapman, "look what she did with the hydrangeas") operated through WiFi transmissions and exchanging identical bags. I check the clock on my phone. A little

142

early for my date.

Time to follow her.

I pretend to be absorbed in my phone as she passes me—all-purpose cover that works almost anywhere. Galina marches past, like I blend in with the furniture. I wait to make sure she doesn't glance back, then I turn on my heel and pursue.

She starts toward the dance studio, but I doubt they're rehearsing, not with Galina dressed for business. I hurry to keep up with her before she can slip out of my sight completely.

She crosses the street and turns the corner toward their studio. Maybe she's rehearsing after all?

I make sure not to fall too far behind. By the time I catch up enough to see her, she's already past their studio, maintaining the same purposeful clip. Exactly how I'd walk on my way to make an exchange.

Careful not to get too close, I keep my focus on Galina. She doesn't ever check her back—poor tradecraft. (Unless you *know* you're surrounded by spies. But she has no reason to think anyone suspects her.)

And she keeps going. One block, two, three. (In those heels?!) I'll be late for Danny. Sheer length of a surveillance detection route can sometimes compensate for not trying to detect anyone. Is that her game? I scan the oncoming crowd for matching black bags. An undetectable brush pass with something that size isn't easy, but possible.

Then I see it: the oncoming black tote. My heart rate hops higher. I dodge the man who stops abruptly ahead of me—accomplice?—my gaze jumping between those two totes.

Galina and the guy with the matching bag approach each other. A cordoned off pothole in the sidewalk drives them closer together—closer than strangers-walking-down-the-street distance. Far enough back that they won't notice, I halt to concentrate on watching them.

Until the man who'd stopped ten feet ago passes in front of

me again, blocking my view as Galina and the guy pass each other. I gasp and try to move forward for a better vantage point, but it's too late. I get a good look at the guy with the tote. From the shape of his face to the life-sucks-and-then-you-die-and-that-sucks-more set to his jowls, he's so stereotypically Russian the whole exchange is suspect. I snap a quick photo and send it off for an ID.

Galina turns and marches into one of the brick Victorian bungalows on our side of the street. A multicolored striped flag hangs out front—an embassy. (I should know the flag. Some-where in Africa, for sure.) Doubt these guys are helping with a spy ring. Must be an emergency translation on a Saturday night.

I can't follow her in without blowing my cover, and if she's already made the pass, no point in waiting around. I'll report this Monday, and somebody will pick up the slack on watching her.

The photo ID comes back: *neg.* We don't have a record of this guy? I've only gotten a couple negs ever. I guess he could be off-the-grid and Canadian (with those jowls?), but, man—double shutdown.

Guess it's back to Danny's. (Darn.) Somehow, facing his door doesn't help my pulse slow down. I almost can't knock. The nerves are back full force.

Do you know how often I go on second dates—let alone *ask* someone on a second date? I don't keep track, but if I had to guess, I'd say it's been years. I keep my distance from entangle-ments, relationships and anything that might ever turn serious, because I just can't go there. I can't.

Yet here I am, going out with Danny. Heading down a dangerous road?

No. That's crazy. I'm safe for a second date. No commit-ment. Right?

I finally knock, and he answers, smiling. I find myself

smiling back, until he steps out, keeping the door close, like he's hiding something in his apartment.

Behind him, a woman clears her throat before the door closes all the way, and Danny sighs. He backs up a couple feet, opening the door and welcoming me in. A tall, tanned, totally together brunette a couple decades older than us stands in his living room.

"Talia, this is my mom, Kathi Fluker. Mom, Talia Reynolds."

Whoa. Meeting the parents on our second date? I shake his mom's hand, noting the conspicuous absence of a title for me. (Way too fast to say "girlfriend," but "date" works.) Her return smile is tight and disapproving.

It's going well.

Danny's mom fastens him with an intense stare. "Can I talk to you?"

He looks to me, but I can't tell if his wide eyes are begging for help or pleading to appease his mother. Either way, a yellow light.

I move back, a don't-let-me-interfere dance. Danny's mom seizes his arm and drags him down the hall into another room, shutting the door behind him. Which, you know, is super attractive.

As a spy, I can't let a conversation behind closed doors take place without me. Unfortunately, I left my spy gadgets in my *other* jeans, so I'm left with creeping to the doorway and regular old eavesdropping.

". . . no point when you're moving back home," his mother insists.

"Did I say I was going back?" Danny's voice holds a hint of challenge. (*That's* more like it.)

"Come on. You like it here, but where is your *future*? Canada?"

Isn't Danny, like, twenty-eight? Man, I'd hate to find out he's still enmeshed in those apron strings.

"I've got a something good going," Danny says, calm and firm, "and it's just getting started. Of course my future's here. Why would I want to leave now?"

I'm controlling my breathing to eavesdrop more stealthily, but suddenly that's harder. Please, please tell me that means . . . I don't know what, but not me. Anything but me. I'm no one's future.

"Why do you think I came here?" Danny concludes.

"To take a break. To get your head on straight. To come home and pick up where you left off."

Wish I knew him well enough to picture his posture, his expression, his unspoken retort. For all I know, he could be standing there, shoulders slumped, gaze on the floor, the picture of surrender.

"Pick up where I left off? Let's be honest," he finally says, his tone weary. "This is about Kendra. All these months, you've been harping on me to date someone, but what you really wanted was for me to date Kendra again, wasn't it."

"That isn't fair—"

"It isn't happening," Danny cuts her off. "Not now, not ever, with or without the money. I'm sorry to disappoint you, but it's not. My future *is* here, and I'd like to get back to it."

Clearly meaning me. I don't have time to panic. Finality rings through his words—these are his closing arguments. I take the cue to back into the living room. No, too obvious. I hurry to the kitchen where he left me, although it's too clean to pretend to admire at anything. Danny opens the door and strides out, and I look up, the picture of innocence. I can't tell if Danny's flushed from the discussion with his mom or embarrassed I had to see that.

He chooses not to acknowledge the awkwardness. "Ready?" he asks, opening the door.

"Yep." I gauge my reaction by his. He doesn't glance back at his mom as we leave the apartment. We pass the elevator ride with stilted small talk. Danny doesn't say anything about the mom incident until we've reached the ground floor. "Sorry about my mother."

"It's okay. I understand." More than he could know.

"She flew in to present me with a 'gift,' but . . ." Danny grimaces. The money he mentioned?

He holds the glass front door for me, sparing him the rest of his answer—but believe me, I know all about gifts as tools for manipulation. (Surprised Mom isn't still harping on me about her twenty bucks.)

I'm used to closing up shop and hunkering down to weather a storm like this. Seems like that's Danny's role tonight. When my family's storms were bad, one thing brought me out of my shell: Trevor's jokes.

"As long as she didn't fly in to meet me because we made it to a second date," I try.

Danny gives me a half-grin. "Have to make sure you're marriage material, right?"

My gut inches toward the sidewalk, and my brain replays a highlight reel of Elliott teasing me last week. About marrying Danny.

He didn't send that jewelry catalog, did he? I should've spent my time alone in the living room searching for it.

And my silence is making this more awkward. I need to change the subject. "Well," I say like I'm tying that whole ordeal up, "looks like I failed. Pity."

Danny watches me, his face serious. Too serious. "Actually . . ."

Actually? He's turning this into a real discussion? About marriage? A chill bolts down my back.

"Maybe we should talk," he finishes.

"Talk? About—?" I try to speak, but my tongue is dry. I can't even say the M-word out loud.

"Well, yeah." Like it's a foregone conclusion. Like all we have to do is pick the date.

My brain jumps into hyperspeed, flashing memories of Elliott teasing me about catching the bouquet, Arjay proclaiming we'll get married, my parents' story. Each memory weighs on my chest, constricting my rib cage like a python crushing me to death.

My parents dated for three weeks. Today is exactly three weeks since my first date with Danny.

And his future is in Canada. He's started something good. Why his future's here.

He did mean me. He wants me to be his future, and he's bringing up marriage.

The last landslide of memories lands on me like a load of lead. Hate. Resentment. Fear. Fights, tears, screaming, all the venom that ripped apart our family and our lives.

Air. I need air. I can barely make out Danny's voice over the blood rushing in my ears. No idea what he's saying. It finally registers he's a few feet ahead of me. Because I stopped walking.

He finally glances around for me, then hurries to my side. "Talia? Are you okay?"

"I'm feeling—" I pant and try again. "I'm not feeling ... lightheaded."

"You're *not* feeling lightheaded?"

I reach out for the stucco and steel wall next to me, but I'm too far away. My hand finds nothing. I stumble sideways and crash into the building.

"Whoa, whoa." Danny takes hold of my arms. "Breathe."

I drag in a ragged breath, but I can't—I can't—I can't—

"It's okay," he soothes. "I got you."

That's the problem. I try to get another breath, but the air and my nose and my lungs won't cooperate.

"I'll take care of you," he says. I finally focus on him.

On one knee in front of me. Pledging to take care of me. (I think? Did I hear right?)

"No," I gasp. "No—"

"Do you need to lie down? Breathe in a paper bag? . . . Elevate your feet?"

"I need to go home." I manage the five words in a rush of air before I drag in more. "Sorry."

Danny helps me stand—I don't need help—I try to pull away.

"I'll drive you home," he offers.

"No!" Now I'm too forceful, but I don't let anybody from church come to my building. Too risky. Too paranoid.

"Okay." He backs away a step, but keeps one hand on my arm. "I can't leave you like this. Is this asthma? Do you have an inhaler?"

"No. I'm fine." No, obviously I'm not, since every breath still hitches in my chest. "I'll be fine." I fish my clicker out of my pocket and point it at my car, three spaces down the sidewalk. The hazard lights flash. "See?"

Danny's free hand settles on my back. "Let me get you there, at least."

Further protests would look more bizarre than breaking out in a rumba right now, so I snap my mouth shut and go with it, concentrating on my breathing and putting one foot in front of another. I open my door before he can and get in, but Danny lingers there, concern in the furrow of his brows. "Are you sure I can't take you home?"

"Very." I look up at him, standing beside my car despite the traffic passing dangerously close.

They're not the only things dangerously close.

I can breathe a little better, but the walls are still closing in inside my head. I need to go. I need to run. I need to escape. But Danny's waiting. I draw in an exaggerated breath for show. "See? I'll be okay. I just need to rest."

The concern etches deeper, but he doesn't disagree. "If you're *really* sure."

"Completely."

He closes my car door, still reluctant. Not waiting around for him to leave. I start my car and slip into the first gap in traffic. I'm home in my tiny studio apartment, searched, cleared and safe, before my ribs finally relax. I escaped. I'm free.

I sink onto my so-not-me floral bedspread and just breathe. The cool air feels so good in my lungs it takes me a couple minutes of calming down to identify the other feeling there, cold and hard.

Regret.

I really blew it. And he'll probably never talk to me again.

CHAPTER 20
DANNY

MY NIGHT'S BEEN AWESOME. Mom dragging me off to lecture me in front of Talia, like I'm ten. Arguing with Mom and mentioning Kendra. Talia freaking out for no apparent reason and driving off five minutes later.

Needless to say, I don't head right up to resume the argument with Mom. Nowhere else to go, so I spend half an hour, forty-five minutes pacing the lobby and the patio. Saturday night's usual crowd is getting rowdy around the pool, but I keep to my rounds and keep to myself, going over every minute of the Shortest Date in History in excruciating detail.

Is she okay? How did I set her off? Am I a walking trigger for people's psychological problems? What's the matter with me?

Is something the matter with her?

My circuits and my mental circles get tighter and tighter, till I'm wearing a track into the black-and-white tile of my lobby. My phone buzzes, and I drift to a stop to check the message—Mom. *Having fun?*

Nope. I sink onto a low lobby bench without texting back, not yet. But since I've got my phone out, I have to know how Talia's doing. Even if she never speaks to me again, I want to know she made it home all right. So I text her. *Are you okay?*

Yeah, she replies quickly. *I'm so sorry.*

What, like it's her fault she had a panic attack? *Was it something I said?* I hope that comes across as a joke and not clingy—classic Kendra. Talia doesn't respond. Either I missed the mark, or something I said really did set her off.

I settle back on the bench and review our short conversation. When she freaked out, we were talking about Mom flying in. Then we started talking about . . . marriage. On a second date.

Who sounds like the psycho now?

I grab hold of my courage and my phone to text her again. *Is it because I brought up marriage on a 2nd date? I promise I'm not that crazy.*

Probably good to establish this. Exactly how crazy are you?

A joke has to be the best answer. *On a scale of 1 to purple, Bernoulli's principle.*

Ha ha.

Every minute I wait for her responses feels longer. I should just call her. I hit the icon to dial. Takes a couple rings too many, but Talia finally answers. "Hi."

"Hey. Listen, I promise, I'm not insane. And I can explain."

She hesitates. "I'm listening."

No, she was listening when we sat in the half-shadows of a bike tunnel, waiting out the rain, talking about nothing and everything. Now, I can't see her, I can't read her expression, I can't gauge whether I'm explaining it right. "Can we talk about this in person?"

"Two talking dates in a row? What will people think?"

"A gentleman doesn't date and tell."

"You didn't?" She fakes an offended tone, but I know her

better. The shields in her eyes? No way. Even on our first date it took time to push past them.

Then I remember that little moment where they disappeared altogether, revealing a flash of terror: when I said she'd been hurt. Like I have.

If I told her the whole truth, she'd understand. I know she would.

I need to see her. "I can explain better face-to-face. Meet for dessert?" I offer. "You pick the place, I'll buy?"

She hesitates. "Can't say no to that. You know Choconilla? It's on Durham Street."

"I'll find it." Shouldn't be too hard. The street's only a couple blocks over, but she doesn't need to know I've been moping like a loser since she left. "Meet you there in ten?"

"Fifteen."

I consult my mental map and draw a fifteen minute driving radius from the street she picked, but that doesn't do much to narrow down where she lives. "See you there."

Talia reaches the busy restaurant a few minutes after me, and she inspects the crowd like a scared rabbit. I wave, urging her to join me in the long line—last hurrah of summer, I guess—and I *think* the trepidation leaves when she sees me.

"Hey," she says. Hope I'm imagining that she still sounds breathless. "Sorry."

"No problem."

"Have you had frozen custard before?" She gestures at the gleaming silver ice cream machines behind the counter.

"Yeah. Ever heard of Culver's?"

Talia concentrates on that a little too hard. "Don't think so."

I wave it away. "Anyway. It's good."

"Yeah. And I like this place because they're really into keeping the food fresh. Never save the custard overnight and serve it again, fresh ingredients every day, and they're pretty strict about who can touch the machines. Saw a manager yell at a guy for going behind the counter once."

"Whoa." Not a quality I usually look for in a restaurant, but I guess freakish devotion to your food has its pluses. We reach the counter: I get vanilla with crushed Kit Kats, and Talia opts for the flavor of the day, maple cinnamon roll. We take the last open table in the back corner of the crowded restaurant.

"Okay," I start with a deep breath. "I'm not a psycho."

"Uh huh. And Whoever's Principle is your definition of sanity."

"That's not crazy. It's the concept all flight is based on."

She contemplates that and takes another bite of her custard. "Human flight is *not* my idea of 'sane' either."

"No, you know what's insane? How far we've come in just over a century."

"Gonna take more than that to get me hurtling through the air in a pressurized metal tube." She scans the restaurant.

I file her aviophobia away under my Talia tab and turn back to the subject at hand. "I wasn't talking about marriage."

She cocks an eyebrow. "You said we should talk. The topic was marriage."

"Okay, yes." I shut myself up with a spoonful of frozen custard—man, this is good, thick and smooth and sweet—before I restart the topic. "I *was* talking about marriage."

Talia fixes on her bowl, swirling a pattern into her custard with her spoon.

"I was trying to tell you I *don't* want to talk about marriage."

"Sorry, what?"

"I want to take it off the table." I finish with a slicing motion, like I'm knocking that subject off our actual table—and my spoon between my fingers flings a big drop of half-melted frozen custard at her, hitting her square in the chest.

Do I always have to be an idiot? "Sorry." I hop up for napkins, but let her work on cleaning it off.

Talia scrubs her gray shirt for a minute. I wait until she's done—or given up—before I repeat my statement. "I want to take marriage off the table."

She says nothing. She doesn't protest or support my statement, waiting for further explanation.

Here comes the tricky part. "I just . . . I'm not in a good place for that now."

She stares at me for a long minute, then slowly nods. Like she doesn't quite get what I'm trying to say.

I immediately begin editing my story into the safe version, the one I can share, the one I can put into words. "I went through a bad breakup last year—but the last thing you want to hear about is your date's ex."

"Everyone's been hurt." She uses the same words we said on our last date, after that moment of fear when I came way too close to the truth. Too close for both of us. I watch her face, but she isn't trying to tell me my pain doesn't matter just because other people are hurting more. Deep in her hazel eyes, I can see that truth, alongside the fear: she's been hurt, too. She's not judging me. She understands.

No. Nobody quite understands, no matter how much they want to. I eat some custard, and then some more, but my cup's almost gone. I pick out the safest, most neutral way to say it. "My ex was. . . really crazy, and she kind of took it out on me. When I broke it off, she went off the insane-stalker-Richter scale."

Talia contemplates me a long time, like she's seeing through everything I glossed over. All she says is "That sucks. I'm sorry."

I'm not telling her this for pity.

"How long has it been?" she asks.

"Nine months." Nine months. Two weeks. Four days. Like I haven't counted every minute away from her.

Talia's hand, cold from her bowl of frozen custard, lands on my wrist where it rests on the table. "I'm so sorry that happened to you." Her face is sincere and sympathetic, and that means almost more than her words.

Not sure I deserve that. I look away. "Thanks."

"I've gone through some rough stuff, too, and I know how much it sucks. Good for you for getting out of there."

I look to my empty paper bowl and pull away from her grasp. If she knew how it finally ended, she wouldn't say that. "Anyway," I say, like I can lock all these feelings back in their little Pandora's box and undo all the damage I've done to Kendra, to Talia, to me. "I'm not in a place to be thinking about . . . any of that, and I didn't want to get your expectations up."

"Oh. Thanks. But don't worry about me. Sometimes you need to focus on you, on getting your head right first."

Not sure how my letting-her-down-easy speech turned into Talia's letting-me-down-easy speech. "Where does that leave us?" I ask.

"Friends, I hope?"

Holy. Crap. Are you kidding me? I just got friend-zoned. Again.

Maybe she's right—and I could use a friend. "You do know me better than pretty much anyone in the country."

Talia places her hand on her chest, like she's so very touched, though her eyes are smiling. "I'm honored."

"You should be. You've entered the ranks of the privileged few." I'm joking, and I grin back, but Talia catches the truth in that statement. I've really only told a couple people this much of the truth. Even my mom isn't one of them.

"Okay." She looks at the table like she's laying out a plan

there. "I know you didn't tell me this to solve your problem, but, Danny—" She meets my gaze. "You really are a great guy. You can't stay off the market forever. It wouldn't be fair."

Fair to whom? But I don't ask.

"Obviously I'm not a therapist, but . . . I've known a few." She flashes half a smile, like I should understand just how self-deprecating she's being, clearly a hint that she's been to a therapist or "a few."

"When you go through something like this, you keep analyzing what went wrong and why, but eventually, you're running in circles."

Like how I keep trying to start over and keep failing, back at square one?

"I don't want to see you get trapped in that," Talia finishes. "You've got to break out."

There's a way out? Yes, please. Seriously. "Okay. How?"

"One thing: take up something creative."

"Oh, man, I've been trying to figure out what to do with all my old Bob Ross tapes."

She laughs. "Doesn't have to be like that."

I snap my fingers like I'm disappointed. "There goes my happy little tree."

"And his happy little neighbor." She rolls her eyes good-naturedly.

I'm starting to love her eyes.

No, wait, no—I reset myself into a platonic mindset. As much as I can.

Talia leans back in her chair, relaxing into her therapist role. "Painting isn't the only option. How about music?"

"Does playing the radio count?"

"Nope."

I set aside my empty bowl and mirror her relaxed posture, ready for Talia to regale me with options. "Writing?"

"Nah."

"Dancing?"

I shake my head. "I don't dance."

"I won't ask you." She glances up like she's flipping through the files of her mind. "Making ceramic kittens?"

I almost jump to sit up straight. "Yes!"

She raises an eyebrow, a silent *really?*

And I drop the enthusiastic act, slumping back in my chair. "No."

"Okay. . . . Cooking?"

Can't dismiss that one right away. "I like eating."

"Hey, me too! It's perfect."

This solution seems too easy. I'm supposed to cope by tossing a chicken in the Crock-Pot? "How will cooking help?"

"A couple ways—keeps your mind occupied so you don't dwell on it, gives you a new direction to move forward, and you're making something. Isn't it basically doctrine that we *need* to create?"

"Don't remember hearing that."

"Definitely heard that. It feeds your soul." She isn't kidding.

I was kind of hoping to dismiss the arguments and get out of this setup, but . . . honestly, all those outcomes sound pretty good to me.

The overhead lights suddenly dim. I check to see if someone accidentally hit the switch. Nope—the crowd from earlier has dissipated, and we're alone in the shop with the servers. They're trying to close. We both stand and toss our empty bowls, shuffling toward the exit. The air outside is already chillier than August should be.

"Danny?" Talia's tentative question instantly draws me a step too close to her. "I'm not looking to get married either. But if you need help eating all the gourmet meals you're going to churn out . . ."

"I know who to call." Because that wouldn't be awkward. *Hi, girl that I think is cute and cool enough to ask out despite my issues, want to come over for a platonic meal alone at my place?*

Oh—but we wouldn't be alone. Campbell's moving in.

Hm. Not less awkward.

Speaking of awkward, we've reached the "doorstep" portion of our first platonic friend-zone date. I almost wish her work *would* interrupt again to save us from having to figure this out.

"Well," she says. That's it.

"I had fun," I say, like that surprises me. Because it does.

"Me too. And I had ice cream, so that pretty much covers it." She sighs, grinning. Then she turns serious. "You know, if you ever need to talk, you can call me for that, too."

I start to work up a joke, but the offer's so sincere, I can't tease her about it. "Thanks."

Cue the awkward.

Within a second, Talia holds out her arms, waiting for a hug. I guess that settles that question. I pull her in for a short squeeze. Believe me, I know how to hug a friend-who's-a-girl. Done it plenty.

"Now you know all my secrets," I say. "Except about that gambling habit."

She shoots me a lip purse that says *is that so?*

Why does she have to be pretty and funny and just a friend? Oh, right—because I'm a basket case.

I can do this. I can. "Talk to you later?" I ask.

She holds my gaze an extra millisecond before she nods. "Definitely."

Then I let her walk away. Shooting down my chance with her forever.

You know, par for the course for my second dates.

CHAPTER 21
TALIA

THE NEXT WEDNESDAY, it's still too soon for my knee to have "healed," so I'm once again outside Vasily's barbershop—and I'm still not totally over that conversation with Danny. Always hard to shift out of you're-cute-and-funny-and-awesome-and-I-wouldn't-exactly-object-to-kissing-you mode.

Stupid, I know, but . . . I'm not ready to lose that one little connection I had. I thought *we* had. Reason #109—

Come on. Time to stop tormenting myself. It was never going anywhere, and I knew that. I should be relieved to duck that relationship RPG—and I am. Mostly. At least I kept him from cutting all ties and salvaged a friendship.

Which is exactly what I'm *supposed* to want. No matter how much I actually want more.

"The Latvian." Elliott's voice comes over comms from his position across the street. I get a photograph of Vasily's latest happy customer with my phone and fire it off to our facial recognition servers to verify the identity, though we know it's him. The guy's in here every three weeks, clockwork. The text comes back within a couple seconds: *Juris Ozols.*

Vasily's computer calendar had today highlighted in red. Hope it wasn't for these afterhours appointments with his important clients—and here comes another one. "That the American heading in?" I murmur.

Elliott blows out a breath between his lips. "Looks like it."

"Again?" He was just here over the weekend. I snap the photo and send it to be sure. Yep. Carson Metzgar, foreign service officer. Unwitting spy? Willing? We can't tell from here—until Elliott records their appointment.

Metzgar waits at the barbershop's front desk. Vasily comes to meet him, but they don't start back to his cutting station. They chat for a minute. Then Metzgar hands over a small red piece of paper and leaves.

"What was that about?" I ask Elliott.

"Rescheduled next week's appointment."

"And the paper?" I crane my neck, as if I could see anything from here.

"Explains why, I guess."

Or it's passing off information, or a signal. If we had more people in our surveillance team, we might send someone after Metzgar, but we barely have enough manpower to cover our two big objectives: get that paper and keep an eye on Vasily.

Vasily tosses Metzgar's paper in the trash by the reception desk and heads to the back. I catch a glimpse of him sweeping. Closing up for the night.

The cleaning crew doesn't come until midnight, so we've got hours before we have to get in and get that paper. In the meantime, we'll be on Vasily.

"Fifty bucks says he's going home," Elliott says. "Just because we're here to watch him."

That would be our luck.

I have the better view of Vasily's car, so when he locks up, I'm on alert. He walks straight to his blue Hyundai, and I merge into traffic a couple cars behind him.

So glad I've got backup tonight. Pursuing someone by yourself, all their stops and starts and turns, is a lot harder than they make it appear in movies. But with Elliott here, we can tag team, moving up and falling back—making it harder for Vasily to spot us. Also much easier to pick up the slack if Vasily alters course suddenly.

Vasily doesn't make it super easy, with stops by the dry cleaner, the library and an ATM, but we manage to neither look too suspicious nor lose him. These mundane errands are exactly what I do everywhere I go (which is more than a CIA officer needs to, but, yeah, it's me). You watch for the surveillance team that might be behind you and bore them until they decide you don't have anything after all.

Won't work on us tonight. Vasily's path takes us toward Little Italy. Man, I wish I'd had time for dinner before this. But as soon as we emerge from the underpass decorated with neighborhood-themed murals, Vasily takes a left.

My stomach jumps. I'm too close to do the same without seeming suspect. I relay the route back to Elliott over comms. "Can you get him?"

"Yep."

I round the block and circle back to follow them within a couple minutes. The street looks like a one-way extension into a parking lot. I slow down, cruising by whatever's in here. Just before the end of the brick building, a maroon awning proclaims Ottawa St. Anthony Italia Soccer Club and their banquet facilities. "Thought we were tailing FEATHERSTONE, not shopping for reception venues," I rib Elliott.

"Two birds, one stone. Don't girls like multitasking?" he jokes back. "He's parking."

Several signs next to the last set of doors on the building advertise other uses of the club: off-track betting (so we can gamble on how long Elliott's marriage will last?), club offices with a bar, motor sports club. I put on my oversized sunglasses before I turn into the real parking lot past the building. Vasily walks by my car and heads through those doors.

"He's got a lot of options in there, HAMMER."

"I'm hurrying."

Any of those places might be a good meeting spot with a handler. Not the safest method, but if they're only signaling, it can work. Of course, Vasily could be part of any of these clubs, especially if he's targeting another club member. Either way, we want him out of our sight as little time as possible.

Elliott strolls by me, wearing a medium brown, medium shaggy wig and horn-rimmed glasses.

"Hipsters today, are we?" I ask. One negative to that cover for him: his complete inability to grow a beard, or even a two o'clock shadow. "You need more facial hair. Guess I should've warned you last winter."

Strangely, he has no response. "Hurry up," he murmurs. "Checking the bar first."

"Little early to be hitting the bottle, isn't it?" I whip into a parking spot in the far corner of the walled lot and dig through my disguises. Normally, a real spy would never wear something crazy that would draw undue attention, but for this cover, a pink or green wig might work. Don't carry those on me. I settle for light brown one that really, really needs brushing, tie a bandana around it "vintage" style and adjust my bangs. An old flannel shirt makes my "hipster" uniform. (Or is this grunge? No, I'm doing this *ironically.*) The final thing I need: glasses of my own. I don't have fake ones here, but I pop the lenses out of a smaller pair of sunglasses. Bam.

"What's taking so long?" Elliott asks. "He's in the OTB, waiting to make a bet."

I hurry through the doors. No idea what to expect. Possibly walking into a setup. My heart constricts, but I head downstairs to the off-track betting lounge.

Okay, "lounge" is a stretch. I've passed through casinos here and in Vegas, so I was expecting something more glitzy. Instead, we've got a wall of TVs, a couple rows of tables and chairs, and a lot of sad, desperate people. Which I guess is what you get when you strip away the glamour of a regular casino.

"Finally." Elliott joins me at the entrance. "Come here often?"

I give him a fake glare. "I played the ponies before it was cool." (Just so we're clear: I didn't, and it isn't.) "Who're you betting on?"

"IndieHorse. You probably haven't heard of him."

We manage not to laugh at ourselves and rein in the self-mocking humor. We stake out the corner, taking turns watching Vasily and the rest of the crowd. He knows a few people here, and between the races they joke about results and bad luck.

Are the bets the signals? Just coming here? Is he here for someone in particular? He hangs out with the same four or five guys, but he's not focusing on any one of them.

After an hour, he's placed a couple bets, but Vasily's getting quieter. Maybe he's losing. Or maybe something big is coming up. Like the signal or the message. He keeps checking the schedule in front of him, the TV, the schedule, the betting desk, his wallet. Everything else seems to pause and fade.

Then he stands. My heartbeat takes off like they just fired the starting pistol. I make eye contact with Elliott. This is it.

Elliott gets in line behind Vasily, and I watch the races and the friends. None of them seem to care Vasily's betting.

I glance over as Vasily reaches the old-school desk. He hands his money to the clerk—and that's definitely his biggest bet yet. He gets his little paper and heads back to his friends. But now they're all quiet.

Elliott joins me at the table again, and we monitor the TV screens (and Vasily). "Trifecta: Constance's Luck in first, then

Hamfisted and Wishfish," Elliott says softly. Are these horses? "Practically guaranteed to lose with any bet that specific."

Dropping all that cash on a sure-fire loss? Gotta be a signal. The race starts, and Vasily and his friends cheer for . . . whoever to place first, second and third, exactly as he predicted. The tension tightening my back muscles has nothing to do with the race outcome.

By the final lap, Vasily's quiet again, fingering his bet receipt, which I'm guessing is about to become worthless. Elliott and I scan the floor for anyone paying attention to Vasily, but everyone else is glued to the race.

The winners cross the finish line, and Vasily doesn't move from his table. No winnings to collect. He hasn't won all night.

What was Danny saying about a gambling habit? I believe him when he says he doesn't have one—but someone else might. Someone else who owes a big enough debt to warrant an enforcer.

Vasily's friends drift away. After a few minutes, he hauls himself to his feet and shuffles for the stairs. I wasn't betting, but the drop in the room's energy leaves me cold. If this is a way to signal his handler, that's harsh. The defeat in his posture isn't fake.

Elliott and I let him go. It's possible this was part of an extended SDR—and if so, he went above and beyond to sell it— but spending this long in one place is likelier to get you caught.

"Was this a waste of time?" I ask Elliott.

He gives an I-don't-know headshake. "Let Langley figure it out."

I doubt they'll give us the insight we can't get on the ground, but I take Elliott's answer.

Vasily's handler doesn't seem to be here, but he has to be communicating somehow. And we *will* figure out how.

CHAPTER 22
DANNY

MOM DIDN'T TO GLOAT TOO MUCH when I told her I wouldn't be seeing Talia again, even when we avoided one another at church the next day. Since obviously I didn't need Mom's help packing my apartment, she flew home Monday. With Campbell moving in last night, tonight's my first opportunity to try Talia's cooking scheme.

Guess I'm ready to try almost anything to move forward with my life, wacky as it might sound.

It's not like I've never cooked before. I survived this long, and nobody can eat takeout *every* night. I even earned the Cooking merit badge for my Eagle Scout—though that mostly involved cataloguing the food pyramid and the many ways you can kill someone with poor sanitation.

Hopefully that's not an issue tonight. I fill a pot with water, but the nerves building in my chest feel more like I'm gearing up for a performance the whole world is watching.

I put the pot on the burner and brace myself. As long as I follow the recipe, I should be fine. Fish isn't that hard to cook.

No reason to get worked up. With Campbell out on a date—on a Wednesday—this is my chance to screw up without an audience. Not that I'm planning to screw up.

I'm prepared. I make sure I have all the ingredients set out, arranging them on the counter by my laptop. I check the recipe again, inventorying once more: bag of fish fillets, head of garlic, jar of peppercorns, bunch of parsley and canister of bay leaves. Buying all this stuff makes this meal twice as expensive as it would be in a restaurant, but that would defeat the purpose. I'm supposed to create something. Other than a mess.

The recipe only uses some of the garlic, so I take it apart and peel off the papery skin. I count out the right number of peppercorns—man, I love the precision of this recipe. Clearly it was written for an engineer.

The lineup's looking more like a meal than a grocery list. I rearrange the ingredients on the stove around the pot in the order I'll need them: cloves of garlic, handful of peppercorns, sprigs of parsley, bay leaf, bag of fish. Yep, prepared.

Awesome. Doing good. I turn the knob, but the ancient stove makes an electric zapping sound from the burner. Not good. I test to see if it's heating up. Nope.

Great.

I change the pot to the next burner and switch it on as I read through the other half of the recipe: what to do with the fish after I've cooked it. I get the ingredients for round two before I get the stove started. Once again, I set aside the ingredients by the waiting plate: salt shaker, olive oil, jar of capers, lemon. Just have to wait for the pot to boil, add the flavorings and the fish for five minutes, and I should be in business.

While the water heats up, I'll work on the side dish. Should've gotten canned green beans, but I was already in the freezer section for the fish—wait, is the fish supposed to be thawed? I pick up the bag and read the back. No answer. I return the bag to the stove and scan the recipe again, but it doesn't say, either. I have to ask "Chef Google."

I scan the first three results. If it's frozen, just have to cook it a little longer. Can do.

I get out the frozen green beans, pour them in a bowl and throw them in the microwave. I consult the pot. Barely a bubble. Plenty of time.

What else would go well with this? Rice? Do I have rice? I search the tiny pantry and come up empty-handed. As soon as I turn back to the room, an acrid smell hits me, like an industrial accident happened in my kitchen while I wasn't looking. I know this smell: burning plastic, and something else.

I hurry to lift the pot off the burner. Nothing on the burner underneath. I examine the bottom of the pot. Clean.

I set the pot aside, but the fumes are growing stronger. The stove knobs—oh, no no no. I snatch the bag of fish off the "broken" burner, and the plastic melts away, stuck to the burner. Frozen fillets clatter onto the stovetop, and two plop into the poaching water. I fish the fish out of the water but I have nowhere to put them, and they're freezing to my fingers.

And then the garlic cloves burst into flames.

I shake my hands, flinging the fish across the kitchen, then grab the garlic off the burner.

I swear I had a plan when I picked this up, but now I don't know what to do, and *it is burning*. So I drop it in the nearest water—the poaching liquid.

Where was I the week we earned the Don't Pick Up Things That Are On Fire merit badge? Apparently the same place I was when we earned the Cooking Without Inviting The Fire Department merit badge.

The recipe made it clear that the fish would pick up any off flavors in your water, for example, blackened garlic. I stifle a groan, throw out the ruined liquid and gather up the fish filets from the counter. I can still do this. I am an Eagle Scout. I am an engineer. I am an adult. I can cook a simple dinner.

Dinner, take two. I triple check which burner I'm using and where I've put the refilled pot. I prep a few more cloves of garlic and add those to the pot with the peppercorns, parsley and bay leaf *before* I turn on the heat. This time I switch on the *right* burner and watch the water.

After a minute, I remember the green beans in the microwave. I open the door and take them out. Too late, I realize once again I picked up something *really* hot. The pain receptors send the message to the brainstem first, and my hands jerk away instinctively.

The bowl of green beans drops into the poaching pot. A wave of lukewarm water and hot green beans splashes onto my shirt.

It takes a few deep breaths and a few minutes of clenched teeth—and a change of clothes—before I'm back in the kitchen, psyching myself up to give this one more shot.

Engineer. Eagle Scout. Adult. Top of the food chain. Not going to let frozen fish fillets defeat me.

Dinner, take three. I finally get the poaching liquid to a boil, turn down the heat, and add the fish fillets. It's been almost an hour since I started cooking, so I'm starving. The promise of perfect, tasty fish in a couple minutes is making my stomach growl.

More than a couple minutes. Have to add time for them being frozen.

I'm watching the stove clock when my phone rings. Mom. I answer. "Hi."

"What's wrong?"

That's a mom for you. "Nothing's wrong."

"You sound annoyed."

"I *am* annoyed." Recounting the pratfalls of one simple meal will only make me more annoyed.

"What are you up to?"

"Poaching fish."

Silence. "That's illegal." She's not kidding; she's horrified.

"Not that kind of poaching."

Again, she hesitates before she answers. "Oh, right. The cooking kind."

"Yep." This is where I got my chef genes. I check the stove clock. Two more minutes. Plus frozen time? I make sure the slotted spoon's handy to remove them from the pot.

"Anyway, I was calling to apologize."

I instantly perk up. "You were?"

"Yes—I think I came across wrong this weekend, and I wanted to say I'm sorry."

"That's okay." I turn around and lean against the stove. Are there new strings?

"I didn't mean to upset you," she says. "About Kendra."

I manage to keep the wince mostly mental. What am I supposed to say? "Thanks."

"And I hope you're not still mad at me."

I sigh. "I'm not mad, Mom."

"You're not annoyed with me?"

"No, with dinner."

She laughs. "Then you're probably doing it wrong."

"Believe me, Mom, I've done everything I could wrong tonight."

"Aw, honey, I'm sorry."

It'd be nice if she shared a story of how she ruined dinner once—I know it had to have happened, but like I was ever picky about what she fed us. "So," she continues. No funny stories. "About the money."

I let my hopes rise a centimeter. The cash isn't what I care about—it's Mom admitting I can run my own life. "Yes?"

"Your father and I do want you closer."

After a few seconds of silence, clearly she thinks she's finished. "That's it?"

"Excuse me? What do you mean, 'that's it'? I think that's

quite a bit."

"So you're calling to say, 'Sorry I made you mad, stop being mad, but I'm still not giving you this "gift" unless you give up your life and move home with Mommy and Daddy'?"

"Danny," she says with a warning in her tone. Bet she regrets not naming me Daniel.

I pull back on the attitude. I'm not fifteen. "Listen, it's really nice of you to offer, but—" I've got nothing.

"I have an idea," she finally says. "A compromise?"

I should say no. If she doesn't want to give me this "gift," that's fine, but I can't move back to Michigan, no matter what she wants.

Still, how can I slam the door on my mom? I have to listen. "All right, let's hear it."

Then I remember the fish. The two nice fish fillets that were poaching a minute ago are now ten thousand little fishy bits. "Crap," I mutter. Shifting the phone to my shoulder, I grab the slotted spoon, like it'll salvage this mess.

"We'd like you to get preapproved for a loan," Mom says. "It'd give you a budget amount, and you could see how far our gift would go toward a down payment."

"Uh huh." Yeah, I'm at my most articulate as I'm scooping up my ruined dinner with the phone at this awkward angle. This would be why speakerphone was invented, genius.

"Is that an 'uh huh, that's true' or an 'uh huh, I'll do it'?"

"There's a difference?"

"Of course there is." Mom's voice verges on exasperated.

"Okay, sorry, a little distracted here." I need her off my case—I can say yes, and for all I know, they'll reject me for a loan, and that could be the end of it. She's giving some; I can too. "I'll look into it."

"Great. I'll let you go. Love you."

"You too."

The front door of my apartment swings open. I whirl

171

around to see who's there before I remember I have a room-mate now—and my phone slips from between my shoulder and my cheek. It lands with a plop. In the poaching water.

"Hey," Campbell says. He's alone, carrying a box to the counter. "Why don't you have any music on?"

I barely contain my frustration with him, my mom, my phone, the fish, the whole freaking night and turn back to the pot. I scoop out my phone, covered in flaky bits—and it's off. Bad sign.

"Okay," Campbell practically chirps, apparently unaffected by my non-answer. He plugs his phone into the speakers he left on the counter. Are they supposed to be a permanent fixture there? He flips on something loud and upbeat I sort of recognize from the radio.

"I don't know why you only own two plates—" Campbell's observation is enough to trigger a memory, or maybe a flash-back, all the rest of that set crashing and breaking. And when I tried to stop Kendra—I grip my phone tighter just to keep me tethered to the present.

"But I got some more." He pats the box he carried in and heads to his room.

Awesome. I set my phone on the counter. Is there anything I can salvage from this? I barely dare to taste one of the watery fish flakes. It's like eating bland fish soup with a fork. Plus my phone won't turn back on.

Dinner, take four. I nuke a frozen burrito. Not sure what flavor it's supposed to be, but it tastes suspiciously like they were going for freezer burn. I reach for my pocket to text Talia to remind me why I'm doing this—but my phone's dead. And I might've just lost Talia's number.

Full. Of. Win.

Things I've cooked for dinner: a plastic bag. Two cloves of garlic. My phone.

Things I'm throwing away: the fish. The poaching water.

Possibly the ruined burner.

Things I may or may not keep: trying. Dignity. Hope.

Not sure which I'm dreading more: this meeting with my boss Carol or my next attempt at cooking tonight. The logical side of my mind has spent the last week arguing that cooking failed as a psychological reset button. But that rational side also hasn't come up with a better plan and—I've let the past rule my life long enough.

First I have to make it through this status update. "And de-icing?" Carol asks.

Is this her pet project? "Going well. I think Lucas has a full report ready for you."

"Already? Hm." She doesn't seem impressed. "AeroTech-Canada's wingtips?"

I open up the last model she approved on my monitor, complete with its testing results. Carol leans over me, frowning at the failures. "It did make it all the way to the testing phase this time," I try, like that helps.

"Well, I guess that's something." Her tone makes it obvious it isn't.

Okay, we've run out of standard options. Time to show her what I've been working on for months. I've run the math about eight thousand times, gone over every spec and angle, getting everything ready for modeling and testing. If she approves it.

"I do have one more idea." I switch to view my hybrid wingtip design. I'm not 100% clear how much Carol knows about aerospace design, so I don't know how much to delve in-to the details. I point to the upper section of the wingtip device. "Obviously, this is akin to the winglet, how it flips up at the end of the wing." I trace to the bottom of the sideways V. "And then it's like a fence, extending above and below the wing. Also combines some of the sweep from the raked wingtip design we started with."

Carol stares at the computer model and puffs out a breath.

"Ready for modeling, testing and Transport Canada."

When she straightens instead of expressing the tiniest amount of approval or suggesting the next direction we might go—I could name four, easy—that's probably enough humiliation. I close the window.

Leaving up my browser, on a mortgage rate search. "Looking for a home?" Carol asks.

"Sort of. Need to get prequalified for a loan."

For the first time since she came in, Carol doesn't look like she wants to fire me. "You know, my husband's a real estate agent. He has a guy who does prequalifications. They could get you a letter in a day or two."

Easy, convenient—though I don't know if a Canadian loan approval will please my mom. But the way Carol offers makes me want to say yes. Like it's my last chance to do something to impress her and keep my job safe for another week.

"Sure," I say. "That'd be great."

"I'll have him email you tonight. And I'll think about your wingtip." She actually smiles before she leaves.

Yeah, that's only a true victory for one of us. I definitely need something to move this day to the "win" column for me, too. I finish up at work and hit the grocery store.

This time, I'm going even less ambitious than poaching frozen fish. I'm only doing a side dish. Supposed to be foolproof, and it's bacon. I think I've challenged the definition of "fool" when it comes to cooking.

Not totally sure "creating something" is helping.

Once I get home, I lay out my ingredients, just six of them: asparagus, bacon, balsamic vinegar, olive oil, pepper, and a lemon. After watching a video courtesy of Chef Google—wish there really were such a thing—I'm ready to try.

How did I let the Internet talk me into eating asparagus? I glance at the bacon and remember. That's how.

I restart the video and follow along, snapping off the end of one asparagus stalk and using that as a guide to cut off the tough parts of the others. Not slicing my fingers feels like cheating the cooking gods. They'll probably exact vengeance soon.

The next step is easy, too: wind half a piece of bacon around each asparagus stalk, and set them on a foil-covered pan. Some pieces of bacon or asparagus aren't as cooperative, but within a couple minutes, each stalk is encased in a spiral of bacon goodness. I drizzle on a tablespoon each of the vinegar and olive oil. A little black pepper and they're ready to go in the oven.

Oh. Except I forgot to preheat the oven. Could that really be my only kitchen disaster?

Once the oven's hot, it does take twenty-seven minutes to get them nice and crispy on both sides, but that seems to be the only mishap tonight. No fire, no change of clothes, no bloodshed.

And no one to celebrate with. Even Campbell isn't around, with his constant companions, friends and music.

I try an asparagus spear, and it's surprisingly good. The tang of the vinegar, the salty crunch of the bacon, and the heat from the pepper actually make asparagus worth it. Maybe not a whole pound of asparagus, but . . . it does feel really good to say I made this.

Not as good as saying it to someone other than myself. I could get away with a platonic text—if I hadn't broken my phone and lost her number in my last attempt. Like Arjay told me weeks ago, her number's wrong in our church directory.

Is there a "platonic" way to ask for someone's digits? Without using the word "digits"?

Wait a minute. I know exactly how to get ahold of her.

CHAPTER 23
TALIA

'M FINISHING UP AT THE OFFICE (Terfort & Sutter) Friday night when I get a text. In Urdu. *Where have you been? When are you and Danny getting married?*

My stomach dips automatically—but yeah, pretty sure that's out of the question. (Whew.) *I missed you too, Arjay.*

Where are you?

Work. I check my email once more, double-check my court robes are ready for Monday (you have no idea what a big deal it is to appear in federal court as an articling student, even if I'm only there because I studied all the depositions for this witness), and triple-check my phone. I haven't heard from Danny since our "unbreakup," and . . . I miss him. I barely know the guy, but I've had to stop myself from texting him kitten photos four times a day.

Which is for the best, right?

I'm at Danny's, Arjay replies. *Thanks for asking. Why aren't you here?*

Does he want the real reason? *How do you say "baggage"*

in Urdu? No need to get specific about whose.

You don't want to see him?

For a second, I worry Arjay's reflecting this conversation back to Danny, going from wingman to puppeteer, but then he'd text in English, right? *I don't mind seeing him*, I reply. *We're just not dating.*

Baggage. Gotcha.

Hope he drops it. But at the same time, I hope he *doesn't* drop it.

Great. Even more issues.

He doesn't text again until I'm at my car. *Come on, it's my last week of freedom.*

Freedom? Then my heart sinks—right. Because Arjay will be a missionary soon, which means no TV, no video games, no un-churchy books, no Internet, no dating, no nothing. You find other ways to have fun, and it's worth it, but yeah. I have to say goodbye.

But wait. *Your last week of freedom and you're at Danny's?*

Campbell invited me to play video games.

Since when can Jonathan Campbell invite people over to Danny's house? No idea. I ask Arjay.

Since he moved in a week ago. Joel's here too.

Well, if it's a party . . . I toss my phone on the passenger seat and start the car. I'm one short surveillance detection run away from seeing Danny. In a totally platonic, hey-how's-that-baggage-mine's-about-the-same way. But honestly? Even that sounds good.

In fact, it sounds good enough that when I reach his door thirty minutes later, my heart's sprinting (and not because Galina might be here—I checked; she's busy at the dance studio). This won't be awkward, will it? Church was kinda weird, but that might've been because his mom was there, and I didn't dare get too close.

No, it'll be fine. I'll play it cool, and he'll play it cool, and it'll be . . . cool.

I know he lives here, but Campbell answering the door (and the loud music) is still a shock. He's even more surprised to see me, his eyes wide open, lifting his brows enough to wrinkle his forehead. "Hey, Talia. Do you need something?"

"No." I subtly crane my neck to peer past him. "Arjay invited me. For his last hurrah."

"Oh. Cool." He moves back to let me in. "Look who's here, guys."

Please, please, I *so* want to make an entrance. I walk in, folding my arms. But I don't let myself scan the room for Danny, like I came here for him.

Not *just* him.

"Talia!" Arjay bounds over to me. "You've got to try these." He holds out something, and I take it before I see it's a spear of asparagus wrapped in bacon. I don't normally eat asparagus, but with bacon? Sure. I take a bite. Probably better warm, but it's still pretty good. It's encased in bacon; of course it's good, but there's something else going on there, too, something complex and tangy.

"Did you make this?" I ask Arjay.

He jerks his chin to indicate someone behind him, then steps aside to open my path to the kitchen—and Danny, leaning against the counter, ankles crossed.

"*You* made this?" I point the asparagus at him.

He half a modest smile flickers across his lips. "First thing that's gone right."

The full implications dawn in my mind: Danny's cooking. Like we talked about. And if this is the first thing that's gone right, this isn't his first attempt.

Well, I guess that answers the how's-your-baggage question. Sort of. I take another bite to hide the grin like we're sharing an inside joke. "It's good," I say.

Arjay slaps Campbell's shoulder and heads for the living

room couch to resume their video game. Danny lingers in the kitchen. I didn't come for the gaming, so it's only natural to join him, right?

I pick a semi-neutral distance and mirror his posture, kicking back against the counter. I gesture at the speakers blaring behind him. "Bowie fan?"

"That'd be the 'Space Oddity' over there." He shoots a pointed glance Campbell's direction and lowers the volume.

"How have you been?"

"Not bad. You?"

"Busy." I finish off the asparagus. "Thought you were supposed to call me to help eat."

"Sorry—cooking mishap killed my phone and lost all my numbers. Would've posted on Facebook, but you know."

I laugh. "If this is your cooking, I'd better make sure you have my number. It's really good."

"Thanks. Surprisingly easy, too."

"How does it feel?"

"To convert vegetables into a viable heart-attack method?" He smirks, but softens quickly, looking past my shoulder. "Good, actually. Pretty proud of it."

"You should be." I nod to one of the last two spears on the tray to ask permission; he holds out a hand. I have to maneuver closer to get it, but neither of us object. "It's a feat to get me to eat asparagus. I had a bad experience."

"Sounds like something I do *not* want to hear about."

I pretend to roll my eyes. "I was supposed to feed my little brother asparagus, and Timo—well, it's a family legend."

You'd have to hear a lot more of the story to get the joke, but instead of asking, Danny slips into thought, focusing behind me again. "Didn't you say you're the youngest?"

I nearly choke on my food. Did I let that slip?

Crap. Now I have to tell more of the truth than I like to. "I am—I—um." I meet his gaze, and he's waiting, free of judgment.

"I mean," I try again, "I *was* the youngest for twelve years. Until my half brother was born."

"Ah." He nods slowly, but I see the pieces fitting together in his mind. He knows what that says about my parents' marriage, about Timo, about me. So much he could pry into with that one little detail. "Are you close?"

I shrug one shoulder. "He doesn't remember when I lived with them, so not really. I try, but . . . guess that's the biggest drawback of not being on Facebook."

I don't talk about this stuff, not with Arjay, not with Elliott—but despite the change in our dating status, it's not (all that) weird to talk to Danny. He doesn't pester or push or press for clarification. He accepts whatever I want to share without giving me grief or guilt.

Except I kind of do feel bad for keeping so much from him. It's my job to deal in secrets, but honestly, I take that to a whole new level when it comes to my personal life. This relationship was always going to be a dead end for me, with everything I don't dare say, to anyone. Secrets always carry a high price.

Before I can figure out which direction to go in the conversation, Campbell, Arjay and Joel pile into the kitchen, raiding the pantry. Rather than going back to their game, the three of them join us in the kitchen. Now it's a party. Yay. But Campbell starts sharing mission stories, and we all join in.

Another area where I have to tread with caution. We're alternating between ragging on Arjay and encouraging him, but I have to be careful how much of any story I share because no one in this room knows I really served my mission in Russia. So Aleksei becomes Alex and Katya becomes Katy, and I have to leave out tales of the extreme cold and heat, the history, the culture. The others, even Danny, tell stories with enough enthusiasm that my silence isn't that noticeable.

We're getting into the stupid pranks Joel and Campbell

pulled—they're mission buddies, so talking about this stuff makes them act like nineteen-year-olds—when my phone chimes. My stomach slowly sinks. Either my mom or work, and either way, it's bad.

Yep. Elliott: *You busy? Another red letter day in Mr. Featherstone's calendar. Could use you in case we need a distraction.* I glance back at Danny—and Arjay. This is my last chance to see the guy for two years. "Hey, guys, I gotta go. Apparently I forgot to close out my files at work."

"Do you need someone to walk you out?" Campbell offers.

"I'm good, thanks." Though I don't know if I could have turned Danny down that easily. Arjay follows me to the door, but I can't exactly hug the guy with an audience. "Be good, kid. Live by the rules, no matter what these idiots tell you."

"I'll try." He grins, and I punch him in the shoulder to say goodbye. Like he's Timo, or how I wish things were with Timo.

I suppress the urge to cast one last look at Danny. Yeah, most of my relationships are nothing like what I wish.

Pursuing a shadowy figure down a dark street is a spy movie cliché, but once in a while, we do it in real life. Fortunately for me and Elliott, we can finally bring the rest of our team in to help—Eric running comms, Justin tailing on foot and Rashad with vehicle support. As long as we keep one another apprised of Vasily's movements and change disguises, we can stay on his tail for hours if necessary.

Which is good, because we've already been at this for ninety minutes, and I'm getting really cold. Especially since we stopped moving when he entered the Pine Grove "tree plantation" (huh?)/forest. Eric, feeding us information from a safe distance, cheerily told us the marked paths alone are over eighteen kilometers (that's eleven miles) when Vasily disappeared into the woods. We'd be in trouble if Elliott hadn't packed infrared/night vision binoculars.

And that leaves me pacing alone in the parking lot of a beige brick church—St. Bernard, no joke. A safe distance from Pine Grove, I'm still close enough to swoop in if they need me to run interference. Vasily and I have rehearsed all of twice, but that's enough of a connection to use me as a diversion.

"How's it coming?" I ask into my minimicrophone, wired into my jacket's top button.

"Hasn't done anything interesting," Eric tells me. Which means Elliott's too close or too preoccupied to answer. "Coming up on Athans Park."

Half a mile away. "Want me to move in?" If I get to him and get him talking, that should give Elliott time to check any drops he might've made in there.

Eric doesn't respond right away, so I start across the street past the Russell Boyd Park sign. A paved path from the parking lot skirts the trees, running in roughly the right direction.

"He hasn't made a drop yet," Eric finally says. "Take cover."

Trees will have to do. I leave the path and duck into the shadows. I don't know exactly where he is, so I watch the part of the street I can see. Empty. Quiet.

"Breaking off," Elliott reports. He followed Vasily through Pine Grove and then this adjacent park. Only so many marked paths in there, so it might've seemed like a coincidence for Elliott to be behind him the whole way, but until Elliott changes disguises, he'll look too suspicious tailing him longer. "He's leaving Athans Park on foot, taking a left on Eureka."

"OTIS is on Athans Avenue," Eric responds. "Headed to intercept."

Hope he doesn't make a drop while we're blind. It's just a minute or two, but that's long enough. Rashad catches up and follows Vasily down Athans a minute

"Left on Sixth," Rashad says.

"Coming your way, FOXHUNT," Eric reminds me. Oh boy. The trees along here are thick enough I can barely make out the street—but not nearly thick enough to hide me safely. My shoulders start to tense, but I remind myself to stay loose.

"I'm behind him," Rashad says. "About to pass him."

"I got it," I barely breathe.

But I don't got it. I weave between the trees—can't risk a flashlight. Vasily would see.

"Passing," Rashad says. "I got him in the rearview."

CIA officers spend so much time practicing the skill of watching behind them while driving—and Ottawa streets are so well-lit—that I'm not *too* worried.

Except about being spotted myself. My heart echoes in my ears as the seconds slide by.

Vasily appears at the edge of my view, walking along the shoulder, thirty feet away. I'm in the shadows, but he could still see me if he looked. I sneak behind the biggest tree I can find. As he nears the corner of the park, the trees between us grow thicker, and I lose sight of him.

"He's turning again," Rashad announces. "What street is that?"

"Saint Bernard," I murmur. "On him."

I slip through the trees again until I have a clear view of Vasily. The trees afford *way* less cover from this direction, and my pulse throbs in my throat. He'll see me. All he has to do is turn his head.

"Heads up." Elliott's hushed voice comes over comms. "We've got a chalk signal." He describes the line on a lamppost back by Athans Park. Now we have to figure out if Vasily made a drop in the seconds we were blind or if we missed something—or if he isn't done yet.

I stay well behind him, and the trees grow even more sparse. He marches past the brick school across the street. Before he reaches the pedestrian crossing at the parking lot entrance, he veers off the sidewalk. His hand slides from his pocket, and a small black object tumbles out. He barely pauses long enough to kick it into the drainage ditch then continues to the crosswalk.

"And a drop!" I whisper. I describe the site, and Justin and Elliott signal they're on the way.

Time for my part, too. Vasily continues down the block. I hope he turns on the street just after the church so Elliott and Justin will have that much more privacy to dig in the ditch. But Vasily continues straight down St. Bernard Street.

Okay. My job: make sure he's distracted. I hurry across the street and past the church, hunching my shoulders like I'm trying to get out of the cold. Yes, it's only September, but an early cold snap makes a leather jacket not enough warmth, and I'm really feeling it. I pass Vasily, barely looking at him—and then I slow down. "Vasily?"

"Joanne?"

I make my face light up. "What are you doing here?"

Probably shouldn't ask him that, but I want to see how he'll answer. "In the neighborhood, visiting a friend. You?"

"Helping at the church." As soon as I say it, I realize I don't know what "helping" constitutes in the Catholic church—but this is usually a safe bet. "Putting away tables and chairs, you know."

"Oh, do you live around here?"

Yep, that's a lie we should've backstopped. How can I back it up now? "Yeah, on the next street over." Wait—if someone he knows lives nearby, they'll change his drop site. "Well, until we move next week."

"I'll make sure you get there okay."

"Aw, thanks."

On one hand, this is great—I can get him off this street and give Elliott and Justin more time. On the other hand, this is bad—what will I do when I get to my "house"?

I need to use this opportunity to my advantage, to look like a potential agent for him. "This week's just been crazy. Big stuff on the Hill. But I suppose you've heard about all that."

He shrugs. "I watch the news when I can."

I puff out half a laugh. "The news? They're so clueless, you might as well listen to *This is That*." Um, if he doesn't know the satirical radio news show, I've just confused him.

But he nods. "I can imagine. You must know a lot more about the inner workings than you ever anticipated."

Almost an attempt at eliciting information from me. But before he presses further, Vasily changes the subject. "Have you been practicing?" he asks.

"Not as much as I'd like." Or as much as we both know I need to.

We near the street I said was my home a minute ago, and I see the yellow sign: No Exit.

Great. As if I wasn't doomed enough.

"Are you enjoying dancing?" Vasily asks.

"Yes, of course." Then I see my opportunity. I enunciate very clearly, the message intended for more than Vasily: "But obviously I need a lot of help."

"I can tell you're trying hard."

"Thank you." We reach the corner, and I point down the street. "This is me, Treetop Court." I give the name for Eric's benefit. Hope Vasily will buy me being able to afford rent in one of these two-story brick houses. "See you soon."

"Oh, I can't let you go now."

I swallow hard.

"A pretty young woman walking alone at night? I have to see you to your door."

Why is it the spies threatening your homeland always have to play the gentleman? I scramble for a strategy, an excuse, an escape. We near the end of the cul-de-sac, and I pick a house with lights on. "Oh." I pat my pockets. "Guess I forgot my keys.

Good thing my roommate's here. Thanks for walking me."

Again, I've dismissed him, but he isn't going anywhere. Testing my story? Running into me *is* a pretty big coincidence.

Gotta play this cover to the hilt. Vasily waits on the driveway, and I march up to the front door and knock. While I wait, I make my expression scared and innocent and work up to shallow, panty breathing. Someone answers quickly—a middle-aged woman with gentle eyes. "Can I help you?"

Good thing her voice is soft, too. I grab her forearm. "Don't look behind me," I say in a stage whisper, "but there's a man following me. Help!"

Her gentle eyes widen and, against my orders, she glances behind me where Vasily waits. Fortunately, she also pulls me into the house and closes the door. "What happened?"

"My car broke down by the school, and I was walking down to the main road to take a bus, but this guy started following me. He gave me the creeps."

"Oh, you poor thing! Should we make a police report?"

"I couldn't describe him. He just . . . freaked me out."

"Can I give you a ride anywhere?"

I shake my head. "No, thanks—have to make sure he goes away. Could I call a friend to pick me up?"

"Of course."

I give Rashad a ring. He takes his time, since we don't want it to seem too obvious. I spend ten minutes I parked in Mary Devereaux's quaint living room, avoiding her benign interrogation. She's only curious, and I deflect the questions back to her. (She's divorced, mother of two teenagers who are still out for the evening, and she likes to paint. She decorated the living room herself. And her favorite flavor of coffee creamer is hazelnut.)

The poor Samaritan's reluctant to release me until Elliott comes to the door. Probably a good call—not sure how Mary would react to a big Black man here to save me.

Rashad's driving, and Elliott and I pile into the backseat. "Nicely done, FOX."

"Thanks, HAM."

He beams, and I roll my eyes. The nickname's perfect.

Once we're out of the neighborhood, Rashad drops me and Elliott off to split up and execute our surveillance detection runs. No surprise that Rashad, behind the wheel instead of hoofing it half his SDR, beats us back to the office, already leaving as Elliott and I arrive.

"I don't think I told you the other day," Elliott starts. "We tracked down that red flyer the American gave FEATHERSTONE. School thing for his kids. Looks legit, sent it in for analysis."

"Oh." I'd kinda hoped something more important would come from our "adventure," but it seldom does. Spycraft is a numbers game, a minimum level of time investment necessary to get the smallest intel return. Which I bet Vasily knows all about.

"How're rehearsals?" Elliott asks.

"Grueling. Don't know how much longer I can keep them up."

Before Elliott can reassure me, my phone chimes in my pocket. Not sure who'd be texting after ten (especially not when the most likely culprit is standing in front of me). I pull out my phone.

My mother. *call me.*

Uh oh. It's an hour earlier where she is, but this is never, *ever*, good. I bring up the icon to dial, but first, my phone rings. She's calling.

"Hello?" I answer.

"Talia, terrible news." Her voice carries a dramatic hush.

Don't know how to respond, since my mom thinks a houseguest canceling on her is "terrible news"—and she *thrives* on terrible news.

"Tyler's getting divorced."

My brain refuses to process that information. "My *brother* Tyler?" As if she'd be calling about some stranger who happened to be named Tyler.

"Yes!"

I can feel the blood draining from my face, leaving my skin cool and clammy. Elliott cocks his head, one eyebrow arched. Yeah, no. I wave him away and cover my other ear, starting for my car.

"What—what happened?"

My mom spills what details she knows, as if she understood anything about why marriages fall apart. If she did, she probably wouldn't have let it happen to her three times, would she? And whatever she's talking about—Bianca always hated my mother, Tyler couldn't take the anti-Mom venom—it's all filtered through her insane lens on the world, where she's the only person who matters.

And when it comes down to it, that's why Tyler's getting a divorce. Because we were raised to do nothing else. Between my parents arguing for more than a decade and the insanity my mother worked so hard to instill in us, it's no wonder Tyler's marriage is falling apart. Like Troy's did. Like Mom and Dave's did. Like Mom and Peter's did. Like Mom and Dad's did.

Because we're doomed to fail. The sick truth rolls over in my stomach, triggering a tide of nausea.

"Why is this happening?" Mom wails. "What haven't I done for you guys? Why do you always do this to me?"

Yeah, Mom, because Tyler's getting a divorce to punish you. But I'm too numb or too upset to give my mom the pity and feedback she thinks she deserves—as if she's the only one affected here. I sink into my driver's seat, saying nothing. What about Tyler and Bianca's daughter? Mom never mentions Ruby. Typical.

"Talia?" she finally tries. "Aren't you listening to me?"

"Sorry, I'm working late tonight. Thanks for letting me know, but I've got a lot going on here."

"Talia! I need you! Think of what I'm going through here." But she's almost crowing, triumphant at Tyler's tragedy and how I'll have to pay attention to her.

"We'll talk later." I end the call.

I wanted—I needed to get away from her voice. But suddenly it's too quiet, and my thoughts bounce around the car. Tyler. Bianca. Ruby. What each of them must be going through.

What all of us went through as kids.

I try to dodge the thoughts, to focus on the drive and the extra surveillance detection run on the way home. But every time I stop moving, the nagging begins to creep in.

Tyler. Bianca. Ruby. They're the latest casualties. Troy. Heather. Dave. Peter. Dad. Trevor. We've all fallen under Mom's control, and we're all screwed up.

One more name for the list: Talia.

After more surveillance detection stops than I bother to count, I find myself staring at my building, unwilling to go inside my apartment, alone with my thoughts. But what can I do? Intrude on Tyler's pain? Call Troy, who's still reeling from his own divorce? Talk to Trevor, who thinks I had it easy because I hid in my room most of the time when we lived with Mom?

Then one last alternative pops into my mind. Before I stop myself, I'm nearly running to my apartment. I dash through my standard search for intruders. Only takes a minute to clear my teeny studio apartment. Then I pull up the contact on my phone and hit the icon to dial.

"Hello?" he answers.

"Danny?"

"Talia, hey."

I don't have the time or the will to try to read into his tone, whether he wants to talk to me or not.

And I don't know what I was planning to say. "Sorry to call so late."

"Only eleven," he says. "Everything okay?"

I release one shaky breath. "No. It's not—but I don't want to talk about it, not yet." I'm more surprised than he is to hear those last two words. Would I ever be okay with telling someone else about Tyler, my crazy family, my mother? It's all one tangled knot.

"Okay."

"I just . . . I need to be distracted for a while."

"I can do that, I guess. But I don't have any pictures of kittens."

In spite of myself, I smile. "I think we'll manage."

"Did I tell you what happened to my phone?"

"Cooking mishap?"

"Better tell you the whole story." He sighs. "I think it's been long enough I can laugh about this, but I don't know."

Danny continues, and I stretch out on my bed, grateful for this little anchor to a place where cooking your cell phone is the punchline, to a world where I don't have to think about my messed up family, to sanity.

To Danny.

CHAPTER 24
DANNY

TUESDAY, I LEAVE WORK EARLY. I can only take so much frustration in a day, and my favorite place to unwind closes at five. Luckily, the Aviation and Space Museum is just a couple minutes away.

The familiar sight of the Arrow doesn't do enough to erase the stress of work. I don't think Carol has any intention of letting my wingtip design move forward, though modeling is going well. I stare up at the chopped up jet. My design could end up axed too. Sometimes it's hard to make progress.

Speaking of progress, I'm supposed to cook again tonight. I head home and put the crusty, dried breakfast dishes in the sink to make room on the counter for the tortilla chips. I forgot how much you have to get used to with a roommate: someone else's leftovers, someone else's dishes and someone else's music. All the time.

Maybe I was getting too used to silence. And there are other advantages. Campbell does my dishes sometimes, and he doesn't mind if I borrow his food occasionally. Especially not if

I cook with it.

That didn't work out so well with the pork chops or the panko chicken, but the grilled shrimp, steak with gorgonzola, and sweet and sour meatballs were good enough to share. So I did. Just like she promised, Talia's come to help eat whenever she didn't have work over the last three weeks, even when the food was awful. But with Captain Third Wheel hanging around, it takes twice as long to lower her shields.

Tonight, however, he's still at work, and Talia came here as I was finishing up. I think the only caution in her expression has to do with my latest kitchen experiment. Can't blame her. "Not really sure about this one," I explain. "I didn't have time to go to the grocery store, so I had to make it up as I went along." And I burned some of it. Not mentioning that.

"That's okay." Talia gets plates out of the cabinet. I mentioned she tried the pork chops, right? "But if you ever need anything, I'm at the grocery store like every day."

"Oh, cool. Thanks."

She sets the plates on the counter, and *now* she looks at me. This whole platonic thing would be a lot easier if I didn't have to see her, and her eyes and her lips and—best to look away.

"How're you doing?" She asks like she really wants to know. Obviously that question only brings up the exact reason this definitely isn't a date. Even after . . . what, almost two months of talking, there are still a couple things I know better than to dump on her.

Talia frowns in sympathy. "That bad, huh?"

"No, just frustrating. My mom."

"Ah." She loads her plate with tortilla chips. "Still pushing you to move back home?"

"We compromised on seeing if I could get approved for a loan. My boss is married to a real estate guy, and he took care of it. Apparently having almost no debt and a good job qualify you for huge piles of cash."

"Hard to say no."

"Yeah. Guess I was hoping *they'd* say no, and Mom would back off, but that backfired." Yep. Resistance is futile. "And now," I almost laugh, "he's sending me real estate listings. I've told him I'm not looking, but he's relentless."

Talia sighs and turns to the pan of peppers, onions, tomatoes, black beans and slightly blackened corn. Who am I kidding? This isn't dinner; it's glorified salsa. Seriously needs meat.

But Talia doesn't complain. She spoons some onto her plate, scoops it up with a tortilla chip and takes a bite. She pauses, and my stomach tenses up. Is it that bad?

"Wow," she says around her food.

Crap. It *is* that bad.

She chews and swallows. "Have you tried this yet?"

"No." Really don't want to now.

She picks up another tortilla chip, scoops up the veggie mix and holds it out to me. Fitting punishment for afflicting her with this garbage, I suppose. I lean down, like it's totally not awkward for her to feed me—and I pick the totally wrong moment to make eye contact.

I said platonic, right?

She raises one amused eyebrow. "I meant for you to take the chip."

"Oh, right." I take it and take a bite, and whoa. That isn't bad. At all. The vegetables mix really well together, and instead of tasting burnt, the char on the corn adds this awesome smoky flavor to the whole thing.

My face must show my reaction because Talia nods. "I know, right? It's really good."

"It's *really* good." I snag another tortilla chip and salsa from her plate. "Could use some meat—steak."

"Oh yeah. But it's good without too, and you made this. I mean, you made this up."

"Yeah." I look back at the skillet of salsa, and revel in the accomplishment. I. Made. This. And it's—I'll say it—amazing.

Talia's right. This does feel good. I turn to her again, my smile still lingering.

Then I realize we have the whole place to ourselves, and we're standing two feet apart, sharing one plate of food. Alone in the apartment.

It's really quiet. Quiet enough I can hear my heartbeat. Maybe Talia's too.

Before I think about my next move—or whether I should make a next move—the door opens, and Campbell and Joel troop in. I try not to act guilty, though I'm not sure what I should be guilty for. Nothing happened.

Was I thinking about something happening?

"Hey, guys." Campbell brushes past us. Talia backs up a bit to accommodate the bigger party, as nonchalant as Campbell and Joel.

Campbell goes right to the bag of chips and scoops salsa straight out of the skillet. Impressive manners in front of a guest. Who's a girl.

"Sorry," I mouth to Talia.

She holds up four fingers. "Four brothers," she mouths back.

As always whenever she mentions something about herself, I correlate that info with everything else she's told me: three older brothers, one much younger half brother named Timo— which probably means either her parents are divorced or one of them died.

With someone else, I might want to ask about that, but with Talia, I'm learning to take what she's ready to share. Six months ago, I would've freaked out that there might be a lot more to her than what I see—but now I'm pretty sure "a lot more" doesn't mean "a lot more insane."

"Good stuff." Campbell points in the pan with his chip

before scooping up another bite. "You make this?"

"Yep."

Campbell nods his compliments. He takes out his phone and plugs it into the stereo speakers on the counter. Been home all of two minutes, must be time to flip on music. He scrolls through the playlist and starts something loud and Latin.

Joel tries the salsa, also right from the pan, and nods his approval too. "Takes me back to the mission."

"I thought you guys served in Nebraska," Talia says.

"Spanish speaking," they answer together. Then Campbell starts singing along to the song, dancing in time.

Talia glances at me. "You don't speak Spanish, too, do you?"

"French."

"Right. Came in handy in Québec, huh."

"Hey!" Joel exclaims. The four of us are all together in this little kitchen, so I shouldn't be annoyed that he's jumping in our conversation, but I am. "You should make poutine next."

Good idea, actually. I tell him so, but I glimpse Talia's grimace. "What?" I ask her. "Don't like poutine?"

"Can't take more than a couple fries at a time. Eating them two meals a day for a week straight cures you for life. And then gravy, which is, what, fat and flour?"

"That's why it's good!" Joel insists.

She wrinkles her nose. "And squeaky cheese—that's a texture thing."

Joel gapes at her. "Are you kidding?"

She shakes her head, her lips twisted in a *sorry, dude*.

"But . . . first of all, the gravy is supposed to be hot enough to melt the cheese curds."

At the mention of the apparently offensive food, Talia shudders. I guess the shiver ended with a little shake of her hips—okay, it did, and yes, I noticed. We're friends; I'm not dead.

Campbell takes that movement as his cue to cut in. He takes Talia's plate and sticks it on the counter next to me, then grabs her hands. She falls in step with his dance. He holds up his arm and pivots her underneath, then pulls her close.

I'm not jealous.

"This what you did on your mission?" I ask Joel, though we all know this wasn't allowed.

"He learned to dance in high school. To meet girls." Joel's extra loud, like he's trying to embarrass Campbell. Don't think it'll work, but definitely worth a shot.

"Ah," I join in the mocking. "The only thing he's got going for him."

Talia laughs. Good.

"Is that why you learned to cook?" Campbell shoots back.

Talia laughs harder. Bad.

I'm not jealous.

The song finally ends, and Talia and Campbell exchange compliments. Her cheeks are pink. I don't know if that's from dancing, or dancing in front of people, or . . . something else.

Talia checks at the microwave clock. "Better go. Have fun, guys." She pauses to reach around me for one more scoop of salsa from her plate. I can't help this little inhale just because she's *really* close again. Then she looks up and meets my eyes. "Good job on dinner."

"Thanks." We share a smile, but only for half a second before she turns to Campbell.

"Thanks for the dance, Cam."

Cam? He winks at her, and she leaves.

Despite what the heat rising in my chest would indicate, I'm. Not. Jealous.

I'm still telling myself that four hours later as I'm getting ready for bed. Not sure it's working. First piece of evidence: it's been four hours, and I'm still telling myself that.

I finish brushing my teeth and head back to my room to

find Campbell stretched out across the ugly '70s afghan my mother insisted I put on my bed.

"You need something?" I ask. Despite my not-really-best efforts, my tone's short.

Campbell either doesn't pick up on it or doesn't care. He sits up. "Is there anything going on between you and Talia?"

Only in my dreams? Yeah, can't say that. "Why?"

"I want to ask her out. Just wanted to make sure I wasn't stepping on your toes." There's a subtle question in his tone at the end of the sentence, like he's double-checking Talia and I aren't secretly dating.

I could tell him to back off. I could tell him to get lost. I could ask Talia out for real again.

Until I remember her dancing with Campbell. Smiling at him. Blushing. Calling him Cam.

I may have successfully cooked a few things, but am I ready to date her myself—when she could be into Campbell?

"Go for it, man," I tell him, like I'm not hating myself for every syllable.

"Awesome. We can double."

Ooh, can we? "Sure. Now get off my bed." I manage not to actually, physically kick him out and shut the door behind him with a little too much force.

Okay, I *am* jealous. But I can't hold Talia back, either.

CHAPTER 25
TALIA

I'S HARD TO CATCH SOMEONE doing something they shouldn't without twenty-four-hour surveillance. Tonight we won't even have four-hour surveillance until I've got to go rehearse with Vasily, but somebody's got to pick up the slack with Galina. She finishes work at the US Embassy Wednesday evening and I tail her to a coffee shop. I put on a honey blond wig and a spare hat from my emergency disguise stash (AKA the glove box) before I follow her in.

The coffee shop isn't Tim Hortons, but the chain has more than personality this place. Nondescript furniture, generic art—even the baked goods selection is boring. The whole shop could be a front, but that's more elaborate than I think Vasily's going for. Galina gets a latte; I get a chocolate chip muffin to not eat. She takes a table by the door to set up her laptop.

That better not be sensitive US information. The Illegals spy ring used a similar setup to broadcast intelligence from their computers to Russian diplomats parked nearby. Should I check the street? My cover purse has my most-used tools, but no Wi-Fi scanner.

Have to monitor Galina. I take a seat at a table diagonally behind her, close enough to kind of see what she's doing, but not suspicious-close. I get out my phone to use as a cover (again) while still observing Galina.

She's playing a farming game. Seriously? For ten minutes straight, planting crops, working the fields, harvesting, feeding animals. Is this the job of an international spy? (Definitely hasn't come up in my line of work.)

I could've gotten to my seat too late. Maybe she started a transmission and is playing as a cover. Or they might be using steganography, hidden messages in images or files.

Another patron brushes by my table, knocking my napkin to the floor. "Oh, sorry," he says as we both lean down to pick it up. I almost avoid his gaze, but just before he straightens, I recognize his eyes. The last person I expected to see here.

Mack. Head of our Canadian counterparts at CSIS.

Oh boy.

He sets the napkin on my table for me and walks away. I'm no idiot. After a few minutes, I pretend to use the napkin and discreetly check the underside for a message. (He doesn't write that fast; he switched them out.) *She's taken.*

Either Mack's targeting her, or he's already using her as an agent. (To spy on us? Or her Russian friends?) Mack tosses his cup in the garbage and heads out. I stall before I pursue and find him waiting at the corner, patting his pockets.

We're alone. Mack starts around the corner and I follow, trying to look like we're strangers matching pace. "We've been together for three months," he murmurs. And I know "together" doesn't mean they're dating, since Mack's been married forever.

If Mack's recruited her, unless she's playing him, she's not spying for the Russians—she's spying *on* them. "Trust her?"

"Passed a poly. Everything's corroborated." His answer's

clipped to keep the communication discreet, but the meaning's clear: Galina's not guilty. At the corner, Mack turns the opposite direction. Like how my case is veering off on another course.

A surveillance detection run takes me to Vasily's. As with all our rehearsals, my pulse steadily climbs the closer I get. I'm dancing with the enemy, trying to convince him I'd be a great asset to his spy ring. If he even suspects I'm not who I say I am, I'll blow the whole op. I've got to focus on more than my footwork.

After forty-five minutes of rehearsal, focus is still not my friend. I check the floor-to-ceiling windows in the dance studio mirror again for someone I recognize on the street. Another drawback to Campbell moving into Danny's spare bedroom: now two people who know the real me live around the corner from Vasily's studio. I'm four times as cautious as I was before. Which is fifty times as difficult because Vasily's convinced he's found me a partner, so we've doubled up on practices. I had to leave Danny's to come here (with a few surveillance stops) last night, and here I am again. Tomorrow might be my only night off this week.

"Joanne, please," Vasily says for the fourth time. "Stay with me."

"Sorry." I keep my Canadian cover firmly in place with my accent and refocus on Vasily.

Not thinking about Danny.

Okay, yes I am. I'm thinking maybe if he's making this much progress with cooking, his creative activity, maybe that whole baggage situation is getting better.

You know, the opposite of mine, so the point's probably moot. But pretty soon, Danny might be ready to date. Anyone but me.

Vasily clears his throat, and I once again draw my attention to him. "Rumba is a dance of passion," he begins. But my concentration immediately begins to dissipate, and not just because I've had this lecture from him twice in the last week, and four times from Elliott before that.

Sorry if I can't stare at you like I want to tear your clothes off. I'm too worried about keeping my feet moving in the right direction.

"What are you passionate about, Joanne?" Vasily cuts into my thoughts with a detour from the usual course of his lecture. "What is your passion?"

"Ballroom." The cover was never intended to be scrutinized, so I need to be careful what I say here.

"You enjoy dance," Vasily says, "but I do not think it is your passion. Is there anything you enjoy as much as dance?"

Eating. Sleeping. The five minutes a day I'm not working. (Oh, and working. That too.)

"How about your job? With Parliament, yes?"

He remembers my cover job. Could he hope to recruit me as an agent, or milk me for intelligence? "My job's good—although, man, sometimes people need to talk sense into those MPs."

Vasily's attention wanders away. Considering what I said? But then he changes the subject. "You're not married, are you?"

"No." Covers are single. Safer for them, too.

"Dating anyone?"

"No." I take a split second to check the street in the mirrors again.

"Hm." Vasily screws up his lips, concentrating. "There must be someone or something you love. Your family?"

I roll my eyes. I love them—even Mom—but I'm most passionate about avoiding that mess.

"Someone you would like to be dating?"

"Not really."

Vasily smiles slowly, and I already know why. That was the world's least convincing lie. As if he could read my mind, I carefully keep far away from any thoughts about Danny.

Um, beginning now. Or now. But seriously, now.

"Sorry, Vasily, but the reason I started dancing was to *not* think about my personal life." No more words come. I physically can't tell him any more. It's too close to the truth for a cover, and even then—I can't. "That's all."

He nods like an old sage, and I feel like I've climbed Everest. "Why don't we work on paso doble?" he suggests.

"Sounds good." Not sure whether the guy's giving up on me or senses we've gone somewhere I don't want to. I try to convince myself this is good for the cover—if Joanne had no issues, no personality, no concerns, Vasily would see through her a lot faster.

But I feel like I've given away too much.

We spend another half hour on traveling spins and the chasse capes figure, one of the most advanced set of moves in the dance. Vasily has me count the steps with him. I stare down at our feet on the floorboards as we walk through the step, together, step, step, crossover, spin of the first half. When I've got that up to speed, we add the "leg hook," lifting my knee. It's a complex sequence, but once I can watch myself in the mirror instead of fixating on our feet, Vasily seems satisfied with my progress. We move on to the twist-kick-step-twist-kick of the coup de pique. (Don't ask me why the moves of the paso doble are in French.)

My leg muscles are practically humming by the time we finish. Between Elliott and Vasily, I've been through my own personal *Dancing with the Stars* these last few months. Unfortunately, beating Vasily and Galina isn't part of my goal for the long term, so this doesn't feel like progress.

I grab my bag from its spot by the stereo and change into my street shoes. Vasily, already changed and packed, waits by the wall with the ballet barre (ugh, bad memories). I tug on my jacket, and we head through the office together.

"Does dancing help you escape your problems?" he asks.

"For a while." I look at Vasily. He bites his lip, staring at the floor as we cross the tile. He wants to say something, but doesn't know if he should.

I pretend the anticipation building in my system is nothing. Vasily could be bugged about a cute girl or family problems. But I'll never know if I don't ask. "Is something the matter?"

"Just . . . a friendship. It's been stressful."

I stop short at the front doors. Normally, half a block from my friends' apartment, I'd be trying to get rid of Vasily, but we're finally making the smallest bit of progress—*if* his friend is his handler and not, say, his bookie. "Stressful?" I ask. "Mind if I ask what's wrong?"

He doesn't answer. But spies are part confidant, part counselor, part confessor. I key into my most sympathetic expression, like I understand exactly what he's going through, and all he has to do is open up and spill his deepest darkest secrets to relieve that burden.

Heck, for all I know, that's how it works.

Vasily focuses on the door handle, but meets my eyes at last. "I—I couldn't—"

"After all you've done for me? Listening's the least I could do."

He draws in a deep breath. "It didn't seem like much when he first asked me, but now, I worry I'll hurt someone."

Not a bookie. I furrow my brow slightly. "How could you hurt someone?"

"My friend has asked me to give him . . . information. That might hurt someone." He pushes through the doors before I respond, to leave that confession and all its implications behind in the foyer.

I match his pace on the sidewalk. "I see why you'd be stressed."

Vasily glances over. "Yes. Well. I'll figure something out."

"If you ever need to talk about it, I'm here."

One side of his mouth tilts up. "Thank you, Joanne."

We reach the street corner and wait for the light. My car's the other way, but I'm not giving up this first connection. Too soon to push him our direction, but if he's an unwilling agent, this might be easier than I thought.

The light flashes for us to cross the street—toward Danny's building. Okay, creating this relationship of trust or not, I may not be able to continue this direction and keep my cover. We reach the other sidewalk, and I turn to Vasily to say goodbye.

"Talia!" shouts a familiar voice.

My stomach plunges faster than the mercury during the last cold snap. Crap. I fight off the instinct to see who's calling me. (Though I've got the tiniest bit of comfort: not Danny.) Instead, I keep my gaze glued to Vasily. "Did you want me to meet the man who needs a partner?"

"Absolutely—if you think you're ready."

Chances are low, but might as well ask. "This isn't your friend who's stressing you out, right?"

"Right." He dismisses that concern. "Forget I mentioned him."

Aaand we're back to where we started. So I start over. "I'm not sure I'm ready."

"How about an informal meeting? To see if it's a good fit—Saturday at eleven? Here?" He gestures back at the studio.

"Hey! Talia!" shouts my friend that I might seriously have to hurt. (It's either Campbell or Joel, and believe me—I would.)

"I'll be there."

Vasily grins, because this is supposed to be a major triumph, instead of a defeat. If Vasily succeeds in getting me a partner, I have 0 reason to see Vasily again.

Maybe we'll have to *not* succeed.

"Talia!" Campbell/Joel's close enough to be sure it's me. He should also be sure I'm *ignoring him*, but I shouldn't put it past

204

him to ignore that right back.

But we're about two seconds from a very bad showdown. My mouth goes dry as Vasily hesitates. What if he wants to talk about the stressful friend again?

"See you Saturday," he finally says.

"Great."

Vasily turns—heading away from Campbell/Joel. I breathe a sigh of relief and start in the direction of Danny's building, not looking at Joel as I pass.

"Hey!" He jumps in front of me, and I fake a startled hop back.

"Oh, hey—you scared me."

"Sorry. I've been calling for you."

You don't say. "Really? I didn't hear you."

He changes the subject. "Are you doing anything tomorrow? Danny and Campbell were talking about getting a group together to see a movie at the Diefenbunker."

I bite back a smile. Last time I went to the city's declassified Cold War bunker, I was running surveillance for a dead drop pickup. (Yes, it was Elliott who wanted to use such a goofy drop site. Just once.) "What movie?"

"*From Russia with Love.*"

Oh. Goody. Sean Connery notwithstanding, Bond films from the era of camp aren't my thing. But hanging out with Danny is (and unfortunately, my work is just beginning for the night, so I can't go do that now). "Sounds like fun. I'll try to make it."

"Great. The movie starts at seven, so we'll probably meet around six."

"I'll try," I say again. I don't have any agent meetings scheduled (that's tonight), but sometimes they come up at the last minute. "See you later."

Joel finally gets the not-really-a-hint-anymore I'm done with this conversation and starts for Danny's building, leaving me to tally my losses for the night. I did manage to avoid Joel till Vasily was gone. But my only progress with Vasily is on my dance technique—and now we've got a deadline to end even that side of our relationship.

I've got a long way to go.

With Vasily and Galina rehearsing (and Elliott listening in), I can't do a whole lot to make progress with Vasily the next night, and I was formally invited to Danny's this time. Once I'm done at Terfort & Sutter (and a surveillance detection run), I'm knocking on Danny's door.

Yep. I'm pathetic.

No—I'm a friend. Heaven knows I could use one.

Danny answers the door. Looking confused. "Hey." Well, that's what he says, but what he obviously means is *What are you doing here?*

My stupid little mind instantly springs to the conclusion: he must have a date. He's taking someone else to the movie. Which was why he didn't ask me in the first place.

Okay, I can salvage this. A group's going, supposedly, so I won't seem like a total idiot. Other than standing here staring at him for a full minute. "Joel said something about a movie tonight?"

"Oh, yeah, they left ten minutes ago."

So much for saving face. "Ah."

"Did you want to go?"

That won't be awkward. Goody. "I don't—"

"We can go." He ducks behind the door and returns with jacket in hand. Before I reassure him he doesn't have to go anywhere, he's locked the door and is walking down the hall.

"Wait, why didn't you leave with the others?"

"Not enough room in the cars. Not worth driving and pay-

206

ing to watch someone else's screen."

I fall in step with him and shake my head at that engineer pragmatism, but I can't argue. "We don't have to go."

"Nah—it'll be fun with you there."

Yep. I'm the fun friend. "So everyone else going was lame?"

Danny hits the button for the elevator and considers my question. "Anything else you'd like to do?"

That's a joke, judging from his bright tone. "Depends. Who else went?"

Danny lists off half a dozen people from church. I don't know any of them well, but I don't avoid them at all costs either. On the drive, Danny fills me in about his day as an engineer (yeah, still not clear on how he spends eight hours rocket-sciencing, but I'll take his word). I get to tell him all about appearing before the Master (just to get a case delayed for a day, but it makes me sound good, even if I don't have to wear robes in a lower court). We're halfway to the Diefenbunker when his phone rings. He frowns at the screen. "Hello?"

After a pause, he continues. "I can't tonight—" He listens again and sighs. "I don't know."

I lift an eyebrow, and he glances at me. "Hang on," he says to the person on the phone. He turns to me. "That real estate guy I told you about wants to show me a house. Now."

"Sounds like slightly more fun than paying to watch someone else's screen."

"Listen, I'd better go—he's my boss's husband, and he says it's just this once—but I can take you back."

"Where's the house?"

Danny frowns again and switches back to the phone. "Where is it?" He checks with me. "Aylmer?"

"It'll take twice as long to take me back." And I'm not ready to give up the rest of my night with him. "I'll go with you."

"You sure?"

"Yeah. It'll be fun."

Skepticism flickers over his features, but he gets back on the phone for the address. I get him turned around and headed across the closest bridge into Québec, but his phone's GPS has to guide us to the house. Can't tell what color it is in the dark, but the stone façade looks nice, and the lights in every window make it seem homey. Bay windows, a two-car garage, two stories . . . How much of a loan did Danny qualify for?

But Danny isn't in the market for a house—is he? "Remind me why we're doing this," I say as we walk up the stairs to the glowing French door.

"He's my boss's husband," he tells me again. Not much of a reason. Guess it's enough for him, though, because he knocks.

The door swings open, and I suck in a gasp. I know this guy, the real estate agent. Mid-forties, short, graying on top. I rack my brain to figure out how.

The recognition shows in his face. My heart dives. I'm in trouble.

I got it—he showed a house to one of my potential agents, and I was posing as an interior designer. Who was I that day?

The real estate agent moves back to let us in. Danny, oblivious, starts into the tiled entry, but I grab his elbow and walk with him. "You want to have fun? Run with this." I turn back to the agent, hold out my hand and hope I've got the right identity. "Hi, Georgia McBride," I say in my broadest Southern accent, stressing both syllables of the surname so it sounds like Mack-Bride. (I went to middle school with Georgia for two years. Trust me, I know how she says it.) "I'm Mr. Fluker's designer."

"Roger Anderson." He glances at Danny. "I didn't realize you'd hired an interior decorator already."

This gives me the first natural break to check Danny's reaction. He's eyeing me like I'm crazy—but a good crazy, I think. "Kinda fell into it," he manages.

He shakes Roger's hand, and I introduce him, "My newest

client, Daniel Fluker."

"Just Danny."

I flutter a hand to my chest. "Didn't want to presume—"

"Not presumptuous. My legal name is Danny."

Interesting. I pat his arm. "Iddn't he just darlin'?"

"Uh . . . yeah." Roger starts the tour without comment.

Danny leans close enough to me to mutter, "Darlin'?"

"'Course you are, darlin'. I'm the fun one, right?"

He gives me a whatever-you-say expression and follows Roger past the staircase into the living room. I keep up a commentary on the hardwood floors and bay window, but lament how hard it'll be to effectively use the open space. We continue to the dining room, and then the kitchen, all dark wood, stainless steel, granite and tile. It has another eating area and sliding glass doors out to a dark deck. From the eating area, there's a family room with a fireplace. We make our way back to the entry, with a detour for the side door, laundry, half bath and garage.

Okay, honestly? I'm impressed. I'm half-tempted to buy the house, if I knew I'd be in Ottawa a few more years—but I don't think I make enough to afford it with my jobs combined.

Danny looks impressed, too, and I think Roger's noticed by the time he starts up the stairs. "The owners have already moved, so they're motivated to sell. I think we could get a good deal, and they'll want to close quickly."

Danny heads up the dark wood stairs. We peek into the full bath and three decent-sized bedrooms before Roger practically runs ahead, as if he's preparing for the big reveal.

"Sure you don't want to buy a house, darlin'?" I whisper to Danny as we stroll after Roger.

"You know, I never said that." A smile fights to get past his poker-face defense.

That would certainly send a message to his mom. We reach Roger, and he flings open the double doors to the master.

Danny and I stand in stunned silence. "Oh my," I finally murmur. "That's—that's—"

"Chartreuse," Danny names the hideous yellow-green all over the walls.

I look at him with wide eyes. "Apparently you don't need a designer if you know what color chartreuse is."

The smile he was fighting is gone. He doesn't even smirk at my joke or my accent. He fixates on the carpet and doesn't move to go in the room.

"Danny, darlin', don't you think you'd better take a peek?"

He doesn't answer, but steps two feet into the room.

I come to stand next to him. "I take it you don't like the color."

He shakes his head without looking at the walls. His lips compress, his whole countenance grim.

No idea what's going on. "You're right, honey, it's the ugliest thing I ever did see. But a little paint can fix this. A nice greige or maybe a navy—"

"I'm done." He wheels around and walks out of the room. Roger and I exchange a mystified glance before I go to snap some quick photos of the master bathroom (corner tub *and* a corner shower?) and walk-in closet.

Danny's waiting at the door. He tells Roger he'll call if he's interested, but it's obvious he's not, not after the master bedroom. Roger gives me his card (I pretend to have forgotten mine), and we make our escape.

After five minutes of heavy silence, I'm totally at a loss. I haven't seen Danny like this, ever, not even when he was talking about his bad breakup. "I take it you don't want to talk."

He stays focused on the road. "And say what?"

"For starters, you could tell me what that color ever did to you."

He clams up.

"Look, I know that color just existing is a crime against

fashion and good taste and humanity—"

"Don't." He interrupts without cutting me off; his tone is firm but gentle. I stop and look out the window, like my CIA-trained land navigation skills will help me in this conversation.

Nope, still lost.

We're on the Ottawa side of the river before Danny parks (not all that far from my apartment, but I'm not volunteering that info). He seems to brace himself before he looks at me.

I could use all those tools I used on Vasily yesterday, even if they didn't work so great. I could pretend to be whoever Danny would be most likely to talk to.

Or I could just *be* someone Danny can talk to. So I turn in my seat to face him and wait.

CHAPTER 26
DANNY

TALIA'S SITTING THERE, and I don't know what to say. I've tried, I've tried to work through this, but suddenly coping with time and cooking seems pretty pitiful.

No. I've coped. I just haven't talked about it. With anyone. Ever.

I look at Talia again. She's waiting, patiently, for some explanation of why I freaked out over a freaking paint color. I know it doesn't make sense. I know it's stupid. But when I saw it, the memories fell on me like a ton of titanium.

And to explain, I'll have to open all those wounds.

Come on, man. Rip the Band-Aid. "We were engaged."

She barely blinks. "You and Kendra?"

Have I told Talia her name? "What, are you Facebook stalking me?"

"You mentioned her once. This was your bad breakup last year?"

"Oh. Yeah."

After a long silence, Talia takes a stab in the dark. "And

chartreuse is her favorite color?"

Yeah, that's why I shut down. I'm that unstable. "She picked it as our wedding color. I didn't even care, but my sister hated it. I just wanted everybody to be happy. So one night, I suggested maybe it wasn't the most flattering color, and . . ."

I clench my fists, my whole body tensing like that'll be enough to will back the wall of memories and emotions threatening to crush me.

Maybe I haven't coped with this. Maybe I've just tried to ignore it and push it away and move forward like it never happened.

Talia's hand lands on my wrist. I pry my other hand off the wheel, place it over hers. I can do this. "Suddenly, I was the worst human who ever walked the Earth. Everything I said made it worse. She said I didn't want to get married, I was looking for any excuse to get away, I hated her. . . . It was like someone flipped a switch."

I pause for a minute. Is that enough? Do I have to tell the rest?

"Danny," she says. "Seriously, that sounds like a symptom of mental illness."

"Yeah, I picked up on that sometime between when she started throwing all my plates at my feet, and when I went to stop her, and she punched me in the face. Or maybe it was when she said if I told anyone about that, she'd claim I tried to rape her. Yeah, that was probably the time."

Talia doesn't say anything at first, but her eyes grow wider. "What did you do?"

"Said something like, 'You're right, I don't want to get married,' and walked her out."

"I mean, what did you do, like, in your life?"

I focus on the steering wheel. Still don't know how to pilot through all this. "I . . . I couldn't go to work with a black eye 'not' from my fiancée. I called in sick for two days, and worked from home for another couple weeks." I stop for a second, remembering how trapped I felt—but at the same time, I wasn't. "Then I realized what my life had become with her. I mean, at first, everything was awesome. I was the greatest boyfriend she'd ever had, and everyone else she'd dated sounded like a long stream of creeps who'd hurt her and morons who never appreciated her. I was *everything*, the best thing that ever happened to her, and I thought she was the same thing for me. I thought this was it, this is why people get married."

Talia scoffs, pulling me back to the present. I glance at her, and she realizes her mistake. "Sorry. I'm . . . kinda cynical about why people get married."

"*You're* cynical?"

She holds up her hands, surrendering the point. What was I saying? Why I thought it made sense to marry Kendra? "I only wanted her to be happy. I wanted everything to be perfect, and maybe she was a little dramatic. Then out of nowhere, she cheated, and I took her back, and she dumped me and begged me to take her back two days later. We had a fight—*I* wasn't committed enough—and she 'accidentally' broke my Xbox. But I thought I could prove I was committed if we got married."

I wait for Talia to object again, but she just gives me a tiny, pitiful frown.

Pitiful sounds about right. "She was in charge of everything for the wedding. Seemed normal to me. Whatever she wanted, I went along with. What difference did it make to me?"

"Well, sure."

"But when she was gone—and after I kicked her out—for a while she went total silent treatment, not even wondering if I was okay. I should've been crushed, and I was, but . . ." I take a deep breath and sigh it out. Feels almost as good now as it did then.

Talia leans forward in her seat, ready for me to continue.

"I felt free. I saw how small my life had become, always

walking on eggshells, always trying to make her happy, always falling short. I had to take her side on everything or I was the villain. I couldn't play video games or go to my sister's or talk to my mom if we were together—all the focus had to be on her. Suddenly, I didn't have to constantly reassure her I loved her, she was wonderful and everything else."

"And then you felt bad for feeling good."

I check with Talia again, but this time I'm surprised for a different reason. I wasn't expecting her to *get it*, but for a minute, I realize her shields aren't just down; they're gone completely, like never before.

This is all of her—the person who was hurt before, who still doesn't want to be hurt again, who's open and waiting and willing and scared but *here*, listening, understanding.

I nod slowly. "Still do, sometimes."

"Have you seen her again?"

I grimace and shift against my seatbelt. "No. After a few weeks, she tried to contact me. She called; I changed my phone number. I blocked her on Facebook; she messaged me from a friend's account."

"Hence no Facebook."

"Yep. Scorched earth. She kept coming to my apartment, so I moved. She tracked me down again. Then I moved back to Michigan. She followed me, tried to come see me at my parents'. When I wasn't home, she got my number and left a message saying she'd kill herself if I didn't respond. I didn't, and she did."

"She committed suicide?"

I make a sound to say *sort of.* "She tried. Ended up in the hospital." I pull my wrist free from Talia's fingers, folding my arms. "The worst part: I know I could've stopped it. I could've prevented it, and I—I did nothing."

"Danny, you know she needs help."

I turn to Talia. "*I* was supposed to help her. I was ready to spend the rest of eternity with her, taking care of her, and . . . I failed. She begged me to help her, and I couldn't. I. Failed."

She lets the words die, and then stays on her same track. "She needs *professional* help, and until she gets that, she's in no shape to be in any relationship."

"I don't know." Everything she says makes total sense, but I'm still having a hard time buying it. I've tried telling myself the same thing, but . . . I still feel like it's my fault.

"Have you thought about talking to someone about it?"

"What do you think I'm doing?"

She shoots me a smirk. "Seriously. Couldn't hurt."

Famous last words. "Talia, I've never told anyone this. Ever. Not even my mom."

That makes her smirk fall away. "Why—?" She cuts off her own question, her eyes trailing away toward the windshield. "You were keeping the family secret. Because maybe *you* were the crazy one. The bad one."

"Not making me feel real good."

Her gaze tracks back to me. "Sorry. I'm . . ." Her focus moves away again, like she's thinking or remembering something. "Did you have Family Home Evening growing up?"

Okay, abrupt subject change. "Yeah?"

"What's the worst one you can remember?"

I have to scan my memory of the weekly spiritual lesson from my parents. "One time my brother and sister and I ended up wrestling on the floor, fighting. Why?"

"When I lived with my mother, our *best* Family Home Evening was when she sat us down in a circle. She pointed to my brother Troy and told him three things he was doing wrong. The way he chewed was one. Then we had to go around the circle, everyone telling Troy why he was bad. If we couldn't think of something, Mom screamed at us until we did. No matter how long we cried—and if you cried, it was your fault, and you didn't love Mom, and you were a horrible person. Then it was Trevor's turn."

I can feel my jaw slowly dropping. The tangent's starting to make sense. My mom's overbearing sometimes, but this is straight evil. "Why would your mother do that?"

"In her twisted mind, it made her feel like she was doing something right—doing everything right. She thought she was perfect and couldn't stand to see us do something right half the time—or worse, doing something wrong. I begged her to put me in ballet but she pulled me out after a year because she thought I was awful and making *her* look bad."

I can't even—"Why?"

"Because she's insane. Really, truly mentally ill. And she'll never get help, because the last person who thinks they need a psychiatrist is a narcissist. Everything we did was wrong. We never did enough. We never loved her enough. We bent over backwards to be perfect, and we weren't enough. She spent years breaking us down until we couldn't function without her."

Every word sounds eerily familiar.

Then it dawns on me. When Talia said everyone's been hurt, I figured she had a scumbag ex. Her scars run much deeper. Deeper than mine. "How did you survive?"

She shrugs. "Kids are resilient. We ran away after five years, and Dad won custody again." Though I don't know how she can, she smiles. "Years of therapy helped, too."

"Yeah, I guess it would."

For the first time since she started talking, Talia meets my eyes. "I've never told anyone—*anyone*—about that. Because it was *my* family secret. I spent five years not knowing that kind of life wasn't normal. I spent five years thinking *I* was the crazy one. I spent five years believing I'd done something wrong. But most of all, I spent five years hiding, trying to kill off my emotions, withdrawing." She sighs softly. "Know what? It never really helped. It never solved anything."

I sit there for a minute, absorbing everything she's told me. How does anyone survive that type of abuse?

That word hits me like a shockwave. Abuse. It's the word for what Kendra did to me, too.

And even with all Talia's been through, she's only tried to help *me* heal.

"Hang on a sec." I unlock the doors and get out. Talia leans forward to watch me round the car, raising an eyebrow when I go to open her door. She accepts my hands and stands, and I wrap my arms around her.

"It's been thirteen years, Danny. I'll be okay." But her voice quavers a tiny bit, and she slides her arms around my waist, laying her head on my chest.

"I know." I'm holding on for me, too, and she doesn't let go. Because it just feels *right*. Not like *hey, I'm attracted to you, let me find any excuse to touch you.* More that she *gets* how I ended up in this bizarre mirror world and understands how that breaks you—and she doesn't think I'm stupid or weak or anything else. No judgment. Just—

"Danny?" she asks after a minute.

"Yeah?"

Her shoulders fall, and she pulls back enough to see me. "Thanks for telling me. Trusting me." Her eyes add an unspoken postscript: *thanks for letting me trust you.*

"Oh, you know, anytime."

Talia maintains her serious eye contact. "I know." She steps back to lean against my car frame. "Can I say something?"

"At this point, you can say pretty much anything."

"I'm not a psychiatrist, but everything you said reminds me of a personality disorder, like my mother. But diagnosis or not, what happened with Kendra was *her* fault. Her responsibility. All of it."

I shove my hands in my pockets and pivot to face my car. "Yeah."

"But—"

I turn to her again.

"—it might not hurt to do a little digging to figure out *why* you stayed with her when you knew she was hurting you."

"Because I'm an idiot."

Talia pushes off my car and moves closer, waiting for me to look at her. "You're not an idiot. I think there's another reason."

"You going to start dropping hints?"

She gives me a frown-smile. "If I knew, I might. That's on you."

I sigh and hold her door for her. Intellectually, I know about the cycle of abuse. Even as someone who's been so mistreated—abused—I still can't quite wrap my brain around why you'd stay with a person who's hurting you, no matter how great that initial honeymoon period was.

I only wanted to take care of her, to make her happy. I thought I loved her.

Maybe I was wrong. Or maybe that wasn't enough.

I get in my side of the car and buckle my seatbelt.

"Danny?" Talia tries again. "Telling me about this—it's big."

Yeah, knew that.

"You've really moved forward."

Doesn't feel like it—feels like a jumbo jet pushed me back nearly a year—but she might be right.

Now I just have to figure out what's wrong with me.

CHAPTER 27
TALIA

’M STILL PONDERING my last conversation with Danny as I huddle on a park bench two days later, pretending to know what I'm doing with some needles and yarn. On one hand, how can I not feel good Danny confided in me and let me confide him? I've never been able to tell anyone, not even my therapists, about the finer points of Mom.

But on the other hand, a selfish part of me doesn't want Danny to make strides toward healing. Because if he moves on, he'll be ready to think about dating and marriage. And I won't.

And on a third hand, I need to focus. We're intercepting a dead drop, not worrying about Danny.

Next to me on the park bench, Elliott updates Eric on our position: backs to the school where Vasily made his last drop. (Rearview mirrors in fake glasses are the best invention ever.) (That may be an exaggeration.) Vasily's on his way this direction, and friendship stress or not, coming here means one thing: he's making a drop.

"We've got a signal," Eric reports. "Probably five minutes

away."

Elliott switches off the minimic in his lapel pin and snaps his newspaper. I click my needles together. "Doing anything fun tomorrow?"

"One last desperate attempt to book Shanna's dream spot." He groans quietly.

I choke back a scoff.

"How about you? Any plans for the weekend?"

Wish I had plans for right now instead of sitting here, but all that's left of the weekend is tomorrow. "Just church."

Now Elliott scoffs. "Okay, you've gotta tell me. Why do you bother with church?"

"Excuse me?"

He turns to me. "Is it the social life? A lot of hot guys in your parish?"

"We call it a ward. And I don't have time for a social life."

Elliott checks his rearview and the empty park. "The food?"

"No food."

"Then what?"

I stare at on my mess of yarn and needles. "Why do you care?"

"I don't *care*, I just don't get it. I mean, you claim to believe in the Bible, following all these extra commandments about sex and coffee and smoking, but we run around every day, lying through our teeth and doing everything the Bible says thou shalt not."

"Everything? Last I checked, we're not killing, adultering, coveting—in fact, I'm pretty sure I'm good on nine of the top ten commandments."

"What, you use the David Letterman Version of the Bible?"

I stifle a laugh. Fortunately, we're still alone enough I can talk. "There are spies in the Bible, you know. On God's side."

Elliott's silence seems to suggest he didn't know.

"I know I don't have to lecture you on the morality of our

job." We both know the CIA needs people not necessarily with religion, but with a moral code, people they can trust completely—and that means people who won't turn around and lie to them. "Soldiers kill. Spies lie. I'm pretty sure God gets that. I hear He's smart."

He shifts on the bench, flipping another newspaper page. The quiet shifts into the awkward range. "Sorry," he finally says. "I didn't mean—"

I interrupt his apology. "I know."

"Just seems like you'd be better off—I don't know . . . without that stuff holding you back."

I break off watching the street behind us to look at him, really look at him. Elliott has delighted in tormenting me like a brother would for over a year. He's already betrayed my trust, my security in this friendship, with that stupid kiss. But this is the first time his words have actually cut.

On a logical level, he's right. My life would look a lot easier if I didn't have these "silly" rules "burdening" me. If I didn't obsess over doing the right thing all the time. If I let that all go.

But on a deeper level, Elliott truly doesn't get it. Being Mormon—the real reasons I believe—isn't something I can toss out like a scratchy sweater. I didn't spend over a year in Russia preaching the gospel, risking my life a couple times, for kicks, and I certainly didn't do it to go and give it up now because it's inconvenient. It's who I am. I know Elliott doesn't *get* it, but I thought he respected that.

Elliott may be one of the few who knows what I'm really doing in Canada, but he has no clue who I really am. None whatsoever.

"FEATHERSTONE's about to turn," comes Eric's voice over my earpiece. "You got him?"

We both face forward to look backward and Elliott twists his lapel pin to switch his mic back on. "Not yet."

Five seconds later, I pick up the movement in my mirrors.

Vasily's short, svelte silhouette walks into view under the streetlamps, highlighting his light blond hair where it sticks out of his dark cap. A lot more subtle than his favorite red dancing shirt. "Got him."

Elliott and I don't make a move, not even to breathe, our eyes glued to the guy behind us. Vasily veers off the sidewalk for the drainage ditch. We have to turn our heads slightly, the opposite direction, to keep watching, but the tiny splash by his ankles gives us our answer.

"He's done," Elliott murmurs. "Moving out."

We sit there, watching Vasily's retreating figure in our rearviews. Elliott switches off his mic again. "Listen," he says. "I wasn't trying to say—"

I hold up a hand. "It's fine. Let's focus."

We turn to the park in prickly silence, me pretending to knit, Elliott pretending to read, both watching the road behind us. Vasily's long gone, and we listen to Eric and our team coordinating surveillance on him, getting farther and farther away.

Could be hours or days before a courier comes to check for his signal and pick up his intel—or it could be minutes. Once Vasily's far enough away, Elliott and I go to work, dropping off our props in the car. We pull on gloves and head to the drainage ditch, ambling like we're not we're aiming for it. We've been watching long enough to know nobody's around, but that could change any minute.

I watch for Vasily or his courier while Elliott fishes the container out of the water, a small black sphere. We casually walk away, taking the left just past the church. Once we're out of sight, he unscrews the sphere halves and opens them. Inside is a USB flash drive. This time, we're doing more than copying. We're on the offensive.

"Let's see what he's got," Elliott mutters. He gives me Vasily's drive, and takes up scanning the street for me. I wedge my thin-bladed screwdriver into the seam along the side of the USB drive casing and pry out the circuitry inside. Elliott hands me a replacement, and I snap the whole thing back together.

Whatever Vasily's handlers expect, I think they'll be disappointed to find two corrupt files infected with a Ukrainian virus. Elliott and I split up, him going back to replace the dead drop, and me to rendezvous with our team and pass off Vasily's intelligence to be analyzed.

We're closing in on him.

I'm grateful to be away from Elliott for my surveillance detection run back to the office. At least he can't pin me down for another "soul-searching." I like the guy, I do, but . . . I thought we were really friends.

Apparently I've miscalculated that relationship in more ways than one. And that cuts worse than anything Elliott could say.

I finish up my SDR at the office, where my car waits. Of course, Elliott's leaning against my door. I check my phone, like I can get out of the conversation that way, and find a voicemail waiting. I hit the icon to listen so I can brush past Elliott without talking.

It's my mom, and that would be the "insanity" decibel range. I can't even make out half the words through the distortion of her screams. I yank the phone away and touch the button to delete the message.

"What was that?" Elliott asks.

"My mother," I mutter, trying to reach behind him for my car door.

"Oh." He groans. "Don't tell me you've got 'mommy issues.'"

His derisive tone knocks the wind out of me. As if the first blow tonight and my mother's attack weren't enough.

"Move," I order him.

"Hey, wait—"

"Now, Elliott!" My words hold enough bark that Elliott backs away, defensive hands raised. I get in and whip out of the parking lot fast.

I'm used to taking risks—I have to do it all the time. But now, I feel . . . exposed. Because the people who should know me the best don't know me at all. Or don't care.

I go through the motions of an SDR, gradually angling for the place a paranoid spy feels safest. I don't realize I'm not driving to my apartment until after my last stop. Instead, I'm headed to Danny's.

Despite all their (conscious or subconscious) efforts, I know I'm not invisible—because there's one person who *sees* me, the real me, the me I have to hide even deeper than my CIA connections, and he cares.

I debate the wisdom of this choice the rest of the way there, but I don't talk myself out of it. As soon as Campbell answers the door, the noise from inside attacks me almost like my mother did.

Exactly what I don't need after tonight.

"Hey!" Campbell greets me. "You're here for the party!"

Before I back out, Campbell grabs my wrist and pulls me in. A party it is, mostly people from church. Danny's in the kitchen, leaning against the counter, laughing with two girls I kind of know, Maddi Burton and Jenna Overson. Both of whom probably would've made it onto my "Girls from church over 25 without major, obvious issues" list. The list for Danny to date.

He should. It's an arrow to the heart, but he should. I came here because I need him, and soon he won't need me.

Campbell's dragging me to the living room, but I get free. "Actually, I can't stay. Just wanted to stop by and say hi, but you guys are busy."

"Oh, okay." Campbell's brow crinkles like he couldn't possibly understand how someone could resist a party, but he walks me to the door.

225

And follows me out. I turn back in the hall as he closes the door.

"I can make it to my car okay," I assure him.

"Of course you can." He stops walking, and I wait for him to talk. "Danny and I are going dancing next Friday—not together, as a double date. Want to go?"

I'd wonder why Campbell's arranging Danny's dates for him, but it did look like he was busy. (With other girls.)

We've pretty much established that if you mention Danny, I'm down. Movie I have no desire to see? Sounds good. Viewing a home neither of us want to buy? I'm in. Walking over a bed of hot coals for the chance to just see him? Here, hold my shoes.

"Sure."

"Oh, and do you think you could find someone else to go with us? Somebody cool."

I raise an eyebrow. He wants me to line up his date?

This is Campbell we're talking about. He's gone out with every girl over twenty from church (and half the teenagers). He isn't picky. "I guess."

He beams. "Great. Pick you up at seven?"

A year of telling him to meet me at church for home teaching every month, and he still hasn't figured out I don't give out my address. "I'll be here at seven."

"Oh, okay. That works."

He flashes one more quick grin and ducks back into his apartment. I'm in the elevator when it hits me: we'd better not go to Rahim's on this date/not-a-date.

There have to be other places to go dancing in Ottawa, right? And it's not like Vasily hangs out at Rahim's every week.

I hope.

With two full-time jobs (have I mentioned that?), one of which requires a lot of time out-of-office, it's not hard to avoid Elliott for a couple days. But Wednesday afternoon, I'm back to file reports, and Elliott acts like everything's fine.

Sure. Fine.

He stops by my desk and nods at my computer. "See the analysis on FEATHERSTONE's files?"

"Yeah." I don't look away from the monitor.

"Apparently the USB drive he gave to Galina was music."

"She's already off the list."

"And I compared his cryptonyms to our surveillance records," Elliott singsongs like this is the world's most tempting intelligence.

World's most tempting? Maybe not, but I have to bite. "Identify anyone?"

Elliott squints slightly. "Not exactly." He steps to his desk to wheel his chair over and plops down. "This week and two weeks ago, he reported intelligence from someone code named STRAUS."

I don't know the term right off. Doubt he'd use someone's real name as their cryptonym. A quick search shows *straus* is Russian for *ostrich*, and I report that to Elliott.

"Lame," he mutters. He pulls out a file folder with lists of Vasily's customers. "I looked for overlapping customers from those two weeks." He lays two pieces of paper on the desk and waits for me to draw the conclusion. I'm not going to comb through the alphabetized lists, but clearly no name is circled, and at a quick glance, I don't see anyone listed twice.

"Find someone?" I ask.

He offers his empty hands. "Nope."

What does that mean? "Did he make it up?"

"Looks like it."

Making up intelligence is a dangerous game. Then again, Vasily might want to be cut loose. "We can't take anything he's said in these reports at face value."

"Nope." Elliott grabs a list of names and passes the folder to me. "You know the guy. Could he be useful to us?"

I ponder that a minute. "He's talked to me about a stressful friendship. Sounded like it *might* be his handler."

"If that's got him manufacturing his intel. . . ."

I meet Elliott's gaze. "Maybe we could manufacture it for him."

He grins. "How close are you to pitching him?"

Crud. The wind dies in my sails, and my shoulders fall. "Not close."

"Well, let's get that way."

I turn back to my desk. We both know that's easier said than done. But if Vasily's making up stuff, we'd better get to him before his handler catches on.

CHAPTER 28
DANNY

'M DESPERATELY TRYING TO FIND A REASON to *not* regret this double date. Talia and whoever she picked for me aren't even here yet—can't believe Campbell asked her to do that. Meanwhile, Campbell's so happy to be going out! Having fun! Dancing! That he's practically bouncing off the walls.

Maybe I should work on getting out of this instead. But before I start, there's a knock at our door, and suddenly, I don't regret this idea, because Talia's here. Even if it's for a date with Campbell.

I beat him to the door—no, I didn't run. Much. I open it to find Talia, extra hot in black and jeans, and . . . Maddi, I think? "Hey," I say.

"Hi." Could be my imagination, but I want to believe I only see that light in her eyes when she's talking to me.

Maybe we can ditch Campbell. Though I guess we probably can't lose Maddi too.

"You know Maddi, right?" Talia gestures at the blonde next to her.

"Oh, yeah, hi."

"Hi."

Talia takes over the conversation, fighting back a grin. "I thought you didn't dance."

When did I say—oh yeah, in our search for a "creative activity." "You didn't ask me."

"Ready to go?" Campbell jumps in. "Don't want to be late for the lesson for you guys."

Goody. Campbell insists on driving as well as dominating the discussion on the short ride to . . . a brick church.

It's not *too* weird. We have dances in our building; we just hold them ourselves instead of hiring them out. By the time we walk in, the dance floor is nearly full of people for the lesson.

Talia's fidgeting, scanning the crowd. Does being around this many people bug her? It's not that many more than at church.

Campbell scopes out the crowd, too, and frowns. "I think we'll sit out, and you noobs can get all the help you need."

Maddi giggles. Yeah, he's hilarious. Fortunately she's a good sport—neither of us are great dancers—but we make it through the lesson with a rudimentary understanding. We find Talia and Campbell in the chairs ringing the room. "Ready?" Talia asks.

I try not to grimace. "Not really." I turn to Maddi. "You?"

"You guys'll wipe the floor with us."

"Is that a challenge?" Campbell hops to his feet, puffing up his chest like a bantam matador. He holds out a hand for Talia, and she jumps into the part, striking a Latin pose, placing her hand in his with an extra twist of the wrist.

My stomach falls to about my feet. This is what it'll be like all night.

"I give." I raise my hands in surrender, then check with Maddi. "You give?"

"Definitely." She nods for extra emphasis.

"Aw." Campbell thrusts out his bottom lip to pout, but decides to show off anyway, moving closer and lifting Talia's hand. She pivots under his arm, and he spins her twice, finally bringing her in for a slow dip.

No, *this* is what it'll be like all night. Now *I'm* Captain Third Wheel. I fight to unclench my jaw. "Still giving," I mutter.

Campbell rights Talia, and the host takes the microphone to welcome us. First, he introduces a couple who performs an impressive solo. Talia's still watching the crowd, but Campbell keeps whispering to her through the show—and is she giggling? I'm not a fan.

At last, the DJ starts the music for everyone to dance. I don't always like to be right, and tonight I'm sorry I am. The definition of torture: watching Talia in Campbell's arms. I knew I was lying when I told him I didn't care if he dated her, but I wasn't betting on having to watch, either.

Watch I do, whenever I remember to *not* ruin Maddi's evening. That isn't often enough, though, because I see Talia walk away from Campbell three times—coming our way?—and he pulls her back at the start of the next song. After the first hour, he finally spins Talia over to us.

"Mind if I cut in?" Campbell grabs Maddi and twirls her away before I answer, leaving me and Talia partnerless and surprised.

She recovers first. "Shall we?"

Hm. Let me think. "Are you asking now?"

"Yep." She takes my left hand and shifts closer. Nerves buzz in my brain. It's one thing dancing with someone else who's clueless. A hot girl who moves like a pro is another.

"I don't know what I'm doing," I admit, a preemptive strike.

"That's okay." She takes my right hand and places it on her back, on her shoulder blade, resting her arm on top of mine. "They forgot to mention 'proper' arm form in the lesson."

"Bet that drove you nuts."

A smile sneaks out, and Talia looks up at the beams on the ceiling, feigning innocence. "Let's just say if I were teaching, there are a few people whose form I would've corrected."

"Mine?"

She laughs. "No." She lifts my left hand and spins underneath, pulling away until our arms are extended, then spinning back to me. I try to put my other hand back where she had it. Talia nods her approval. "What I'm trying to say is ballroom's ruined me," she sighs.

I roll my eyes. I'm barely managing to keep my feet moving here. "What made you start dancing?"

Her focus moves over my shoulder, but finally she speaks. "It was *my* creative activity."

"Oh." Did I make fun of it when she suggested it for mine? Either way, I feel like a jerk for bringing it up.

"It's okay." But as soon as she starts to reassure me, her eyes track over my shoulder again, and she tenses in my arms. Her gaze lowers to my shoes. I check our feet too. Did I do something wrong?

Her hand leaves its place on my arm. I look back up to see her press her fingers to her temple.

"You okay?"

Talia shakes her head, still bowed.

"Let's sit down." I steer her toward the closest chairs, fifteen feet away. Once we're sitting, Talia lays her head on my chest, still holding her temple on the other side. Only makes sense to put an arm around her shoulders. I lean closer to ask, "Headache?"

"Mm hm."

"This happen a lot?"

"More than I'd like," she says, "but not really."

"Do we need to go?"

Talia hesitates. "Can't ruin everyone else's night."

Not having to watch her with Campbell again would be the

polar opposite of "ruining." "We can't torture you."

"Is she hurt?" A short, skinny guy with bright blond hair and a glaring red shirt stands over us, casting Talia a concerned frown. Might be my imagination, but it seems like Talia buries her head against my chest more.

"She's fine," I answer. "Just a headache."

"Would you like me to get something? Water?"

Talia shakes her head again, covering the whole side of her face now. I don't know if she knows this concerned dude or not, but his hovering isn't helping.

"No, thanks. We should go." I half-haul, half-help Talia to her feet. She keeps her cheek pressed against me and slides her free arm around my back. I hug her close and guide her away from this guy. Where's Campbell?

I finally spot him across the floor. "I'm going to leave you here for one minute to get Campbell. Okay?"

"No." She clings to my back. What am I supposed to do, drag her through the dancing crowd? I wait until Campbell cycles closer to signal to him. As soon as he sees Talia, he practically runs over, Maddi in tow. "You okay?"

I signal for him to keep his volume down. "Headache."

Campbell glances at Maddi. My date. And I'm standing here holding another woman.

A woman who's my friend and isn't feeling good. Not just a woman I really want to be dating.

"Let's get you home." Campbell takes Talia's elbow and the three of us walk out, Maddi trailing behind. Once we're in the parking lot, Talia shrugs us off to rub her temples.

"I'm sure we've got something for you at our place," Campbell says. "And I think some ice cream. What do you say, Maddi?"

"Actually, I should get going. Seven AM shift."

I should remember what she does, but I don't. Can't blame her for wanting out of this date.

We drop Maddi off at her car and bring Talia upstairs with us. Though she seems a lot better, Campbell digs through a cabinet and produces a bottle of Tylenol PM. Talia shoots me a wary look, but takes two.

"We should wait to make sure it works. You might need more."

"I guess," she says. We settle into our usual spots for dinner: me and Talia at either end of the couch, Campbell in the chair by her. He starts a movie, but focuses his attention on Talia.

Why did I agree to a roommate? How much would I have to pay him to move out?

I pretend like the movie, an action flick I've seen before that substitutes a series of explosions for a plot, absorbs my full attention. I'm not sure whether Talia and Campbell's conversation fades or I do, but the next thing I know, I'm waking up to the credits. I glance around—Talia's out, too, and Campbell's gone, probably bored with us. I suppress a yawn and check the time. After midnight.

Seems creepy, but I watch Talia for a minute. Like I need the reminder how beautiful she is after watching her dance with another guy all night. Instead of looking peaceful in her sleep, she seems smaller. Vulnerable. Like someone who needs shields.

It's late; what she needs is to get to bed. "Hey," I say—or I try to say, but just after waking up, my voice is only a whisper. I shake her knee. "Wake up."

Her eyelids flutter, and she moans softly. "I *am* awake." To prove it, she snuggles into the couch cushion.

"C'mon. You should get home." I pull myself to my feet, and a slight rush of dizziness tells me I did that a little too quickly. I pause to keep my balance. Once I'm good, I take her hands.

She slowly opens her eyes and sighs like she's resigning

herself to being kicked out. I pull her up and let go. The second I release her, Talia wavers, her arms flying out like she stood too fast, too, and might topple back onto the couch.

I catch her to steady her, cinching one arm around her waist. Her hand lands on my chest, and her gaze locks on mine.

Yep, we're both awake. And very, very aware of her body against mine. All I can hear is my pulse beating in my ears, telling me exactly what I should do.

I've hugged her, held her, danced with her—but this is different. Because there's only one thing to do now.

Kiss her.

I don't know whether I feel or sense her take a tiny breath, tilting her chin up a centimeter.

Definitely going for it. It thrums in my heartbeat: kiss her, kiss her, kiss her.

As I start to lean in, a door in the back opens. Campbell—the guy who took Talia on a date tonight, and who I gave the go-ahead with her.

I draw back, steadying her by the elbows instead. "You okay there?"

She fixes on the floor. "Yeah. Fine."

"Good." Just like my stomach sinking is good. Right.

"Oh," Campbell says. I finally release Talia and turn to him, standing in the hallway, holding my T-shirt quilt and a tacky afghan from my bed. "You're up."

"Yep," I say.

Talia nods, still staring down. "Better go."

Campbell gives me this look that's indecipherable but bordering on scary. How much did he see? Talia books it for the door. She lets herself out before Campbell or I can get there.

"I was only gone for a minute," Campbell says, "so I know nothing that serious could've happened. Right?"

I glance at the door, then look back to him. I have no idea what just happened, except that it wasn't what I wanted. I turn away, and that's when I see Talia's coat on the counter. Without consulting Campbell, who, again, was technically her date, I grab the jacket and jog after her.

"Talia," I call down the hall. She looks back but steps onto the elevator, holding the door for me. She looks . . . tired.

Brilliant assessment.

I reach the elevator and hold out her jacket.

"Thanks," she says.

"Are you okay?"

"I'm fine," she says again, not quite meeting my eyes. "Long day."

I let that lie hang between us. "I'm sorry—"

"Don't worry about it." She finally looks up—and lets go of the elevator door. "Good night, Danny."

The door slides shut and it's quiet in the hall. I'm alone in a way that feels much worse than being caught alone with my roommate's date.

Did I totally misread this situation, or that moment she wanted me to kiss her? Or was she confused by sleep and the drugs Campbell gave her?

Campbell's waiting when I get back. "Tell me you didn't just kiss my date."

"I didn't kiss your date." I wanted to. I should have. But I didn't.

Campbell says nothing else, so I push past for my room. A cadaver would've kissed that woman. Why didn't I? Because she was on a date with my roommate?

I shake my head at myself and start getting ready for bed.

I told Campbell he could date her, that I didn't have anything going on with Talia. And I didn't. But I wanted to. Now I want to even more. I *think* she wants to, too. Yeah, she's flirted with Campbell a little, but I don't see her sharing her secrets with him.

I'm going for her.

I toss my shoes in my closet, and they hit the floor with two decisive thumps.

Is this a good idea? Getting friend-zoned again? Even I'm not that much of a glutton for punishment. I go to brush my teeth, but I end up staring at my sorry self in the mirror. Maybe Talia will be happy with Campbell. He'd be happy I didn't go after her when I told him he could.

Yep, Campbell will be happy. Talia will be happy. At this rate, why don't I go ahead and make Mom happy too? How about Kendra?

Everybody's happy except the guy in the mirror. I wash my face just so I don't have to look at him any longer.

I am so tired of making everyone else happy. I just can't—I couldn't make Kendra happy. I never could have, either, because Talia's right. Kendra was mentally ill. I tried my hardest to make her happy, and it wasn't enough, and that's not my fault. It wasn't my job.

I'm drying my hands when it all comes together. I couldn't make Kendra happy, and I didn't have to. I don't have to make anyone else happy. Ever.

I march to my room and open my laptop. The latest email from Roger-the-real-estate-agent is already in the trash, but I undelete it and click reply. *Is that house we saw still available? Let's make an offer.* We. Me and "Georgia MacBride." I don't add that before I hit send.

Now I just have to find the right way to tell Mom.

CHAPTER 29
TALIA

THE LAST THING I WANT TO DO today is dance. Because dancing will remind me of Danny, which will remind me of how I haven't texted him back all morning, which will remind me of how he didn't kiss me.

Why didn't he kiss me?

The only good thing about last night was avoiding Vasily. (Russian spymaster seeing me out with my real-life friends? Less than ideal.) He hasn't said anything about seeing me, and now here I am, around the corner from Danny's, dancing with Marcel, Vasily spectating. We don't have a routine, so we're going over basic steps, but my footwork is precise, my lines are good, and I even remember to smile. I feel like I've been doing this for years (instead of *not* doing it for years). Whenever I turn, I catch a glimpse of Vasily grinning. Yep, everything's going perfectly according to his plan.

Not mine, unfortunately.

Vasily moves to his iPod stereo and stops the song. "Looks like you're doing well."

Marcel nods, and so do I. But if this works out, how can I stay close to Vasily afterward? Have him choreograph with us? Unlikely he'll want to help out the competition that much.

"Let's try the rumba." He's saved this dance for last, for obvious reasons. Always been my weakest, and it's not the footwork that trips me up.

"One minute," Marcel says. "My laces need adjusting." He kneels.

"Joanne." Vasily beckons me to where he stands by the stereo in the corner, and I obey. He places his hands on my shoulders. "Close your eyes."

I indulge him.

"Think about the person you want to be dating."

"Vasily—"

"Please."

I pinch my lips together to hold in the protest and pretend.

"Picture him taking you in his arms, holding you close."

Despite my best efforts, my brain replays the seconds Danny held me and almost—*almost*—kissed me.

"Think about what you'd like to have happen next."

I try to distract myself, thinking of my objectives here, thinking of the waiver I need to rewrite for Mr. Terfort himself, thinking of Mom and Tyler and all the reasons I shouldn't think of Danny.

But his eyes, his lips, his arms keep pulling me back into that memory.

What would I like to have happen next? Duh, I want him to kiss me, but I want more than that. I want to date him without worrying, without my baggage, without pressure. I just want to be in that moment, kiss him, love him, be with him, not worrying about all the moments to come. I want to close my eyes for his kiss and never have to open them again.

I want the impossible.

"Now," Vasily interrupts. "Imagine that you know this is

your final chance to be with him, but if you say a word, you'll break this spell. Tell him what you want with your eyes."

"They're closed."

Vasily laughs and turns me around. I open my eyes, and Marcel's waiting there. An inch or two taller than me, blond, blue eyes. The opposite of Danny.

But I know what Vasily was trying to do, and I'll give it a shot. Marcel escorts me to the center of the floor. Vasily starts the music. Marcel pivots me into a closed dance position.

I lock my gaze on his, pretending he's Danny, and we start. Marcel's obviously a good leader. He starts with the basic walks, rocks and twists, then guides me into the open position. We work up to the more advanced figures, turns, and fallaway.

We finish, as always, with a flourish. Vasily cuts off the music, applauding. We chat with Marcel a minute, gathering our stuff and changing our shoes. I should offer to take one or both of them to lunch, but that would make it harder for me to go see Danny.

This is getting sad.

"How'd I do?" I ask Vasily once Marcel leaves us alone just inside the doors.

"Very well. You'll give me and Galina a run for our money with a decent routine."

I laugh and push open the first set of doors. "How was the rumba?"

His eyebrows draw together, and my heart sinks half an inch. "It was better," he begins. "The intensity was perfect— but . . . your expression was not quite there. Next time, let's work on showing more lust, less love."

Love? That word rockets into my chest. He catches the next door for me, peeling off with a wave, but I drift to a stop on the sidewalk.

Then it hits me: I used that word, too. The pieces click into place. He's become the person I want to see every day, the person I come to when I need help or to talk or to escape—the one person I can trust with the truth. Instead of hiding from him, I want to hide *with* him. And that floating feeling when we're together, like my heart's high on helium, that's not normal.

My heart raced when he held me—not just because he's attractive and I'm human. Because I love him.

I love Danny.

I wander a few steps down the sidewalk, numb, and not from the cool fall air.

I love Danny. I love Danny. Duh. And—once I do an SDR—I can run up there and tell him, and we can finish what we started last night, and it'll be amazing. Wonderful. Perfect. The person who's been there for me whenever I needed him, who knows exactly how to encourage or distract or help me, who I can trust with everything, who sees me. Of course I love him. As long as last night was a fluke, there's nothing, nothing at all, to keep us apart.

I turn to start my SDR, ready to practically skip away, but before I take a step, my phone rings. I pull it out—my mother.

I shouldn't answer for her. But there's always that one tiny chance this time she'll care. So once I check my back—clear—and slip back into the studio, I do. "Hey, Mom."

"Talia Rosalie Reynolds!"

Middle names. They exist either to embarrass you, let you know your mom's off-her-rocker angry, or both. Guessing this call isn't because she cares. "Valarie Marie Tyler Reynolds Westing Davies."

She sputters without actual words, because listing off all her married names implies she's failed not once, but three times.

Finally she recovers. "Talia, I know you're ignoring me."

From the woman who's gone up to a year without contacting me? That's rich.

"How dare you? After all I've done for you?"

"Yeah, Mom." I cover my face, not bothering to hide the weariness in my voice. "What would the boys and I do without our matching sets of baggage?"

After half a second of silence, she unleashes a sarcastic cackle. That sound's more blood-curdling than any movie villain's evil laughter, because her anger has chilled into pure hatred.

Yelling I know how to handle. This mood is a different beast, unpredictable and dangerous, even if I'm out of range of her physical blows.

"You've always had a vivid imagination," she says. I can practically hear her sneer.

"Sure, Mom." I've been away from her for thirteen years. She'll have to try harder than that tired old line.

And try harder she does. "I guess I should've seen this coming. You've never appreciated me. I always had to be so careful how I treated you. I walked on eggshells your entire childhood."

This isn't true, I repeat to myself over and over. Not true, not true, not true. She lies. "Our memories are apparently different, then."

"I'm sorry you feel that way."

Don't know how that makes sense, but fending off her mental attacks is quickly sapping my strength. I lean against the wall next to a poster of Vasily and Galina. "Was there a reason you called?"

"Don't pretend you don't know."

Uh, okay. I wait for her to elaborate.

"I know you clicked 'Ignore request' when I tried to add you on Facebook."

My spine straightens. "Wait, what?"

"You. Are. Ignoring. Me. And I won't tolerate it."

I have to scoff at that *classic* narcissist statement. She ignores me, goes weeks without thinking about me, but the minute I don't hop to when she wants my attention, I'm the bad guy.

The situation only makes the irony richer. "Mom? I don't have a Facebook account. I deleted it after college."

"Oh really?" she snarks. "Then whose profile did I find?"

That. Is a very good question. Ice drizzles down my spine. I'm not the only Talia Reynolds on the planet, but is someone impersonating me? And if so, why? "Was the profile picture of me?"

"No, it was a photo of a waterfall."

One count of safety. "Did their info match mine?"

"Yes, it said your hometown was Temecula."

I would never, ever list Temecula as my hometown. I barely lived there a year, and it's a year I'd love to forget. (The closest I get to a hometown is where I went to college, and . . . sorry, Rexburg, I had a blast, but I'm not claiming you.)

"And it said you were in med school."

Wait—what? I straighten, but Mom keeps talking before I gain my mental footing. "In Connecticut. So I know it's you, ignoring me—"

"Mom!" I cut her off. "Do you really think I'm in med school in Connecticut?"

"Yes, of—"

"Is this a joke?"

That makes her mad. "Why would I joke about this?" she demands. "I've tried to reach out to you, Talia. I've been calling you for months, and you never reciprocate, you never visit, you never email."

"Mom—"

"Now that I know what kind of person you've become, things will never be the same between us." Her words carry a note of finality, like she's cutting me off forever. "I'm done worrying about your feelings. Your self-centeredness destroyed this relationship."

I can't hold back the scoff. Is she *kidding me*??? *My* self-centeredness? Can we say "projection"?

"You've always been so distant and hard to love," she continues. "You can see that's why you're all alone."

My back grows cold, and I know she's won. I made the mistake of giving her that one piece of information months ago, and she's turning it against me. I am alone, and I want to blame it on her, but maybe I can't.

My phone beeps to tell me the call's over. She hung up on me, driving her point home. She's wrong about me and my memories—I know she is—I hope she is.

I step out onto the street, stopping at the corner to let the few pedestrians march past, not noticing me. No one notices. No one knows. No one cares. I am less than invisible. I am nothing.

I *am* alone. I was about to run back to the man I love, and then this phone call, this abuse—this reminder of exactly why I have to stay away. Why I never believed it could work out, and I was right.

The screaming I lived with through my whole childhood echoes in my ears, only now it's not my mother's voice. It's mine, screeching hurtful, cruel epithets, tearing apart our family and our lives

I can't be in love. I can't. I don't even believe in love, especially not for me. I'm not that delusional—and three more seconds in his arms and I'll lose myself inside that illusion.

This wasn't supposed to happen. Yeah, he likes me. (I think? He didn't kiss me.) I like him. That would make everything easy—if I were anyone else.

I'm not anyone else. Danny's working to overcome his baggage and move forward, but for me, there are some things you never escape.

I stare down the street at the awning to Danny's building. That's where I go when I'm lost. I could run up to his apartment and kiss him now—but the minute after we kiss, we *will* have to open our eyes, and my reality? It's ugly. I will hurt him, ruin everything, break his heart. I'm a Reynolds; there are no happily ever afters.

Danny doesn't deserve that. With a final glance at his building, I sigh and walk away. I have to. Because I *do* love him, I have to stay away. For good.

CHAPTER 30
DANNY

I FINISH EXPLAINING THE LATEST DESIGN Thursday afternoon and watch Patrick, the AeroTechCanada exec, for his reaction. He turns over the wing's scale model. "You say you've tested this at speed?"

"Yes. Not only did it hold up, but our tests suggested a 2.6% decrease in fuel consumption—on top of your other efficiency improvements."

"It's also approved by Transport Canada," Carol adds. News to me. I figured she was sitting on the project because it was too "out there."

Patrick presses his lips together like he's impressed. I allow myself the tiniest sense of relief. This is the closest we've come to fulfilling his company's request.

"The design's . . . unusual." He looks at the wing again with the V-shaped wingtip device sticking off the end. "Not quite a fence, not quite a winglet."

"Kind of a hybrid. Raked wingtips weren't cutting it, so we had to think outside the box."

He nods. "That you did. Well," he sighs, standing and collecting the model. "Sounds good. Send the specs over, and we'll get on making a full-size prototype."

"Really?" I'm so used to leaving these meetings frustrated and disappointed, I don't know how to react.

"Of course. Nice work." He holds out his free hand, and I stand to shake it.

Finally. I walk Patrick to the door, where Carol waits, probably expecting to reassure him. Before she can start, Patrick holds up the model. "This'll make quite the impact."

Carol agrees. As soon as Patrick turns away, she shoots me an approving look. Even better. She escorts Patrick out, and I head back to my office. I'm shutting down to go home when Carol leans in the door, knocking. "Great job with AeroTech-Canada."

Probably the closest I'll get to her approval on my design itself. "Thanks. Took us long enough."

"How it is sometimes."

"You know," I begin before she can turn away. "I don't feel like I'm contributing on the de-icing project. I'd like to focus on my other projects."

"If you feel that way, sure. I just thought they could use your insight." She steps all the way in my office. "Did Roger tell you about my transfer?"

"What?" I've been in contact with her husband nearly every day over the last few weeks for some bit of house-buying paperwork or another, but he hasn't mentioned anything outside of business.

"A director position opened up in Vancouver, and I had to take it."

"Oh." Why is she telling me this? Am I supposed to throw her a going away party?

"And," she says, drawing the word out, "I recommended you as my replacement."

I'm too stunned to say anything for a minute. I've only been here six months, and things have gone well other than AeroTechCanada—but design lead? Over all the design teams? I'd get to pick my own projects and get a taste of everything else. With a halfway-competent manager, we could really move things forward. "Thank you," I finally manage.

"You deserve it. I know you've been frustrated with the AeroTechCanada issue, but you've handled it well, the rest of your work is stellar, and you're great with your team."

"Thanks," I say again.

"The decision's up to the bigwigs, but I hear you've got a really good chance."

"Wow. Thank you," I say yet again, because apparently I've run out of other words.

"Have a good evening." She leaves, and the reality sets in. Even if the promotion doesn't work out, some people think I deserve it. That feels good.

It still feels good by the time I walk into my empty apartment, toss the groceries on the counter and sink onto the couch. When I agreed to have Roger preapprove me for a loan, I had no idea I hired the fastest real estate agent in the province. In the last three weeks, I've opened an escrow account, gotten homeowner's insurance, gathered bank statements and pay stubs for the last three years, signed off on the home inspection's minor problems—I think I can fix a slow drain and missing banister on the garage stairs—and reviewed the final closing documentation.

I knew buying a home took a lot of time and money, but I didn't realize it took this many dead trees. Still, we're ready to close tomorrow.

Not only am I possibly getting a promotion, I'm buying a house without my parents' bribe, six hundred miles away from them—and Kendra. That feels like more of an accomplishment than Carol's recommendation.

I get out my phone. Wish I could talk to someone about this. No, not just "someone." I want to talk to the person who understands how much this house means to me, but she hasn't been answering my texts. Not even a picture of kittens, and then a real act of desperation, a picture of a grinning baby hedgehog, has gotten a response beyond *Sorry, super busy.*

Apparently I freaked her out a little with that *I want to kiss you* moment.

I contemplate my phone in my hands. There's someone else I need to tell, too, but I don't think she'll be quite as happy for me. But with eighteen hours until we submit the final paperwork and down payment, it's now or never.

"Never" sounds good, but it won't solve anything. I hit the icon to call my parents' house and listen to the phone ring.

Dad answers, and I kick back on the couch to chat for a few minutes. We commiserate about the woes of managing people, though I only "manage" a small team—for now, maybe. I'll hold off on telling them until I know for sure. Once we've run the topic of work into the ground, I ask for Mom. I grit my teeth to hold back the nerves building through the small talk before I drop the thermonuclear warhead.

Finally, there's a lull. My chance. I sit up. "So, Mom," I initiate the subject change, "about the house."

"What house?"

Oh. Better back up. "A few weeks ago, the real estate agent who prequalified me talked me into seeing a house."

Mom pauses long enough to convey that she's *not* happy. "In Ottawa?"

"Technically across the river, but yes."

Silence again. "I don't like where this is going."

"Picked up on that."

"So you're calling to ask for the money though you won't even consider our conditions?" Annoyance rings through her words.

She can't see me, but I lift a hand, somewhere between a defense and an attempt to calm her down. "No. I'm calling to let you know I'm closing on the house tomorrow."

"What do you expect me to do, run to Western Union?"

Not sure they have those anymore, but that's the opposite of the point. "Mom. I'm not asking you for money."

She doesn't say anything for a minute, but I think this silence is shock, not fury.

"It's your money, and you can do whatever you want with it, put whatever conditions on it you want. Doesn't mean I'll do what you ask."

"Danny—"

"You can't use it to control me. Period." There's no room for argument.

The tension carries over the line, and I resist the urge to tap my foot. When Mom finally speaks, her voice is subdued. "That wasn't my intent."

I release a silent sigh and lean back on the couch cushions again. "It was the result."

"I'm sorry it felt that way to you."

Come on, Mom. Will it kill you to admit you were wrong?

She takes a deep breath. "I can see why it must've felt that way. I just want what's best for you."

"Don't you think I should decide that for myself?"

The words sink in for a minute. "You're probably right. But Danny, you'll always be my baby."

I can't help a good-natured lip purse. "Of course, Mom. I just have to be an adult, too."

"I suppose I can handle that."

I'll take it. Not quite as smooth as it could've been, but not nearly as hard as I thought. I should stand up for myself more often. Mom gives me an update on my siblings, and we talk about work. She almost acknowledges I do have a good job— we'll see how long she can maintain that position if I get this promotion—and she seems to accept that I'm not moving home. Now that's progress.

When we finish talking, I end the call and stare at the phone for an extra minute. I feel . . . released. All this time, on some level, I've told myself it was my fault that Kendra turned on me. In a way, I was right—because I was so desperate to make her happy, I gave up every little part of me to do it.

But I don't have to make other people happy, and the world doesn't end if I don't. Standing up for myself didn't cause huge rift between me and my mom. I'm just fifty thousand dollars poorer than I might've been.

Self respect? Power? Freedom? Worth it.

All I want is to tell somebody. Someone else who'd get what a big deal this is.

If she cared.

I stuff my phone in my pocket and head to the kitchen to start on dinner, maple-mustard pork chops with couscous. Kinda risky, but I'm on a roll. I'm halfway through when it strikes me this isn't nearly as difficult as those first attempts almost two months ago—but my half-made-up recipe's a lot harder than boiling a piece of fish. Everything's going great until I realize I'm missing couscous.

Yeah, an ingredient actually in the name of the recipe. I check my grocery list on my phone. There it is, not crossed off. Great job.

Okay, everyone makes mistakes. Do I stop cooking and stick everything in the fridge to go get couscous or . . . do I call the person who told me she was at the grocery store nearly every day and she'd be happy to pick up stuff for me, who I conveniently want to talk to anyway?

Hm. Tough choice.

I hit the icon to dial Talia.

"Hi, Danny." She sounds like she's resigned herself to having to talk to me.

What a terrible fate. "Hey, Talia—any chance you're going by the grocery store tonight?"

"Possibly. Need something?"

"Actually, yeah. I could use some couscous. I'll pay you back."

Long pause. "I'll be there in twenty minutes."

"Great. See you then." And I'll tell her about my little victory in person.

Little victory? I'm buying a house on my own, away from my parents, away from Kendra, and far, far away from caring what they think. Nothing little about that.

I turn the heat off and move the pan to the oven. Just before Talia's due to arrive, Campbell walks in.

Oh. Goody.

He plugs his phone into the speakers on the counter and cues up some Smashing Pumpkins. "What's for dinner?"

"Pork chops."

"Sounds good. Anybody coming over?"

Man, the guy's so fixated on social interaction, he could probably live on that instead of my food. "Talia," I say, like it doesn't matter to me. Because I did totally give him permission to date her.

Yeah, I don't have to make other people happy, but I can't kick human decency to the curb. I said he could date her. Until I rescind that, I won't swoop in and steal her away. Much.

Before I can find the right way to settle this with Campbell, Talia knocks. I guess Campbell doesn't hear, because he's still in his room when I open the door to find Talia holding a box of couscous. "Not the easiest thing to find."

"Thanks. Probably why I forgot it."

She follows me into the kitchen. "Thanks," I tell her again, switching on the burner under the waiting pot.

"Said I would," she murmurs. She hovers by the counter like she's uncomfortable. The heat shields in her eyes are the last thing I want to see.

Oh, crap. She's shut me out these last few weeks—beginning right after she went on her first date with Campbell. Then I tried to kiss her? No wonder she's barely communicated with me since then. She's dating Campbell, or she wants to, and she's probably still freaked out to be around me. Not that I blame her.

I pretend watching the pot requires my full attention. I should back off, but . . . I don't want to. At the very least, we're still friends, right? She'll care about the house.

Now I just have to get past those shields again. I've got to tap into something we did together. "Remember the house we saw?" I lean closer to add, "Georgia MacBride?"

"I remember that night, yes." She casts me the shortest glance, but I see the smile hiding behind her shields.

I lean another few centimeters closer. "I'm closing on it tomorrow."

That gets her attention. She whips around to face me. "You bought it?"

I nod, reining in a proud grin.

"Wow." She doesn't fight her shocked smile. "What about your parents?"

"Mom wasn't too happy, but I think I convinced her I'm an adult."

Talia huffs out a laugh. "Can you give me lessons?"

I wish. I check the pot. Simmering. I can't see her, but I can sense Talia move closer to me. "What are you doing about the master bedroom?" she asks softly.

"I don't know." I turn back to her. "I mean, I guess it makes a nice trophy, 'look what I did,' but . . ."

"That color's like living inside a migraine."

We laugh together. "I have to paint it," I decide.

She contemplates me a minute, her expression between pride and nostalgia. "This is big."

I shrug one shoulder to play it off and focus on the finally boiling pot. I dump the couscous in, put on the lid and switch off the heat. Talia's hand lands on my back, not moving away, and I turn to her again.

She looks up, shields down. But her expression is tinged with sadness. "You deserve this, Danny."

"Thank you." I mean it.

Just one more thing I want to talk about. But she beats me to the punch. "Listen, I need to—"

"Hey, Talia! When did you get here?" Campbell practically bounds into the kitchen, and I restrain a groan. Hello, Captain Third Wheel—whom I cleared the runway for three weeks ago. Like an idiot.

Talia breaks off and steps away to let Campbell monopolize her for the next five minutes while the couscous steams. The guy can't stand to be left out of the "party." Even if anyone else would identify the "party" as a "date."

With a woman he might be dating himself. Yeah, I'd interrupt, too.

Don't have to like it. I grab a plate, dish up a scoop of couscous and a pork chop, and shove it at Campbell. "Dinner."

"Thanks!" He gets a fork and attacks it with the same enthusiasm he shows for . . . pretty much everything. "This is amazing!"

Talia takes the next plate from the stack and waits for me to serve her. She cuts one bite and eyes it. "What did you say this was?"

"Mustard-maple pork chops with couscous."

She gives me a dubious lip purse and carefully eats her bite. No time to worry before she makes an approving sound. "Best thing you've made. By far."

I get my own plate and try it. Yep, they're right. You wouldn't think these things could go together but the mustard's bitter tang is perfect against the sweet smoke of the

254

maple syrup, and the pork chops aren't overcooked into meat pucks like the last time I tried to make some. Could my life get any better tonight? I glance at Talia. Okay, I can think of one way.

Can I get rid of Campbell, especially if they're dating? "Hey—"

Before I get his name out, Talia's phone rings. She takes another bite, then pulls her cell out. She looks at the screen, and I swear she pales for a second. As effectively as if she'd pushed a button, shields go up. "I have to go." She beelines for the door.

Whatever that call is, it's not good. I barely make it in time to open the door for her. "You okay?"

She nods, but I can't tell if that's a yes or a goodbye before she slips out, shutting the door behind her.

I file a mental note to check on her in an hour or two, then turn to Campbell, still standing in the kitchen, chowing down. The guy who didn't notice her freaking out and running away. Who can't tell when her shields are up.

"How are things with Talia?" I ask.

"Things with Talia?" He stuffs another bite of pork chop into his mouth. "I dunno."

I can barely keep my jaw from dropping. "You don't know? I thought you said you wanted to date her."

"I did. And I did."

"You went on one date."

Campbell takes another bite and holds out a hand as if to say *duh.*

"You asked my permission to go on one date?"

"'Permission'?" he says around his food. "Are you her dad?"

I fold my arms—which would be an appropriate response if I were her dad.

"Not *permission*, man," Campbell says. "I wasn't sure if you were into her. Better safe than sorry, right?"

"For one date?"

He laughs. "I have a whole year to settle down before I'll be a menace to society."

"Trust me, you already are." I can't believe I've been torturing myself so he could go on one casual date with her. "If you didn't care," I ask, "why were you mad about me kissing her?"

He stops cutting his pork chop. "So something did happen?"

"No, but you were angry enough anyway."

"Since when is it okay to kiss another guy's date, even if they're going out for fun?"

"Since I want to date her."

Campbell waggles his eyebrows, like he'd be just as happy for me to date Talia—go on more than one date with her—as he would to date her himself. "Go for it, man."

"I will," I say as decisively as possible.

He grins like an animated Cheshire cat.

It's as hard to hate the guy as it is to hate a cartoon character. Yeah, they might get annoying sometimes, and you have no idea how anyone could act that way *all* the time, but . . . at least he's entertaining.

"Took you long enough." He starts sawing at his pork chop again. "I think she likes you."

I don't answer, especially not to mention tonight's the first time I've seen or spoken to her in three weeks. And I've missed her. A lot.

Now I don't care if I'm "ready" or not. I'm asking her out before she runs away again.

CHAPTER 31
TALIA

WHEN DANNY CALLED, I should've said no. But I didn't—I couldn't—for the same reason I've said yes to him every other time: I want to. I haven't seen him in three weeks, and honestly, that hasn't helped. I think about him all the time, want to text him every day (why must there be so many cute kitten pictures on the Internet?), search for any excuse to see him.

For a minute there, being around him again, I almost forgot why I ran away from Danny in the first place. Which might make Mom calling a good thing.

After our last conversation, I should know better than to answer—but that little part of me that will never, ever grow up, that still wishes my own mother would just love me forces me to take her call. I duck into the stairwell. "Mom?"

"Talia, what took you so long?"

I have no reply. Guess it doesn't matter how self-centered I am anymore.

"I'm sure you don't care, but we're having a very rough

time, and you could be a little more sympathetic."

Hard to be sympathetic to something you know nothing about, so I still have no response. Not like it's safe to say anything anyway. I sink down on the top stair.

"Tyler's losing the custody battle. Do you know what that means? Bianca will keep my granddaughter from me!"

Lucky girl.

"I have half a mind to sue for custody myself," she says. "Grandparents have rights, you know."

I'm a freaking lawyer. "Mom, if you wanted to do that, I would fly down and represent Bianca myself."

She scoffs, still trying to maintain her superior attitude. "You wouldn't know the first thing about the law, Talia. Custody battles are ugly—I know what I'm doing."

"Which is why you lost custody and visitation of us?"

"I don't know where you're getting that information from, but it's definitely not what happened."

"My father, my stepmother, my own memory?" My voice echoes in the stairwell.

"Oh, sweetie." She turns on that saccharine condescending pitch she only uses when she knows she's lost and she's going for emotional blackmail. "You know how unreliable all of those things are."

I can't listen to this anymore. "Look, Mom, I'd love to talk, but I'm busy. And I'll probably be busy for a few weeks."

"What? I need you now."

"I can't." And that's the truth.

"If that's how it'll be, don't expect anything from me again. Ever."

I keep my tone totally even. "That's fine. Bye, Mom." I tap to end the call.

I draw a deep breath. It feels so good to walk away from her. Yet I can't deny the sinking, bitter feeling in my gut. It's been too long since I lived with her, because for a few weeks there I almost thought . . . I don't know, she cared? Or had some idea who I was?

Of course not. My own mother doesn't have a clue who I am, even on the outside. Who does? Elliott, who normally I'd say was my best friend, proved he can't fathom my faith and couldn't handle my family secrets. Elliott knows what I'm doing in Canada (CANADA, Mother, CANADA!), but that's as superficial as he pretends to be.

I may be keeping one big secret from Danny—maybe more than one—but deep down, he knows me better than anyone on the planet.

No avoiding it anymore: I love him. Seeing him again, I almost had to tell him.

I'm not traipsing back into Danny's to confess my love and my complete and utter inability to have a lasting relationship in front of Campbell.

I'd be Danny's worst nightmare. I can't take him away from real prospects, actual chances of happiness.

As with every conversation with my mother, I need to talk to someone. But I can't turn to Danny, though I want to—I *need* to.

No, I need to keep my distance. Tonight was a mistake.

I finish my surveillance detection run and reach my tiny little apartment. Nondescript furniture. No family photos. Meaningless pictures on the walls. Even my freaking fridge is empty.

I drop on my so-not-me bedspread and scroll through my contacts for the person I should actually talk to. Hope this number's still current. The phone rings, and a familiar voice answers.

"Hey, Tyler," I say. "It's Talia. How're you holding up?"

I manage to get out of Terfort & Sutter early after one of those stupid team-building exercises Friday afternoon. Rather than jump-starting my weekend, I'm at Keeler Tate, jump-starting my *other* full-time job.

Jealous, aren't you?

I finish my last report and send it off, leaving my fingers rapid-fire drumming on the edge of my keyboard. Three weeks of a high-tension holding pattern with Vasily are wearing on my nerves, even if it's let me catch up on my other cases. We've fallen into a schedule: dance rehearsal, negotiating with Marcel, intercepting Vasily's drops, following the pickup courier (dead end), finding gaps and fabrications in his data. But I'm ready to make progress.

Elliott tosses me a report in a file folder. (One of these days—i.e., when I work in the morning—I'll have a chance to get my own reports first.) "USB analysis. Asking his handler for more money."

"Looking to settle up with his loan shark?"

"Wouldn't you be?"

I nod, though we'd all like to believe we're smart enough not to get tangled up in a stupid scheme like this. (No, I pick different stupid things to ensnare myself. Guys, for example.)

"Could be a prime opportunity for us," Elliott points out. "He needs money."

That's one thing we have a *lot* of. Money is a top incentive for agents—mostly because it's such a universal motivator. I flip open the folder. We need more to get to him. "Anything to up our leverage?"

"No."

I twist my lips in a sort-of frown. "Tracked down the name of the loan shark?"

"Nick Sabatini."

Never heard of him. But we're not law enforcement, and this isn't our country (and most Canadian criminals don't run with terrorists), so that's doubly not our department. I scan the office, like staring at the same half-dozen guys will help me figure something out.

Then I see Rashad, talking on the phone. Tall and broad-shouldered, he loves to joke about how edgy white people act around a physically imposing Black man (when, of course, his job is protecting them, albeit indirectly). A short loan deadline would increase the pressure on Vasily—and make him more susceptible to our pitch.

"What if a *new* enforcer tightened the deadline?" I say. "And increased the interest rate?"

Elliott tracks my line of sight, then we smile at one another. "Liking where you're going."

He heads to his desk, pointing at me to make it clear I'm supposed to recruit Rashad. (We do have that "token" camara-derie.) I'll have to wait until he's done on the phone, so I turn back to my work, too.

"Hey, T?" Elliott ventures a minute later.

I look up, and Elliott's right there again. Maybe I was too into researching Sabatini, but I didn't hear him come back over. "Yeah?"

"You seem kind of . . . off lately. With me."

I shrug away the way-too-close-to-home observation.

"Just . . . if it's what I said about your church and every-thing, I didn't mean anything."

Can we not talk about this, especially here? "Okay. We're good. Don't worry."

"What, me worry?" He slaps on an obnoxious imitation of the even more obnoxious *Mad* magazine mascot. But the stupid grin fades. "It's *your* personal life, so—I mean, if it works for you, great. Ignore me."

"Like with everything else?" We don't do serious talks, so we'll both pull humor hits as often as possible.

He rolls his eyes and actually continues to be serious.

"And—when I mentioned mommy issues—I was going to say Shanna's mom is becoming our bridezilla. Total control freak."

He was trying to commiserate?

But something about his words nags at a corner of my brain. As he turns away, it hits me. Maybe he doesn't care whether I'm cheering his wedding plans along, but scoffing whenever he mentions them isn't better than him slighting my religion. "Hey, E?"

He looks back. "Yeah?"

"Did you get Shanna's venue?"

"Crystal Gardens? No; she lined up some mansion. Her second choice."

I offer an encouraging smile. "I bet it'll be great. Mother of Bridezilla or not."

"Yeah." Elliott grins back. "Oh, almost forgot. Sabatini's traces—with profiles of his known thugs." He hands me another manila folder.

"Thanks."

Elliott returns to his desk, and I put away the first folder he gave me, sliding the report on the latest USB drive into my desk drawer.

On top of a file labeled "Fluker, Danny."

It's been, what, months since Elliott gave this to me? I still haven't opened it. I don't need to know any of this to know Danny. And yet some sad, sick part of me has to see exactly what I'm giving up.

I take out the folder and page past his photo. Transcript from University of Michigan: Flight and Trajectory Optimization; Control of Structures and Fluids; Avionics, Navigation and Guidance of Aerospace Vehicles—A, A, A. Accepted into an accelerated Master's program. I knew he was smart, but I didn't realize he was a freaking genius. There's a short-but-spotless credit history, a CSIS background check from getting his job with National Research Council Canada complete with interviews from old roommates and mission companions, and his Eagle Scout certificate.

The guy is way too perfect. He'd make a terrible target. I'm used to poring over traces like these to find potential vulnerabilities, and on paper, Danny has none.

I know him well enough to know his real weaknesses. And I've only told him about half of mine.

I snap the folder shut and stuff it back in my desk. Why did Elliott give me this file, anyway? What am I supposed to do, target Danny? Trick him into dating me though I'm the exact opposite of what he needs?

This is stupid. I . . . I can't run away from this anymore.

I sigh. The reason—one of the reasons—the #1 reason I love Danny is because we're friends. Best friends. He's told me everything, and I've held back the most important thing. He knows about my messed up family, but he doesn't know that I will *never, never* be the one to help him move forward like he needs. Like he deserves.

He deserves to be happy. To get married. To have a life. And marriage—a happy marriage—is not going to happen for me.

I need to tell him the truth. As soon as he's started to heal from Kendra and take charge of his life, I have to go and kick his teeth in. But it'd give him more closure than ignoring him.

Closure? Yeah, right. I want to do more for him than talk and run. I want to *do* something, I want to show him that these months have meant a *lot* to me. But how do you show someone you love them?

The saddest part: I don't even know.

CHAPTER 32
DANNY

ON THE ELEVATOR TO MY APARTMENT for one of the last times ever, I slide my newest key onto my key ring. I'm a home-owner. Well, the wire transfer has to go through, but I have the keys, I have the paperwork, and in a few short hours, I'll have the mortgage to match. I get off at my floor and walk in my apartment. Campbell calls out a greeting over his music, his phone plugged into the speakers on the counter as always, blasting "Wonderwall."

I toss him an extra key. "Doing anything tomorrow?"

"Moving, apparently. I'll get some guys. Not against your religion if I post it on Facebook, is it?"

Yep, his first thought's making this a social event. But we could use help. "Sounds good."

"Brought home boxes." He points to a stack of cardboard in the corner, complete with rolls of packing tape.

Okay, he comes in handy sometimes. "Thanks. I'm going to get started."

After an hour of filling boxes with books and clothes, I'm

ready for a break. I venture out, passing Campbell packing up his room. "Want dinner? Pizza?" I call from the kitchen. Yeah, I can cook, but we're busy, and it's pizza.

"Got plans later."

Yep, that's Campbell on a Friday night. A *whumpf* sound effect carries through his door, like he dumped an entire drawer in one box. Something tumbles and crashes in his room, and I wince. Don't know how he'll be ready to move tomorrow if he's got plans tonight. I'll barely make it as it is.

Amid the cacophony of chaos, Campbell's phone vibrates and pauses in its playlist to announce an incoming text. I lean over to see who it's from before I interrupt his packing.

Talia.

I hold back the conclusions and swipe to read the text without stopping Eric Clapton's guitar solo. *You bring the pizza,* says the top message on the screen. From Talia.

K, Campbell replied twenty minutes ago. His plans for tonight. Then he texted again a minute later. *Wait, are we telling Danny?*

No. Duh.

My chest tightens. It's been, what, a *day* since the guy said I should go for her and he only wanted to take her out once?

The last message from her says, *Get drinks too. Leaving now.*

I'll kill him.

Maybe there's more context, something that could save this. But the most recent texts before that are weeks old. I press the button to turn off the screen again and back away. I can't believe this—both of them, but especially Campbell.

He emerges from his room, closing the door and setting off another crash. "Gotta go. See you later."

I don't dare look at him. Because then I really will kill him.

Campbell pulls on his jacket, grabs his phone from where it's plugged in and leaves.

I wait until I'm sure he's on the elevator before I snag my jacket and keys and follow. I have to wait until he pulls out of his parking space and stay back in the garage, but I'm on his tail once we're on the street. He stops at a pizza place and picks up two boxes and two bottles of soda. Could be a party, but with the way that guy eats, it'd have to be a pretty small one.

Like a party for two.

I'm not normally a jealous person, but seriously? This isn't me getting mad over something stupid. This is betrayal.

No idea what to do when we get to their little rendezvous, I tail Campbell across the bridge into Québec. Within a couple minutes, it's obvious where he's going: our new house. *My* new house. That I just gave him a key to.

Having a hard time coming up with a reasonable explanation for Campbell meeting the girl he just gave me a green light with, at my house, alone.

Campbell takes a right onto the street. To be less conspicuous, I turn off my headlights before I turn after him. He parks in my driveway. I park down the street, close enough to watch him carry the pizza and sodas in. A faint light glows in the front windows, like the kitchen light or something else in the back of the house is on.

I spend a minute sitting there, trying to keep the anger simmering low enough for me to process this. Talia—well, I had my chance with her, told her about all my problems. What can I say? She made the smart choice, and I've barely seen her in weeks. Although everything seemed okay last night, we only had a few minutes together.

What am I supposed to do? Run home with my tail between my legs? Right. Stand up to my mom only to let this slide?

I get out of the car and march up to the house. My house. I unlock the front door and head in. The house smells like paint and cleaning chemicals, and it sounds like music—The Cars singing "My Best Friend's Girl." After I kill him, I'll kill his stupid phone.

I take back what I said about not being able to hate the guy.

A bottle of soda hisses open. I stride after the sound, toward the kitchen. Campbell's set out the pizza and soda on the island to hunt through the empty cabinets. "You didn't bring cups, did you?" he shouts loud enough to carry upstairs.

"Nope," I answer his question.

He whirls around, his eyes wide. "Uh . . ."

"Yep, dude, you're caught—you *and* Talia. What's your next move?"

He glances at the ceiling and sighs. "Come on." He walks around me, back to the foyer and up the stairs. I follow.

"Hey, Talia?" Campbell calls. He goes for the master bedroom doors, and again, I follow.

"Campbell!"

I can't see her, but she doesn't sound surprised—she sounds worried. Afraid. Next thing I know, Campbell slams into the doorframe and something hard slaps against my chest. I jerk back, a spike of shock automatically pulling my hands up to defend myself. When I hit my chest, it's wet.

I jump again and look down. A thick blue liquid covers my shirt and hands and whatever it was that thumped me in my chest. I may be a Michigan alum, but I don't actually bleed blue, so I'm okay. Talia's standing there, her eyes wide, too. And then I look back down at the paint-covered object in my hands she just threw at me—a wet paintbrush.

Wait a minute. Wait. "How'd you get in here?"

"Lockbox. I'm your interior designer, remember?"

"And you're . . . painting?" Painting my room. I walk in over the drop cloths and supplies. It's still the world's most hideous color, but they've already started painting the edges of the walls a dark grayish blue, not far off Michigan blue.

No, *they* haven't. Campbell just got here. Talia's been working, probably for a while. All the trim is taped off, all the carpet covered.

"Sorry about your shirt," Talia murmurs. "I saw somebody behind Campbell, and no one else was supposed to be here."

I glance at my polo again. Yeah, it's ruined, and my hands and the whole paintbrush are coated with that same blue. But I'm not sure I mind. I was so angry two minutes ago, but now, my roommate and my . . . would-be girlfriend have been sneaking around to do something nice for me.

Nice? Talia knows what this means. This is more than nice.

Campbell's phone must be set to play The Cars' greatest hits, because the next song that comes up is "Just What I Needed." Kinda on the nose, but I have to agree. She is.

"Surprise?" Talia tries. "Like it?"

I turn back to her. Gray-blue freckles dot her cheeks and hair, and her hazel eyes search mine with a mix of hope and concern.

"Yeah," I finally say. "I like it a lot."

Her gaze falls to the carpet and she smiles like I said she's the most beautiful woman I've ever known. I almost want to tell Campbell to get lost—no, I do want to tell him that, but he's already got a roller and started attacking the biggest wall.

At least he's acting like he's not listening. I step closer to Talia, and she looks up again.

"Thank you," I say.

"You're welcome. And surprise, again."

"Sorry I ruined it."

She takes another brush from a multipack. "What do you think of the color?"

"I like it. Much less like the inside of a migraine."

She laughs and starts edging along the tape line of the baseboards again. "You're welcome to stay and watch."

"Especially if you brought plates and cups," Campbell interjects.

"We'll survive," Talia says. "It's pizza."

"And soda."

"Like you've never drunk out of the bottle." She throws me a rag—yet another painting supply she must've brought—and I scrub at the paint on my shirt. Lost cause, so I hit the master bath to wash my hands and the paintbrush handle. I come back to the room, grab another paint can and pry it open with my pocketknife.

"Always prepared?" Talia asks. I can hear the teasing in her tone though she's not looking at me.

"Yep." I use the paintbrush she threw at me and start around the doorframe. Starting that close to Talia means we work in opposite directions, her going clockwise around the baseboards, and me counter-clockwise on the same thing.

Takes until midnight, but the three of us finish the entire room. We stand in the doorway, admiring our work for a while, and I linger a little longer while Campbell and Talia go down-stairs for clean up.

Now *that's* an accomplishment.

I finally head downstairs to join Campbell and Talia cleaning up. I get the job of rinsing out the brushes.

Talia throws the last slice of pizza in the microwave, and Campbell gathers up the empty pizza boxes. "I don't think we'll be ready to move tomorrow," he says.

"Nope." Don't know if I care. I wipe at a streak of paint on the sink. Cooking was fun, sometimes, and I definitely liked eating, but the satisfaction of a job well done in *my* home—and painting that evil color out of my life? Hard to beat.

Talia tosses us rags to dry our hands and brushes. "What do I owe you for this?" I ask.

"It's a housewarming gift."

"No, I—"

"Seriously." She gives me a small smile. "Figured you'd ap-preciate it more than a plant."

Yeah. I look at her, and time slows down enough for a

thought to surface, one that's been lurking in the back of my mind for I don't know how long.

I love her. Though I freaked out at the idea before, suddenly nothing makes more sense, nothing's more rational—nothing's more obvious. Of course I love her.

I turn away before I tell her that. I mean, the woman had a panic attack when I brought up marriage to take the subject off the table. What will she do when I tell her I love her?

Wait—"when"?

I pick up a brush to dry it again, trying to distract myself from that idea. But of course "when." I have to tell her. I glance at Campbell's back. Maybe not right this minute, but this is the woman who just bought all the paint and supplies to redo a room of my house—a room that she *knew* the symbolism of. She knows a lot more than that, and she's still here. Can I really let her slip away because I'm afraid?

Campbell finishes off the Coke and grabs the last piece of warm pizza before heading for the front door. I roll my eyes and pick up the empty pizza boxes. Talia collects the empty soda bottles.

"Hey, Talia?" I say softly before she can follow Campbell out.

She looks back to me. "Yeah?"

"Can I take you to dinner tomorrow night?"

"Danny, really, you don't have to thank me."

Is that all she thinks I mean? Is that all she wants?

"I insist," I say. Have to try to change her mind.

Her gaze travels down and to the side, and I see her release a deep breath. "All right," she says, and she turns to go.

She's already slipping away. Tomorrow night might be my last chance.

Then I'll make the most of it.

CHAPTER 33
TALIA

I WALK INTO VASILY'S STUDIO SATURDAY AFTERNOON, hoping I've gotten the paint off my face and hands. (My hair . . . I gave up.) I've got my mic, my strategically planted backup, and my mark. All I need is an opportunity to ditch Marcel.

Vasily's playing with his phone, probably selecting songs for my last trial run with Marcel. But there's no sign of him.

This could definitely work in my favor. I ask the obvious question. "Where's Marcel?"

Vasily turns around, grimacing. "Joanne, I'm so sorry. Marcel's partner was being transferred to Toronto, but instead they decided to lay her off. He doesn't need a new partner."

"Oh." I let my shoulders drop a little. We worked hard, but partnering up with Marcel wasn't advancing my real objectives. Can't be too upset.

"I'll keep hunting for anyone who needs a partner," Vasily vows. "We'll find you someone. Have you considered Pro/Am?"

Pairing me, the amateur, with a dance professional? "Not really."

"Another possibility."

"Thanks." I look around the studio. Everyone else *should* be in position, but we weren't expecting to put the plan into action for another hour. I have to buy us time. "Might as well rehearse, huh?"

"Sure. Anything you want to work on?" He picks a song and walks with me to the center of the floor. We go over some jive steps, but after half an hour, I'm tired (and so sore from painting), and my heart isn't in it anymore. We change back to our street shoes and pack up.

"It's all right," Vasily reassures me yet again. "We'll find you someone."

I try not to laugh. I found someone. I'm the problem. "Where are you headed?" I change the subject, but not because I'm curious about Vasily's life—I'm trying to signal to my team that we're leaving ahead of schedule.

"I don't have any plans. Maybe watch TV. There's a race on later." We start out of the studio—and I immediately spot Danny at the corner. Coming our way.

Oh crap oh crap oh crap. Before he can see me, I turn away, ignoring the pang in my chest. (Yeah, it's been three weeks, but I've seen him the last two nights and I'll see him again tonight. I need to *work* now.)

"We're a go," Elliott's voice comes over my earpiece.

"Is something wrong?" Vasily asks.

What was Elliott's cover's name? "I thought I saw Gord."

"Oh." Vasily moves to a protective position, scanning the sidewalk, but Elliott's a block away (and Danny looks nothing like him). Doubly effective: avoiding Danny, and I can lead Vasily to the place where Rashad lies in wait.

"C'mon." I grab his arm and half-drag him down the block. We take the corner. Rashad's waiting on the next street.

I glance back to make sure we've left Danny behind. As I check, I see him. Not Danny—a dude I don't know. The grim set to his jaw puts me on edge.

But the real reason my pulse is rising faster than rocket? This guy was behind us before we turned.

Okay, I've seen him twice. Could still be a coincidence. We have to make sure first—if he follows us one more time, we'll know. I send my team the signal that I'm improvising: "Think we'll have another cold snap soon?" I ask Vasily.

"I hope not," he replies.

"Copy, FOXHUNT." Elliott starts coordinating surveillance on us. After all the times he's let me down lately, he'd better come through now. At the other end of the block, Rashad approaches. Hope he got the signal for the change of plans.

I look to Vasily. "Hey, are you hungry?" Without waiting for an answer, I tug him into the street, toward a café on the other side.

Technically, this isn't great tradecraft, and that'll get you caught or killed faster than anything else—when you're facing off with another spy. But something about this guy's crew cut and sharp jaw is a little . . . obvious.

That and the way he's staring at us like prey.

Square Jaw pursues us across the street. We reach the sidewalk, and Vasily checks traffic behind us. He sucks in a gasp. My grip on his arm tightens, and he whips back around. "Quick." Vasily pulls me into the nearest alley.

I'm about to be alone with a Russian spymaster and a hired thug. Panic flashes through my brain like lightning. Are Vasily and Square Jaw working together—and are they after me?

Before I have a chance to turn on Vasily, he's abruptly yanked backwards. Up close, Square Jaw's so massive, I shrink back automatically. He shoves Vasily against the brick wall, his forearm on Vasily's neck. "Where's the money?"

They don't look too friendly.

"I don't have it!" Vasily pushes against his arm, but he's got no leverage. He strains and gasps for air, his face getting red.

I have to help him. "Leave him alone!"

Square Jaw doesn't glance my direction. I reach for the metal rod the size of a pen from the outside pocket of my dance bag—but Joanne isn't a CIA officer. I have to act defenseless. I scan the alley for a makeshift weapon.

"Please!" Vasily rasps. No human should turn that red, ever.

Square Jaw pushes harder. "Sabatini's giving you three more days. That's it."

Vasily's eyes starts to roll back in his head. Square Jaw's cutting off his air supply, or possibly blood flow—a few seconds too long, and Vasily won't wake up. I find a broken 2×4 behind the Dumpster and whack Square Jaw in the lower back.

He releases Vasily, who slumps to the ground, and Square Jaw wheels on me. His jaw's even squarer with his muscles clenched in rage.

My stomach rolls away to hide. I'm in trouble.

But Vasily's out, so I have no reason to hold back (like I ever would in a fight for my life). Square Jaw may be big and muscly, but he's slow. Might be able to beat him if I'm fast.

In one quick movement, I snatch up my metal rod and grab Square Jaw's hand, pressing against the bones. I twist his wrist behind him like I'm executing an underarm turn. He tries to jerk away, but I've practiced these dance moves, baby. I'm just tall enough to wrench his arm up behind his back, and I apply more pressure to the Kubotan weapon.

Square Jaw sucks in air. I tighten my grip. He reaches around to hit me with his free arm. I dodge and clamp down on my weapon with both hands. Something in his hand pops, and he cries out, stumbling forward.

One kick at the knee holding his weight, and he slams down on them both.

"Almost there!" Elliott reassures me through my earpiece. I check Vasily—he's stirring.

Square Jaw either sees or senses my distraction. He throws

his weight backward, and I have to stutter-step to stay clear—losing my grip on his hand. The Kubotan skitters across the pavement.

Crap. But if Elliott and Rashad get here, we'll be okay.

Square Jaw leaps up and turns on me.

Nope, won't be okay.

He moves forward, forcing me toward the wall. Adrenaline screams through my veins. Danger, danger, danger.

I stop before I'm pinned against the bricks. Will this ginormous dude really beat on average-sized me?

Square Jaw pulls back a fist. Guess that answers that question. I duck before he swings. Yep, slow.

He takes forever to recover from that total air-punch. I pop up and throw my hardest jab straight into his face. I was aiming for his nose, but my fist slams into his mouth and chin. Square Jaw reels back, blood flying from his lips.

"Nice shot!"

I whirl around to find Elliott at the end of the alley with Rashad. He came through. I trusted him, and he was there for me, just like always. (Maybe trust isn't quite as overrated as I thought.)

They hurry to help. Square Jaw takes one look at the woman who bloodied his lips and her backup, and runs away. Rashad pursues him.

My heart's pounding, my hand's aching, my head's swimming and I'm panting, but it's over. "An enforcer," I tell Elliott between pants. "Beat us to the punch."

"You were the one doing the punching." Elliott takes off after Rashad and Square Jaw, I'm guessing mostly to chase him away.

I recover my Kubotan and drop to my knees by Vasily, now coughing. "Are you okay?"

He nods, and I recognize the expression he's going for between coughing fits. The closest words would be *I'm still tough.*

I help him to sitting.

"What happened?" he chokes out.

Some girls play dumb. I usually have to play weak. (Though obviously I'm no Square Jaw.) "A Good Samaritan threw him off you and hit him, and he ran away."

Vasily glances the direction they went.

"Who's Sabatini?" I ask.

"Sabatini?" His pitch is way too high to fake ignorance.

"Apparently you owe him money?"

Vasily sighs as much as he can. "Don't get involved."

"Do you have the money?"

His head hangs further. "No."

I sit in silence long enough to pretend to put this all together. "Do you need help?"

"Joanne, I can't ask that of you."

"Not me, but I have this friend—and I want to repay the favors you've done for me."

Vasily's gaze sneaks away from mine. "I don't need another loan shark coming after me."

"He's not a loan shark. And he might be able to help with your other friend, too."

Vasily slowly turns to me. Does he get the full implications of what I'm saying?

He shakes his head. "You don't understand."

My heart's still pounding, but for a different reason. Time for the big guns. "I understand you're playing with dangerous people—people that make Sabatini seem like a small-time thug. You might be able to put off Sabatini, but you can't lie to your other friend forever. And when he catches up to you? *Do svidanya.*"

"You don't know what you're talking about."

"All I'm saying is you could really get back at the people who're using you *and* pick up a second paycheck."

Vasily presses his lips together, thinking.

"Just meet with the guy. No obligations. Tuesday?"

He sighs again. "Fine. I'll meet with him."

"You won't regret it." I help Vasily to his feet.

"He'll pay?" Vasily asks, brushing himself off.

"Yeah—but don't gamble it all away, okay?"

Vasily rubs a hand over his hair. My hand still stings from hitting that guy, and adrenaline's racing through my veins, but it's mixed with the sweet sense of success. Vasily will say yes. He said yes to spy for his friend to get away from this loan shark—and we'll actually solve both of those problems.

I walk Vasily to his car and confirm our next meeting, then head for my own car.

"Hey, Talia!"

I jump and turn around—Campbell's jogging toward me. "What are you doing in the neighborhood?"

"Getting lunch." I point back around the corner where we *didn't* go to a café.

"Whoa." Campbell grabs my wrist and pulls my hand closer. "You're bleeding."

"I'm not—" Suddenly the residual aching in my knuckles makes sense, because blood covers my fingers. Though it could be Square Jaw's.

I jerk away. How can I explain? "I'm fine."

"Fine? You can't drive home like this. Let's get you patched up."

"No, it's okay—"

"You'll get blood all over your car. Danny would kill me if he ever found out I let you hobble home bleeding."

Hobble? "I'm not hobbling." But I *am* following him to their building. He's right that I can't get blood all over my car. Bloodstains aren't covert.

I can take two minutes to wash up. It'll be okay. It's Danny's.

Which is probably the real reason I'm going along.

Campbell takes me to their apartment, now decorated with cardboard boxes, and oversees me washing off the blood. Sure enough, there's a nice pair of puncture wounds, two dashes across my knuckles.

How do I explain teeth marks?

"What happened?" Campbell asks.

The lie comes to me. "Saw some broken glass in the alley. I went to throw it away and tripped."

He sucks in air through his teeth in sympathy, then digs through a cabinet. "I don't think we have any of those knuckle bandages, but we should have something."

After a minute, he comes over with a paper towel and dries off my hands, then applies two regular Band-Aids.

"Danny's not around, is he?"

On cue, a door in the back of the apartment opens. "Campbell? Did you pack the stuff under my sink?"

"Uh . . . maybe? Come see who's here."

Danny walks out from the back wearing a dark gray suit and red tie. He startles to see me (and I can only imagine what I look like from my post-dance-lesson-and-fight ponytail to my faded yoga pants). "Hey."

"Hi."

I've spent hours and hours talking to Danny, and I have nothing to say. Except I love you. But, um, probably not the thing to say now.

"You're early," he notes.

Campbell seizes my wrist and holds it aloft. "I saw her on the sidewalk, and she'd hurt herself. I was helping her get bandaged up."

Danny and I both eye him, but Danny walks over and takes my wrist, examining the Band-Aids. "You okay?"

"Yeah, fine." Danny's holding my hand, why wouldn't I be fine? *Fabulous*, even?

His gaze meets mine. "You're shaking."

I check my hand again—and I totally am. Not like *oh, I'm trembling to be in front of the man I love, flutter, swoon.* Like hypothermic, *I can't stop shaking, somebody get a spoon before I bite through my tongue.* (Because why, why, why would I naturally do something the cute, girly way?)

"Are you going into shock?" Campbell jumps up and runs to the living room. The couch and chairs are buried deep under stacks of coats and blankets. He grabs the top thing, a jacket, and tosses it to Danny.

"I'm fine," I insist (again). "Just adrenaline. From seeing the blood." Or, you know, drawing it.

Danny wraps the jacket around my shoulders, and at the concern on his face, a tiny piece of my heart splinters.

More pain's coming for me tonight, and Danny . . . will be better off.

He glances at the packed couches. "Want to sit down?"

"No, better if I walk it off." This has only happened once or twice, but that seemed to help.

"Okay." Though that wasn't an invitation, Danny gets his jacket and keys and opens the door for me.

"I'll be fine," I tell him.

"I'm taking you somewhere to walk it off."

We've established I have no willpower when it comes to spending time with Danny, right? "All right."

Danny drives me to his "favorite place to walk." (With the amount of walking I do for my job, the idea of doing it for fun is hilarious.) Guess I shouldn't be surprised when we drive up to the Aviation and Space Museum. Museums can be a good place to meet agents, but I can't say I've ever been to this one.

They let us in free the last hour of the day, and Danny describes the more interesting specimens among the exhibits of the main hall, explaining what improvements they made over previous technology. By the time we reach the World War II exhibit, I'm off the adrenaline high. Instead, I'm hooked on the light in Danny's eyes as he explains seventy-year-old innovations.

Because I needed to add to my list of reasons to love him.

He seems to be angling for a specific destination, moving toward the back corner of the museum. But he has to stop to talk up the good stuff, so we're only halfway there when they play the hurry-up-and-get-out-we're-closing-in-fifteen-minutes announcement.

"Come on." Danny takes my (unhurt) hand and leads me to the exhibit we've been working toward. Not sure which of these planes is making him grin like a little boy, but he finally points up at one of the smallest pieces of the exhibit. "The Avro Canada CF-105 Arrow Two."

The nose cone tip is painted black, and the cockpit seems super small from this angle. There are . . . I don't know, engine slots or air intakes or something reading 205 and—that's it. No body, no wings, no tail. "Super experimental?"

Danny laughs. "No—well, sort of. There's more to the plane. And to the story." He explains how the Arrow was designed after World War II, the wings all one piece, giving it an overhead profile like a triangle. "Bleeding edge for the day, and testing was going well, but one day, the prime minister cut the program, cut the funding, and cut up the prototypes." He walks me around to a different angle, showing the obvious burns.

"Why?"

"Nobody knows for sure, not that they admit publicly. Could've been politics." He leans closer to add. "Could've been American influence. Some people think it was the CIA's fault."

My stomach dips more quickly than this prototype fell from grace. I'm pretty sure his conspiratorial look is because we're both American, but I keep my gaze on the section of the plane. I may have to tell him the truth about me, but not *that* truth. The rules are clear: we're not supposed to tell someone we're CIA until we're engaged to them—and that's not happening. Ever.

"Whoever it was, amazing how one person can destroy something like this, forever. Aerospace could've been completely different today. But as cool as the Arrow is, I think most things work out for the best." The conspiratorial look is back, and now over the secret significance of that symbolism. Which confirms my suspicions—that Danny has no suspicions about my real job.

I almost wish I could tell him that truth—no, I do, but the rules are there to keep us safe. And to keep him safe. If I ever told him, he'd be at risk, and I will never do that to him.

He's gazing up at the Arrow with a faint smile. Then he turns to me, and his smile turns real, crinkling the corners of his eyes, making my heart catch and melt. I don't know what it is about this man's smiles, but you can't *not* fall in love with them. With him.

After a minute of soaking in his smile, I realize I'm smiling back. Danny steps closer, not making a move, just to be nearer to me. I want this moment to last as long as possible, but I have to give him the part of the truth he deserves. "Danny, I need to—"

The closing chime plays over the announcement system, breaking our moment.

"What were you saying?" he asks as we head for the entrance.

"You come here a lot?" I change the subject.

"When I need to walk or think," Danny says. "I was already planning on coming today. Nice to have company." He squeezes my hand, and it dawns on me: I never let go. We've been holding hands for fifteen minutes.

I'm leading him on.

I let go of his hand to get the door, though he opened it for me, and it hurts. Because I love him, and I'm already losing him, and he doesn't know yet.

If he noticed my maneuvering, it doesn't show. The conversation doesn't seem strained from his side on the way back. He parks in his underground garage and walks me back to my car.

"Was this our date?" I ask once we're nearly there.

"Are you kidding? I don't wear a suit and tie to the museum. We've got reservations at seven thirty."

"Reservations? Should I change?" Barely enough time to shower and get ready.

He looks me up and down. "You look great."

"Danny, I'm wearing yoga pants. I can't go somewhere that takes reservations in yoga pants."

"Okay, I can pick you up later."

That smile again. For once, I don't want to lie about every detail of my life that I don't actually *have* to lie about. "Got a pen?"

He fishes one from his shirt pocket. I turn his hand over to write my address on his palm. He doesn't say anything, but he seems to sense how big this is. "Thanks. See you at seven fifteen?"

"Sounds good."

He opens my door and watches from the sidewalk until I pull away. He's still smiling.

I love him. And I have to tell him. I need this one thing in my life to be real—or be nothing. Or, most likely, both.

Yep. I have one final date with the man I love, to tell him why he should run far, far away. Fast.

CHAPTER 34
DANNY

DINNER'S SPECTACULAR, but despite the intimate lighting, the tables are too close together to get into a serious *define the relationship* discussion. We can't really talk until we're on our way out.

"You know," I say as we reach the doors, "I think I owe you some thanks."

"Just some?"

I glance over at Talia, like I've been able to keep my eyes off her all night. I hadn't realized it before, but she always wears black and beige and the most boring, blend-into-the-background colors. Tonight, her dress is the bluest blue I've ever seen, her hair is up, and she's got those ankle strap shoes on again—amazing as always.

She's still smirking, getting ready to put on her jacket. I take it and hold it for her. "Okay, a lot of thanks. It was your idea to start cooking."

"Best idea ever."

"Second best. Made me appreciate the actual best idea ever:

really good food *made by someone else.*"

"I have to admit, this *was* probably the most amazing dinner I've ever eaten." She slides an arm into her jacket sleeve. "No offense to your cooking," she adds.

I signal the *none taken.* That's why I picked this place—it's supposed to be the best restaurant in the city. The price tag matches, but if everything goes well now, it's well worth it.

Even if everything doesn't go well, it was worth it to spend the last hour and a half with her. Also, the food. The food was really good. "That risotto," I say. "And the tuna. The duck?"

"The s'more," Talia sighs. "I could eat that every meal for the rest of my life." She puts on the other sleeve and I pull the jacket up around her shoulders, letting my arm linger there. I swear she leans closer to me for a second, but when we reach the door, she smoothly turns out of my grasp. Like she did when we were leaving the aviation museum.

Two points against taking this jump. I've got no flight plan, no parachute, no landing gear.

But I've got to tell her. I try to swallow despite my dry throat. "Okay," I say once we're on the sidewalk, headed for my car. "Maybe I owe you more like a lot of thanks. That barely begins to cover the painting."

"I think we're square."

Cashwise, maybe—even without the wine pairings, the full tasting menu for two is over $200—but that's definitely not what I'm going for. "Really. Can't imagine where I'd be without you."

"With someone else," she says softly, even wistfully. "Someone better for you."

Make that three points against the jump. Sounds like to her, this is ending—this is goodbye. I can't let her go without trying. We reach the light and wait to cross the street. My car's on the other side, but I want more time. I glance around the intersection. Diagonal from us, there's a huge gray stone church.

"Hey, Miss Ottawa Expert, what's that?"

"Saint Patrick's Basilica," she answers. I didn't actually expect her to know, so I'm impressed.

"Want to take a look?"

"Sure."

We cross both streets to get to that corner, but a wrought iron fence keeps us off their lawn. Man, I wish this were a park or something. Not that I like loitering in public parks after dark, but it'd give us more privacy than walking through the city streets. We admire the lights in the church's arched windows and the towering steeple. The fall leaves are nice too.

Yep. *Nice.* Now say something.

Say something.

ANYTHING.

What, standing here in the middle of the sidewalk? There has to be somewhere to sit.

"Cool church." Talia's still staring at the building, but sounds like she's done with viewing.

Still need to find a way to tell her . . . everything. Like that I love her. I start past the three sets of peaked-arch doors. Are there seriously no benches around this church?

Guess they keep those inside. Going in is probably pushing it. Talia walks with me to the next corner. Across the street, a glass façade building mirrors the church's lights. I cross toward the building. Talia seems to hesitate, but she comes with me.

In front of the building, past the sign proclaiming this a government structure, there's a little court with trees in a planter. At last—benches. I lead Talia into the alcove formed by the planters and look up at the reflected glowing twin steeples and the streetlight filtering through the fall leaves. Perfect spot. Now I just need the perfect words.

"How's work going?" Talia asks, filling in the silence.

"Good—I got a promotion today."

She looks up at me with an open-mouthed grin of surprise

and . . . pride? "Awesome—you deserve it."

She has no way of knowing that, but Talia slides an arm around my back and gives me a squeeze for a kind of side hug. I drape an arm over her shoulders and she doesn't move away. "Danny?" she ventures. "Can I tell you something?"

"Sure." Except I'm the one who's supposed to be saying something.

I wait there, and finally she meets my gaze again. She looks sad—no, beyond sad. Devastated. Like she knows what we're about to say will ruin everything.

She pivots and turns the side hug into a full hug, adding her other arm around my waist. I slide my other arm around her, and she rests her head on my chest.

"You know you're my best friend, right?" she says.

Oh crap. I will not be friend-zoned again. Yeah, she's my best friend, too, but if I have a chance to be happy with her—to be happy together, more than friends—I want to take it. I have to.

Talia lifts her head and looks up at me. "I just wish . . ."

I stare into her hazel eyes, and I don't dare fill in her wish with mine. But suddenly I don't need the perfect words anymore. Because I know exactly what to do.

I ignore the fear of rejection filling my lungs, lean in and kiss her.

Just after my lips touch hers, her hand lands on my chest. I realize my heart is doing about Mach 3.2. Will she push me away again?

Before I stop kissing her, she slides her hand up to twine her fingers in my hair—she has no idea how much I love that—pulling me that much closer. Like she was worried I'd get away.

Believe me, I'm not going anywhere.

First kisses are supposed to be tentative, maybe even a little awkward, and short. This is none of the above. Talia kisses me back like she's been waiting as long as I have and wanting it as much as I do, unwilling to let this end.

When that perfect kiss does end, I linger a couple inches from her. Should we talk and then kiss again, or kiss and then talk and kiss again?

"Don't," she whispers, her eyes still closed.

Oh no.

"Stop," she says. Objecting a minute too late? But she kissed me back. Unless I've totally misread this.

My stomach sinks in a death spiral. "I did stop."

Her eyelids flutter open. "Oh, no—I mean, 'don't stop.' Sorry, had to catch my breath."

Wait, what? My gut rebounds. Not only is she *not* upset about the kiss, but she's breathless, just as caught up as me. I'm so relieved I laugh and squeeze her close. "At some point, we'll have to stop."

"I know—I just didn't want to get . . . here."

She may be the resident expert, but I doubt she means this random building. "What's wrong with here?" Personally, I was really excited about the *more than friends and definitely okay to kiss* stage.

She groans and pushes away from me. "This wasn't supposed to happen—I wasn't supposed to fall in love." She keeps talking, and it doesn't sound good, but I replaying those three words in my mind, my pulse revving all over again with every repetition.

How can this night get any better?

"You're in love with me?" I know that's not the only thing she said, but I can't hide my grin.

Talia wheels back. "Yes, try to keep up, rocket scientist."

I fold my arms. "I'll do my best—once you start explaining."

"I don't know where to start."

"I don't have anywhere else to be." I take her hand and tow her over to the stone benches to sit. They're hard and cold, but I don't care. "I hear the beginning's a good place to start."

"I told you how I don't like French fries."

Is she trying to change the subject? Not going to let that happen. "Weird, but not a relationship killer."

She shakes her head, and then the parts of the truth she's always avoided start to come out. "I ate enough French fries to last a lifetime when I was moving cross-country after my parents' divorce, and again after my mom's next two divorces. That and my dad's job changes are why I've lived in nine states. I want to go into family law so no kid ever has to go through what I did."

The pieces of information slide into place in my Talia file—the things I knew better than to ask. The biggest piece I'd already figured out: her parents' divorce. Now it only makes sense that she avoids that topic, with this many painful memories hinging on that one event.

She sighs. Her gaze follows a passing car. "Danny, you deserve . . . everything. You deserve to be happy."

"Funny, my plan for being happy was to date you, so I'm still not seeing how this precludes that."

She's silent for a long minute, staring up at the steeple.

Now I need to say something—not because I've filed away info on her personal life, but because she's helped so much with mine. "Haven't you spent the last month or two showing me I can't change what people did in the past; I can only change myself and how I tackle the future?"

"Can't say I came into it with that goal, but impressive takeaway." Talia wrings her hands. "Thing is, the past affects the future. History repeats itself when you don't know any other way to act."

"We've hung out for three months. I know how you act. Doesn't seem like a problem." She has a rebuttal for every assertion. Does she just not want to date me? I try to push aside the worry.

"No—do you remember a while back when I called you

because something was bothering me, but I didn't want to talk about it?"

"Yeah?" The night I told her about cooking my phone to help distract her.

A breeze rustles the trees, and she shivers. I scoot closer to put an arm around her. "I was upset because my mom called—always upsetting—but this time, she called to gloat that Tyler's getting a divorce."

Her brother? Man, her mother is messed up. "That sucks; I'm sorry."

"Yeah."

And she can't date me because . . . ? "Trying to keep up, but still not quite seeing your point."

Talia takes a deep breath and starts tracing a pattern on the stone benches. "Tyler's the last in a long string of Reynoldses to ruin a marriage. Tyler's getting divorced. Troy's already divorced. My mom has been married three times, and I was there to watch all three fall apart. My parents fought *constantly*, as far back as I can remember."

"That's hard." I squeeze her shoulders. She leans back, and we both rest against the back of the bench, also cold and hard.

"Even tougher knowing the pattern has repeated itself with Troy and now Tyler. It's how things go in my family. No escaping it."

"Well . . ." There has to be some counterpoint here. "What about your other brother, not Timo? He divorced?"

She folds her hands in her lap. "Trevor? Gay. Adds a whole 'nother degree of difficulty to our family dynamics."

I slide my arm from around her shoulders to take her hand. She doesn't pull away—she clings to me like she doesn't want this to end.

Enough to try again. "Are you trying to say you don't want to date me because you think you'll get divorced?"

"Not 'don't want,' Danny. I want to date you—I *so* want to

date you—"

"Simple solution: date me." I grin to show I'm joking. Kind of.

Sorrow wells up in her eyes until they roll skyward to the leaves above us. "Nothing's that simple. Haven't you done all this healing so you can think about dating and marriage again?"

"Sort of, but you're getting ahead of us. I'm not asking you to marry me—I'm not even ready to think about that."

"Isn't that the endgame of dating?"

"I guess, but—"

She releases my hand and stands. Without her by me, it's suddenly colder, and not just the weather.

She walks two steps away, focused on the glowing reflection of the church. "I'm not going to do that. I just can't. I've never even seen a happy marriage up close. I'm not sure I believe in them." She looks down. "I don't, not for me."

"Talia—"

"Danny." She turns around to cut me off, like she's anticipating my *you're being unreasonable* argument. "Other than my dad's second, every marriage in my family has ended in divorce. And not *oh, well, we grew apart* divorce. Screaming, crying, fighting divorce. Five years of ugly custody battles and poisoning the kids against the ex divorce. Can't be in the same room for a decade afterward divorce. The only way out of it— the *only* way—is to not start."

Wow. Yeah, Talia had years of therapy, but even with that help, she's lost all hope for a happy future. At my darkest place, somewhere inside, I still hoped things might work out for me one day—today—and Talia's been hurting like this for years. Her whole life.

I just want to hold her and make that better. Nothing can erase what she's been through—I know that way too well—and I'm not talking about sacrificing myself to make her happy. I

290

only want to be there for her as much as she's been there for me.

One easy way to do that: I stand up and cross the physical distance between us.

"I can't put you through that kind of pain," she finishes, still staring at the church in the building's windows.

"You want to spare me pain?" Logic time. "If you can walk away now without it hurting, then run. Seriously. Get out while you can."

"Are you kidding?" She laugh-scoffs. "These last few weeks away from you have killed me. I wanted to text you *every* day. The kittens, Danny. Think of the kittens."

I'd almost forgotten that inside joke. "I was dying without you and your kittens. It's too late to avoid pain."

"But—"

"Just listen." I take her in my arms, and I start. "Let's think about this objectively: your mom's mental illness is what destroyed her marriages, and it gave your brothers—and you—a lot of baggage that *will* make a happy marriage—a happy *life* tough."

Talia opens her mouth to object, but can't.

"Because of those problems from her, you're breaking your heart now instead of risking it getting broken later—not a guarantee. Doing that is letting your mom win again. You're letting her mental illness control your life and keep you from happiness."

Her face falls, and I don't think she finds my tie this interesting. "You know, my mother called a couple weeks ago, and . . . she told me I'm difficult to love, and that's why I'm alone."

"Are you serious?" I shake my head.

The wind picks up again, the leaves overhead swishing. I pull her closer, but not just to fight the air currents. "Let me tell you, you're not difficult to love. It's easier than breathing. And all the other autonomic body functions."

Her head snaps up, her eyes bright, but a little furrow appears between her eyebrows. "Autonomic . . . ?"

Yeah, naturally, I try to be smooth and end up confusing. I clarify, "Heartbeat, swallowing, pupils dilating, you know, those."

"Ah."

If I'm going to be there for her, I need to start providing antivenin to her mom's poison. "While we're at it, since I don't know what other lies your mother's been feeding you, let's cover all the bases. You're beautiful."

She glances away for a second, like the truth's embarrassing. Or like she doesn't believe me. I reiterate: "You are."

"Okay."

I'll keep working on convincing her of that. "And you're talented and amazing and everything anyone should ever hope for. You don't deserve to be alone."

Her gaze falls again. I've hit home. I hold her tighter, my voice even softer. "You don't have to be alone, and you're not. I'm here."

She looks up, and the streetlight or the church's glow reflects off tears brimming in her eyes.

Good tears, I hope. "No matter what you decide, I'm still here for you—with you." That would suck, but if that's what I have to do to be there for her, I will.

She bites her lip and blinks away the tears. "You have no idea how much I needed to hear that."

"I mean it."

A passing car honks at us. Didn't know Canadians did that. But we're not about to let that ruin our moment. I keep holding onto Talia.

Until she jumps. "Sorry, hang on." She reaches in her jacket pocket and takes out her phone. She scowls. "My mom."

That woman is a viper. But Talia stares at her phone like

this is a major debate. "Going to answer?" I ask.

"She's my mother. She—she's supposed to . . ." Talia sighs. "She's never going to change."

Her eyes plead for me to contradict her, but she knows that answer better than me. She hits the ignore icon. "I guess if you can stand up to your mom . . ."

"Oh yeah, if I can do it anybody can," I joke.

"Exactly. Thanks for making it look easy," she teases back, and a smile sneaks onto her lips.

Better get to the point before I get distracted by those lips. "I've spent way too much of my life trying to make other people happy, and all I want now is to be happy with you. I don't know what'll happen in a month or two or ten, but I'm not willing to miss out on being with you until then. I promise, if I ever *am* ready to think about marriage, I'll let you know—but even if this goes absolutely nowhere, I would rather date you than break up and hold out for someone who's 'marriage material.'"

"Break up?" Talia's smile turns to a smirk, and she tilts back in my arms to cop a teasing attitude. "We're already dating?"

"We've been dating for almost three months—but it was so secret, even we didn't know."

She laughs. I love that sound.

"Other than your date with Campbell," I add.

"What date with Campbell? I never—"

"When we went dancing."

Her brow furrows again. "No, I thought I was *your* date."

Now I have to laugh. "Are you kidding me? Watching you guys dance was *torture*—and you thought you were there with me?"

"Is that why you didn't kiss me?"

"The only reason. You wanted me to?"

She scoffs, sliding her arms around my waist. "Duh? I've

been thinking about it since our first date."

"Nice to know I wasn't the only one." So much for being jealous—I'm done with that. It's idiotic.

I'm done with secrets. I'm done with bending over backwards to make everyone else happy. I'm done with the past.

And, standing here in this little alcove between a pretty church and its reflection, an even more beautiful woman in my arms, I'm finally ready to start over—with Talia. "So if you don't want to break up—"

"Terrible idea."

I have a much better one. I use my fingertips to tip her chin up and lean in. Despite the *kiss her, kiss her, kiss her* cadence in my pulse, I don't quite yet. "Guess there's just one other thing I need to tell you."

"What's that?"

"You were right about me all along. I *was* lying."

Her eyes turn wary, though her shields are nowhere in sight.

"I *don't* like kittens half as much as I claim."

She purses her lips and slides her arms around my neck, playing with my hair again. "Don't see how anyone could."

I hold her closer. "Talia Reynolds, I love you."

"And I love you, Danny Fluker."

I lean those last inches to kiss her, and it's even more perfect than the first time.

Dear Reader,

Thank you so much for reading *Spy by Night*! I never expected to write this novel—it was supposed to be a novella, maybe two! I started writing Danny's story a long time ago to get to know him better. When I came back to write those same scenes from Talia's perspective, I found myself missing Danny's voice and input. I had to include his story here, even if it made the project more than twice as long (and hard) as I was anticipating!

Whether this is your first book in the Spy Another Day series or your last, I hope you've enjoyed the adventure as much as I have. I write my stories because they're adventures I want to read about, but I publish them because I love to share these stories with you. I'd love to hear from you! **You can write me at Jordan@JordanMcCollum.com or find me (and fun bonus features!) at http://JordanMcCollum.com.**

Finally, can I ask a quick favor? **Could you please leave a review of** *Spy by Night* **online, or tell your friends about it?** So much of a book's success depends on friends' recommendations. To make things easy for you, I've got a full list of review site links on my website at http://JordanMcCollum.com/loved-spy-night/.

Thank you again for reading!

Jordan McCollum

P.S. Want to be the first to know about my next release? Join my mailing list at http://JordanMcCollum.com/newsletter/. (I will never spam you!)

I, SPY

Spy Another Day Series Book 1

Canada is probably the last place you'd expect to find an American spy. But even idyllic Ottawa has its deadly secrets—and so does CIA operative Talia Reynolds. She can climb through ventilation shafts, blend in at the occasional diplomatic function, even scale buildings (small ones). But there's one thing she can't do: tell her aerospace engineer boyfriend Danny about her Top Secret occupation.

It worked for a year, keeping Danny in the dark, keeping him away from danger, keeping her secrets. And then Talia finally catches a hot case: Fyodor Timofeyev. Russian. Aerospace executive. Possible spy?

She can make this work, too—until Danny needs her at the same time her country does. And when Fyodor targets Danny? Suddenly her schedule isn't the only thing suffering. Now to save her secrets and her country, Talia must sacrifice the man she loves.

Available now!

Read on for a free

I DON'T DO CATSUITS. The leather/plastic/spandex coatings female spies pour themselves into on TV are ridiculously impractical for actual spy tradecraft: no mobility, reflective in low light, loud colors. Nothing shouts "I'm a covert operative!" like a catsuit.

But I kinda wish I had one now. At least it wouldn't snag on every half-screwed bolt I come across in this narrow ventilation shaft. My clothes are dark, close fitting and comfortable no matter how I have to contort myself, but I can't move more than ten feet without getting caught on something—like now. If I yank my pants hem free, my knee will hit the metal flashing, inches from my targets' neighbors making dinner on the other side of the wall. I suck in a silent breath thick with their garlic and ginger.

I've made it this far. I'm not about to let one more hitch stop me. I keep my weight evenly distributed and lower myself to the bottom of the narrow tunnel. This looks a lot cooler on TV. James Bond never had to deal with wardrobe malfunctions. He also never faced off with Lashkar-e-Omar, or any other terrorist armies bent on killing people just because they were American.

And I'm not going to get a chance to do it either unless I can get to this apartment. "C'mon, Talia," I whisper, like self-pep talks are effective. I wriggle backward, bending my body into an awkward V against the cold metal to grope for my ankles in the dark.

"Talking to yourself, FOXHUNT?" comes Elliott's voice in my earpiece. "T-plus eighteen."

I have to stick to the targets' routine. We should know it; we've timed them every night for more than a week. I have twenty minutes left until our window is narrower than this ventilation shaft. I need to move. At last my fingers find the bolt and I unhook my CIA-issue, top-secret-weave pants. (I'm kidding; they're just pants.)

Finally free from the flashing, I unkink my body and lift into a low crawl for my targets' vent a few feet away. After inching through this tunnel for so long, it feels like I'll never get there. I swear, the movies seriously gloss over how long this entry takes.

I've never met anyone who's done this for a break-in-and-bug, "black bag" op in real life, and the unexpectedness is part of the reason we chose this Hollywood-style clandestine entry. The only woman on our team, I was the only one agile enough, small enough, eager enough for the job.

Remind me not to do this again.

Within seconds, I'm there. The room below me is lit by the moon streaming through the windows. Nothing remarkable: desk cluttered with office supplies, stained mattresses shoved in every corner, rotting bookcase with a single half-empty shelf. Shabby chic it's not, but I've bugged filthier.

I unwrap the twine from my wrist and thread it between the slats of the vent, pulling it back through the other side. Holding both ends, I can be sure not to drop the vent once it's free. A special tool made for unscrewing bolts from the wrong end—sorry, I can't say much more about it than that—makes for quick work and the built-in rare-earth magnet keeps them from clattering to the bare floor below.

Before I move the vent, I have to make sure I know where I'm going. If there's no way out but the front door, I don't want to get myself trapped. Like the catsuit, that's a little less than covert.

I spot my way out of the apartment, a cold air return near the front closet. I'm going in. My pulse measures the seconds in double time, and I pull the vent cover into the shaft. It's tough unless you know the trick to turn it on a diagonal. I lower myself within a couple feet of the clear area on the desk, not daring to breathe. Even super-secret "quiet shoes" make some noise if you jump hard enough.

Luckily, I don't have far to go and I land between the precarious piles of Post-Its in near-silence. If someone were in the apartment, they'd probably come to check. Two quick heartbeats later, I let myself breathe again. No one's home, and watching the door to make sure that doesn't change is Elliott's job. "Status?" I request.

"All clear. Yours?"

"I'm in." Fourteen minutes until I need to leave. I can do that. I reverse my diagonal trick to replace the vent, pocket my twine, then hop to the floor.

Our meticulous preparations give me an odd sense of déjà vu, but I've only "been here" in the safety of our office. Over the last week, we've lived this case: taking telephoto pictures of the apartment, finding someone in these guys' circles to get us closer to them, fabricating the bug. I'm here to place it so we can collect the intelligence to identify and target them. Until now, Lashkar-e-Omar has operated strictly within Pakistan, but if they're expanding overseas, this cell has got to be the cream of their criminal crop.

"Hey," Elliott launches a conversation. "How's it going?"

"Um, fine?"

"Oh, hold on—"

Is he talking to me, or is he on the phone? "Keep the line clear, would you, Ellie?" The last word is out before I can stop it, and I mentally kick myself. Elliott isn't a complete novice, and I'm not a complete idiot, using his name over comms. But Ellie's not a play on "Elliott." It's short for "Elephant," his you-wouldn't-say-that-to-his-face nickname around the office after our last few missions, and some particularly inelegant missteps.

He doesn't react to my gaffe. "Yeah, sorry, FOX." A soft click tells me he's switched off his mic. We're in the middle of an op; if he's making phone calls, there's only one person he should dial right now. Our boss. And if he's not calling Will, I'm waiting for the elephant's other foot to fall.

But I don't have time to sit around. I turn back to the desk. I'd love to put the bug in the smoke detector—we've got one you can wire into the nine-volt and even if they change the battery, they wouldn't notice it—but that's not for this time. The coolest equipment on the planet to back us up, and tonight we're stuck with the good old cliché, the phone.

Yes, they have a landline, one of those gray numbers from the nineties. I lift the receiver just enough to disengage the hook switch. Dial tone. Nice.

I borrow a piece of tape from the dispenser on the desk— double sided? In some ways this is closer to an Office Depot than a dissident den—and place the tape over the hook switch. The dial tone would be a little distracting, but the off-the-hook signal is designed to get someone's attention. Exactly what I don't want.

My thin-bladed screwdriver is perfect to pry apart the receiver. If these guys were dumb enough to plan over the phone, we'd probably already have the intel we need to get to them, but this bug is designed to pick up the chatter whether the phone is being used or not.

I grab the bug and some pliers from my left belt pack. The plastic coating comes off the wires easily enough, and after half a dozen twists, the bug's installed. This design looks like just another black wire in the phone. It's my second favorite. I cover up the wire joins with electrical tape and tap the undetectable microphone.

Elliott's supposed to tell me he's getting the signal, but his end is so quiet I can hear the interference from my tapping. I snap the phone back together. "Still all clear?"

He doesn't answer.

"HAM?" I try the short version of his code name, HAMMER.

"Just a sec."

He should know the answer right off. I don't like this. I put the phone back into place.

Elliott swears. "They're in the building! Get out now!"

Read more in

ACKNOWLEDGMENTS

MY FAMILY IS MY GREATEST SUPPORT. My husband, Ryan, does so much for us so that I can write, and my children, Hayden, Rebecca, Rachel and Hazel, are all so understanding. They aren't quite old enough to read my books yet, but they are my biggest fans, and I love each of them. (I love you!)

My parents, Ben and Diana Franklin, and my sisters, Jaime, Brooke and Jasmine, have always supported and helped me with my writing. They were my first editors and my first audience and so much more. (I love you!)

As always, my critique partners, Julie Coulter Bellon and Emily Gray Clawson provided invaluable feedback and encouragement. This is actually the last book I wrote in the Spy Another Day series/prequels, and they've been there with me since the first draft of the first book, cheering me on and putting me on the right track when I fell off. I especially appreciate Emily's encouragement to tell Danny's story here, too—even if it made the project more than twice as long as I was anticipating! Thank you! (Yep, I love you too!)

My trusted beta readers helped to knock the last few rough edges off this book in record time: thank you so much for your time and feedback, Ranee´ S. Clark, Heather Baird and Sarah Anderson. (That's right, more love!)

Once again, I want to thank Jason Hanson of Escape & Evasion and formerly of the CIA for answering my questions and for an awesome experience in his Spy Escape & Evasion course, which taught me more than any Q&A session could.

Finally, as always, my heartfelt thanks go to you, my reader. Your words of encouragement help me to focus and persevere no matter how difficult it seems (or how much a project rebels!). Thank you so much for joining me on this adventure and making my stories come to life. I hope you've enjoyed them as much as I have!

Thank you!

ABOUT THE AUTHOR

PHOTO BY JAREN WILKEY

AN AWARD-WINNING AUTHOR, JORDAN MCCOLLUM can't resist a story where good defeats evil and true love conquers all. In her day job, she coerces people to do things they don't want to, elicits information and generally manipulates the people she loves most—she's a mom.

Jordan holds a degree in American Studies and Linguistics from Brigham Young University. When she catches a spare minute, her hobbies include reading, knitting and music. She lives with her husband and four children in Utah.

19295381R00176

Made in the USA
San Bernardino, CA
20 February 2015